Carol Margaret Tetlow

W0008955

Faith Hope and Clarity

ACKNOWLEDGEMENTS

Thank you, more than I can say, to Guy Boulianne
and Editions Dedicaces for believing in me.

Thank you so much Helen Norris for proof reading this novel.
You've always being there since the beginning of my writing
journey to give constructive advice, support and encouragement
to say nothing of the mini Stollen cakes and Twirl bites.

Thank you to Mhoire, Samantha and Sonia,
who are the first to read and appraise my novels.

And thank you to Bill, for your never ending patience,
love and good humour.

Chapter One

Faith was having lunch with her mother. The meal had started off innocently enough, the topic of discussion being Faith's new horse, Caspian, on whom she had been out riding that morning. It had been a decidedly scary outing as Caspian, full of too many high-energy feeds and overjoyed to be out of his stable at last, had required all her strength to hold him. There had been rather too many times when this had not been sufficient, including a particularly unnerving and uncontrolled gallop back through the woods where it was more down to good fortune rather than her equestrian skills that had prevented her from falling off. It had been a relief to get back to the stable yard in one piece, her legs wobbly as her feet touched the ground when she dismounted. She felt exhausted but it was clear that only a tiny part of Caspian's energy had been spent as he bucked and cantered around the paddock, head held high, nostrils flared, on being turned out. Faith watched him, with more admiration than affection, as she walked back to the house, pulling off her hard hat and trying unsuccessfully to do something with her hair which had been flattened against her head. She was rather pleased that her mother had not been with her to witness their tussles.

Her mother, Glenda, was herself an accomplished horsewoman. She had ridden for nearly as long as she had been able to walk and one room of their home was given over entirely to the trophies and rosettes that she had won. Having said that, she only kept the red or blue rosettes; anything that symbolised a more lowly position in the final line up was tossed into the dustbin with contempt. Proud of her own success, she was of the opinion that Faith should follow in her footsteps, an expectation that her daughter had tried hard to live up to but never achieved, owing largely to the fact that where Glenda thought that no ride out was complete without several hair-raising jumps, all taken at neck-breaking speed, Faith was perfectly content with a gentle hack, offering plenty of time to take in the countryside views and preferably a country pub half way at which to stop and have lunch.

They were sitting opposite one another at the kitchen table, papers and magazines having been pushed into unruly piles on one side to make enough room for them. A couple of snoring Labradors, Otis and Sam, were toasting themselves in front of the range while a brown and white terrier, Rex, worried at a plastic string of sausages which squeaked raucously in protest. It was a huge room, expertly designed and expensively fitted out, its features spoilt somewhat by the untidiness. Faith watched her mother stub out a cigarette and tilt her head back to puff out the last bit of smoke towards the ceiling.

Glenda had once been a strikingly beautiful woman, but now her face was thin and pinched, with eyes that were untrusting and a mouth tightened by the acrimony of divorce, her complexion a testament to the combination of too much sunbathing and a lifetime of cigarettes. Her greying blond hair, remarkably still thick and naturally wavy, was held back by a black Alice band. She was dressed, predictably, in an old, sleeveless, quilted jacket, with most of the stitching coming undone, well-worn jodhpurs that rather suited her slight frame and a blue and white striped shirt. A selection of gold chains, some with pendants or lockets attached hung around her freckled neck, intertwined and jumbled, looking cheap and tacky rather than glamorous. Her fingers were bedecked with gold, also. Only the third finger of her left hand was bare. On the others were a selection of diamond solitaires, emerald and diamond eternity rings and a large ruby and opal cluster, all legacies from the early days of her marriage to the wealthy Dennis Faber but now just poignant, persistent reminders of how things had been. But despite the fact that she had emerged from the divorce proceedings with a staggeringly generous settlement, plenty for all of Faith's university fees and more than enough for her to maintain the lifestyle of her choice with her animals, the emotional damage that she had incurred still, after nearly ten years, refused to heal. She now found it laughable that she could have been so naïve as to believe that she had the perfect marriage. For nearly twenty years she had lived a life most could only dream of. They had money, a huge country house on a sprawling thirty-acre estate, as many thoroughbred horses as she wished plus designer clothes and jewels, foreign holidays and the latest model of sports car. When she discovered that he had been unfaithful with that mousy-looking woman for longer than she could bear to think, she had been initially distraught, then incandescent with rage that he couldn't even

6

have managed to destroy their marriage with something a little more imaginative than an affair with his secretary. Hell bent on revenge, she had hired the most expensive divorce solicitor in the county and the results had been worth every penny.

Faith was their only child. With the wisdom that comes with hindsight, Glenda often wondered if she should have had more, but at that time, at the height of her success in the world of three-day eventing, another pregnancy was the furthest thing from her mind. Dennis had seemed quite content. At the time she had found this touching and interpreted it as a sign of his commitment to her sporting career, but later she realised that unwittingly she had handed him more opportunity to cultivate and nurture his sordid dalliance.

After the divorce, Glenda had moved out from the marital home and bought what she scathingly referred to as 'the cottage'. This was in reality a five- bedroomed detached property with eight acres of land, including a ménage, an indoor school and a row of looseboxes around a concrete yard. It was a foregone conclusion that Faith would accompany her and live there as Dennis would be continuing to travel all over the world and Faith, having just left Sixth Form College, was due to go to medical school in Leeds. So, unlike most of her peers, Faith had lived at home throughout her student days, commuting into work on a daily basis and thus missing out on the socialising and most of the camaraderie that took place in the evenings and weekends. A shy, and introspective girl, whose sense of security had just received an unpleasant jolt with the splitting up of her parents, she found it far more preferable in her mind to maintain this close link with her mother and all the things in life which made her feel safe. Graduation completed, with honours, she had then come back to work in the nearest hospital and undertake her pre-registration year before her three years of training to become a general practitioner. Academically mature and confident, she remained emotionally naïve and socially gauche, with few friends.

There was not a lot of food on the table – a bowl of cottage cheese, some tomatoes, cucumber, lettuce, low-fat spread and crispbreads. Faith was starving, a morning of fresh air and strenuous riding having sharpened her appetite. She felt her heart sink as she had hoped for some chunks of fresh, crusty bread and a bowl of rib-sticking soup. What was available would barely satisfy a mouse. She concocted a tower of all the available ingredients and started to attack it noticing that Glenda, as usual, was eating virtually nothing. She nibbled disinterestedly at a couple of lettuce leaves in the manner of a distracted rabbit and then pushed the rest of her food firmly to one side of the plate in favour of her packet of cigarettes, a large glass of gin and tonic, with ice and a slice of lemon and a cup of espresso coffee that was so thick and strong that Faith got palpitations from just looking at it. While she smoked and drank, she continually encouraged Faith to do justice to her food. It was an incongruous fact that Glenda had a compulsion to force feed her daughter while she lived on next to nothing (well, nothing of any nutritional value) herself.

'You'll have to spend more time with that horse,' Glenda announced, exhaling after a particularly long drag on her cigarette. 'He's far too good just to leave in the paddock all day.'

'I know, Ma. I will do, especially now the weather is getting better. He didn't go too badly this morning when we were out. He only spooked when you shouted at us, as we came back into the yard.'

Faith tried to look as confident as she sounded. Glenda was unconvinced.

'He needs more schooling, not just hacking out. Do you want me to have a go?'

'Yes please,' Faith replied, well aware that if anyone could get the best out of a horse then it was her mother. 'I'd be grateful if you would. You know it's hard for me to find the time he needs. In fact I wonder if he's a bit much for me. Perhaps I need something a bit quieter.'

'Rubbish,' barked Glenda as she paused to take a swallow of her drink. 'You just need to put in a bit of time and effort. Pull yourself together and be more confident. Oh, by the way, just after you'd gone out riding, there was a phone call for you. Also Jonty popped in for a cup of tea. He'll ring you later. The phone call sounded as if it might be about work. I've left the details over there on the dresser.'

Immediately interested, Faith jumped up to find the piece of paper her mother had scribbled on in her careless handwriting. She was currently in between jobs and hating it. She loved work and felt frustrated and more than a little useless not being in full-time employment. Secretly her ideal had been to find a partnership once she had completed her training but the colleagues she had been training with had all chosen to become locums at a variety of different surgeries, believing that this was a good way of getting more experience before committing to something that was likely to be a job for the rest of their lives. Presuming that they must know more about it than she did, Faith had taken the same path but was irritated by the lack of continuity she had with her patients, knowing that most that she saw, she was never likely to see again. Added to this, there was the paucity of locums available in the area, which meant she had either to travel long distances or fill her time with some shifts in A&E and this was not a speciality in which she felt confident or at home.

'Those jodhpurs of yours are bursting at the seams, Faith. Have they shrunk or have you got bigger?' Glenda asked unkindly as her daughter got up.
Flustered, Faith tried to adjust her clothes to make them look better.

'I think they might have shrunk in the wash,' she suggested tentatively.

Glenda snorted in disbelief.

'Funny how mine haven't then and they're the same make. You shouldn't eat so much.'

'I've hardly had any lunch and I didn't have breakfast this morning. You need to eat more.' She tried to turn the conversation round to focus on Glenda.

'Not hungry,' was the curt reply. 'Here, let me look at you.'

Glenda put a hand on each of Faith's hips, stopping her as she tried to walk past her to get to the message. She studied her daughter from all angles then slapped her playfully on one buttock.

'You ought to lose weight. I can see your cellulite through those jodhpurs −not a pretty sight.'

Faith self consciously pulled her jumper down as far as she could and forced her way out of her mother's grip. Reading the message, she felt her heart give a small hiccup of hope as she leant over to reach the telephone. She could feel her mother watching her as she made her call, through half-closed eyes as she wallowed in yet more smoke, mentally finding fault with her physique.

The telephone call proved to be as promising as she'd hoped. She spoke to a friendly sounding man called Elliot Douglas, the practice manager at the surgery in Lambdale, some half an hour's drive away, where they were looking for a long-term locum who could start as soon as possible. Faith was delighted and assured them that not only was she available but that she was free to come for an interview the following morning. Putting down the receiver, Faith noticed that she was still under close scrutiny and felt the momentary bubble of optimism burst.

'You're fat, Faith. You know that? It's not fair on Caspian. Like I said, you need to lose weight and tone up a bit…well, a lot actually.'

'Thanks for that, Ma. I know I need to lose some weight; you don't need to remind me constantly. Anyway,' she tried changing the subject, 'I've been asked to go for a job interview tomorrow.'

She told her mother what details she knew.

'One of the partners is off on long-term sick leave. She's having a really difficult time, so they're looking for someone who can start now and help out, then hopefully stay on and cover for her the whole time that's she's off. It would be so great if I get it. I'd be there for several months and really get to know the other doctors and the patients. And maybe, if they liked me, they might ask me to stay on even longer.'

She paused, slightly breathless, her cheeks pink with excitement.

Glenda coughed and Faith shuddered slightly at the sound of her mother's sputum rattling in her chest.

'Fingers crossed then. If you're busy you might have less time to eat. Anyway, I'm off out to the horses. Wash up, would you?'

Faith sighed, cleared up the few dishes from the table and took them to the sink. She watched her mother stroll out across the yard, stopping only to stamp out the stub of her cigarette before she reached the stables. Rex cocked his leg on some plants before trotting obligingly beside her, while Sam and Otis lollopped ahead, smiling in the way that only Labradors can.

Faith had a quick look in the cupboards for biscuits that might help fill her up but finding none went upstairs to her room. She thankfully peeled off her riding clothes, cursing jodhpurs for being the unflattering garment that they were and replaced them with some comfortable jeans, a long shirt and an equally long, baggy cardigan. Tidying as she did so, she put away some clean laundry that had been left on her dressing table before turning on the radio, and lying on the bed. She felt ill at ease after yet another difficult meal with Glenda. Plus, she still felt ravenous. Rolling over to open the drawer in her bedside table, Faith smiled to herself a little, she extracted three giant bars of milk chocolate, which she had hidden underneath some medical magazines. She laid them out carefully on the bed, spending a few moments deciding which to have first. Slowly peeling off the wrapper and foil, she snapped off a small piece before sucking and licking on the row of squares.

How delicious it tasted.

Determined to make her secret feast last as long as possible, Faith nibbled daintily before reaching out for more and stolidly made her way through the first bar. Ignoring the fact that she was beyond the point of feeling full, greed took over and she tore open the next bar and started to stuff the chocolate into her mouth in a haphazard and grotesque manner, barely swallowing one mouthful before cramming more, oblivious of the dark brown sticky rivulet that was running down her chin and onto her clean shirt. There was something totally irresistible momentarily about the sensation in her mouth, the sweetness, the smoothness and the comfort it produced but how rapidly this feeling dissipated to be replaced by those of a completely opposite dimension.

Chocolate finished, Faith was sitting on the edge of her bed, nauseous, bloated and regretting every mouthful. She hated herself for having no self control. The waistband of her jeans was digging into her flesh, so she stood up and aimlessly meandered around the room, pausing to look in the mirror. In reality her reflection showed an unhappy but potentially pretty woman who was only a few pounds overweight but all that Faith could see was a fat, blotchy blob who repulsed her. A vision of her mother's admonitory face seemed to peer over her shoulder, mocking her weight and shape.

'This has got to stop,' Faith reprimanded herself. 'I look gross and I feel disgusting. This has positively got to be the last time I do this.'

How many times had she made this vow?

She wearily made her way into her small en-suite bathroom, closed the door, took a deep breath and knelt in front of the toilet. Sticking her fingers down her throat, she forced herself to vomit, an ungainly sight as she heaved repeatedly until she believed her stomach to be completely empty.

Chapter Two

One of the professors at Faith's medical school told her one day, when she was struggling with some of the finer anatomical points of the abdomen, 'The artery to the spleen is tortuous. It's like life, full of ups and downs.' The same could be said for Faith's continuous battle with her weight.

As a young child and continuing into her adolescence, meals in the Faber household never assumed the regularity that they did in most other homes. With Dennis away more than he was present and Glenda, who seemed to be able to survive on next to nothing, too preoccupied with her horses to give anything more than a cursory thought to the nutrition of her daughter, breakfast was eaten on the go, lunch Faith would make for herself from whatever she could find and the evening meal would be either a take-away, a trip to the local pub, which fortunately welcomed children, or a hastily thrown together affair which relied heavily on the use of the microwave and the existence of ready made meals.

Weekends and holidays, particularly in the summer, were usually spent travelling to horse shows in Glenda's vast horsebox, which boasted luxury living accommodation, including a kitchen, though this was rarely used for anything other than boiling up the kettle for a cup of tea. While Glenda was preparing for her classes, she would absent-mindedly hand over money to Faith to buy herself something to eat, knowing from the aromas that wafted temptingly in the breeze that there were nearby wagons selling bacon sandwiches, greasy pork rolls with apple sauce and hot dogs – food that always tastes better when eaten outside.

Faith sat on the ramp of the box, sharing her spoils with her pony, Christmas, before reluctantly saddling up and taking part in a showing class, being led by Glenda who muttered continuously at her, telling her to sit up, keep her heels down and watch the pony's mouth.

In the increasingly rare times when Dennis put in an appearance, he absolved his guilt at not being there for his daughter, of whom he was enormously fond, by showering her with gifts, which inevitably included chocolates, nestling neatly in huge boxes and bags of the sugary confections that he had enjoyed in his own youth. There was nothing that he and Faith liked better than to cuddle together in the evenings, watching television and dipping into bowls of treats in a conspiratorial fashion, knowing that Glenda would utterly disapprove if she walked in.

By the time she was sixteen, Faith was considerably overweight, with a penchant for all the foods that were bad for her but no knowledge that the situation ought to change. She had a new horse, Silas, Christmas having been outgrown and thus sold to some friends and replaced briefly by Alfie, a finely boned Arab cross whose unpleasant disposition resulted in him only staying with them for a few weeks before being re-homed. Faith and Silas had a lot in common. Both were reliable, liked to take life at a leisurely pace and shared a hatred of gymkhanas and all that they involved. Glenda, in her customarily dismissive way wanted to sell him but Faith, with the help of Dennis, persuaded her not to and she spent many happy hours grooming him and ambling around the countryside on him.

Coerced into joining the local hunt's junior members club, Faith unwillingly went along to the social events, despite her appeals that she had homework to do. It was at one of these where she first fell in love, or perhaps more accurately developed her first crush. His name was Paul. Two years older than she, he was tall, slightly gawky in stature but with a potentially attractive face, which was still struggling with adolescent acne. He asked Faith out to a party, following which they became inseparable for several months. Faith, experiencing emotions she had never felt before, lost her appetite and her usual longing to eat was substituted by a longing to hear from, or be with Paul. Without realising what was happening to her, the weight started to drop off and she suddenly found that she needed smaller clothes and that she rather liked her new-found figure. It was decidedly nice to be able to choose garments that clung to her shape and showed it off to its full advantage, rather than resorting to the loose and baggy as she had done before.

Paul went off to university, leaving behind a bereft Faith. All his protestations of love and promises to remain faithful lasted approximately two weeks. The daily telephone calls ceased and

14

Faith was mortified to learn, via a third party, that he was sleeping with not just a new girlfriend, but one of his tutors as well. In her grief, she stagnated in her bedroom, wore black for days on end and listened to morose music, played at a prohibitively loud volume. Glenda made a brief attempt to penetrate her daughter's gloom by putting her head round the bedroom door one morning, shouting at the top of her voice and asking if Faith wanted to go riding. The monosyllabic expletive that emitted from under the duvet was enough to make Glenda give up, go downstairs and smoke two cigarettes in quick succession before picking up the telephone and barking at Dennis to come home and sort out his daughter. But before he had had time to return from whichever part of the world he was at that time working in, Faith had emerged and decided that the road to consolation lay in food.

Back went on all the weight that she had lost and by the time Faith started at medical school she was as heavy as she had ever been. Commuting to her studies on a daily basis did nothing to help as she had to walk past shops full of temptations. Isolated from most of her colleagues who were living in halls of residence or sharing houses, she made few true friends. Determined to work to the best of her ability, she found herself sitting on the front row of seats in the lecture theatre, next to a small group of ardent students who attempted to write down lectures verbatim.

Her socialising rarely strayed further than a coffee and a sandwich at lunchtime or perhaps tea and cake in between afternoon lectures, hardly the best foundation for forming lasting relationships with either sex. There were some bonuses however. The coffee shop at the medical school boasted the best and fruitiest scones on the campus and the hospital restaurant never failed to serve up one carbohydrate-rich menu after another. Chips were available twenty-four hours a day. Sponge puddings, pies and crumbles, thick sauces and custards featured regularly on the menu to fortify the hungry doctors and nurses. Next door in the snack bar, for those not wanting a sit-down meal, there were crisps and sandwiches, the latter made with crusty fresh rolls and thick slices of cheese or ham. Plus each day there was a different sort of cake and it wasn't long before Faith discovered that a cappuccino made with full-fat milk plus a wedge of cake was very restorative after a testing ward round with a draconian consultant.

After qualifying, which she did with honours, and a rather humiliating graduation ceremony to which both Dennis and Glenda came but refused to speak to one another, Faith started her first jobs in hospital, the second of which was on the surgical wards. Living in hospital accommodation while she was on call and with a busy, unpredictable lifestyle, she was almost totally reliant on the hospital catering to sustain her, well aware that when she did go home, Glenda would have only done the minimum of shopping, if any at all. Snatching food when she could, Faith discovered the left-over cakes from the patients' afternoon tea – most of them were too woozy still from their anaesthetics to want food and the fact that the nurses would share out left-over lunches in the ward kitchen once everyone who could eat had been fed. It was amazing how a bowl of treacle sponge and custard would cheer her up for an afternoon in theatre or the outpatient clinic. The patients were also generous to the staff, leaving boxes of sweets and chocolates regularly in their delight at being discharged and these would be left open on the nursing station for everyone to help themselves.

Faith enjoyed the job thoroughly. She loved talking to the patients, examining them carefully and organising all the relevant investigations for the consultant. It was during one interview with a new patient, who had come in for a routine hernia repair, that something upset her. Perched on the side of his bed, she had been through the ritual of asking questions about each of his bodily functions and was inquiring about his home life and whether he smoked or drank alcohol. Smoothing down his new dressing gown, which had been bought specially for this occasion, as had the paisley pyjamas underneath, Derek McNabb was enjoying chatting to this affable young doctor, who was being very thorough.

'So, you've never smoked, that's good. Do you drink at all?'

'Just a wee dram at bedtime,' came the reply.

Faith recorded this fact in the patient's notes.

'Who is there at home? Are you married?'

Derek nodded.

'Yes, I've a lovely wife. She's beautiful. You remind me of her a bit – you're both lovely and chubby.'

Faith allowed his words to sink in, feeling uncomfortable, before hastily bringing her questions to a conclusion, extracting some blood from his right arm and ensuring that he had signed the consent form for his operation. She hurried down the ward, still smarting from his words. She had never thought of herself as chubby. That was another word for fat.

That weekend, after some covert rustling through books in a nearby newsagent's on weight loss, Faith started a diet. Eschewing fruit and vegetables, she consumed vast amounts of protein and drank gallons of water. Though constipated and slightly dizzy, the weight dropped off steadily and as it did, her self-confidence started to grow. Very slowly, she started to hang out more with her contemporaries. She would join them in the doctors' mess for a drink in the evening, go out for a meal and she even braved one or two riotous parties, though left these early. Her improved self esteem also proved valuable at home and much to her surprise she accepted an invitation to a barbecue at one of Glenda's horse-riding friend's home. It was here that she met Jonty.

A piping hot sausage had leapt off the barbecue, burning his hand and Faith was summoned to the kitchen, as the only guest with any medical knowledge, to settle an argument about whether butter or water was the appropriate first aid. Having dealt efficiently with what was in reality a very minor injury, she found that she was monopolised by the young man for the rest of the evening. He was muscular and striking to look at, with the chiselled features that reminded her of Easter Island statues, and it seemed incongruous to her that he should want to spend time with her. To start with she assumed that he was simply being gracious, politely asking about her work and telling her about his new horse (which Faith thought sounded particularly frightening) to while away a few minutes before he could respectably excuse himself and go back to join his friends. But he was an accomplished talker, with the gift of making Faith feel at ease and after a few rather hesitant starts, she was chatting away happily. The evening wore on and he showed no inclination to mingle with or speak to anyone else. Glenda passed them by a couple of times, once on the way to fill up her glass of gin, the second out of raw curiosity, raised an eyebrow, smirked and patted Jonty on the shoulder in what Faith hoped very much he would not interpret as a patronising way.

He interrogated her thoroughly, finding out what her likes and dislikes were, where she hoped to go on holiday and what car she drove. There was also the matter of his arm, which at some point, Faith was not sure when, had become draped casually over her shoulders, something that she found secretly rather pleasant but unnerving. He was attentive to her needs, bringing her slices of key lime pie, wickedly rich and calorie stuffed, which they shared and topping up her glass of wine. As the evening drew to a close, Faith steeled herself for the inevitable let down, when they went their separate ways, predicting that Jonty, who was too much of a gentleman not to, would dutifully write down her telephone number but then somehow never get round to ringing it. There being no sign of Glenda, Jonty invited Faith to share a taxi with him and continued to chat in the same relaxed fashion before dropping her off at the house, where he leapt out to open the door for her. Taking her completely by surprise, he kissed her briefly but firmly on the lips and made sure that she was safely inside before driving off.

Jonty had asked for her number and Faith imagined that she would be waiting anxiously and pessimistically for him to contact her. But, true to his word, he rang the very next morning, asked how she was, hoped she had enjoyed the party as much as he had and invited her to join him in town for croissants, coffee and the Sunday papers. Faith had been horrified. She was dressed in a rather horrid looking candlewick dressing gown which she had had since she was seventeen and had a particular affection for, her hair was sticking up in a number of different directions and most of last night's make up was still smeared all over her face, because she had been too lazy to remove it before flopping into bed.

She tried hard to find an excuse why she couldn't meet up with him, afraid that he would be put off by the sight of her in the cold light of the morning after, but his insistence had been too great to resist. She showered, washed and tamed her hair as best she could, dressed in jeans, a large shirt which she left untucked and an enormously baggy cardigan, which, when wrapped around her was capable of hiding a multitude of corporeal sins. Nervously, she drove to their appointed meeting place, glad that there was no sign of Glenda who might have wanted to know where she was going. On her arrival, she was terrified that he might not bother to turn up, mindless of the fact that he was the instigator of the arrangement. She peered, in a worried fashion, through the window and spotted, to her relief and delight that he was already there, laughing with one of the waiters but keeping a watch out for her.

Jonty behaved impeccably as he had done the night before. He put Faith at ease and after some awkward silences, the combination of freshly brewed coffee, warm pastries and much in the papers to generate congenial discussion –Jonty having cleverly bought a selection of tabloids and broadsheets- Faith knew she was enjoying herself thoroughly and felt more than a twinge of disappointment when it was time for her to go and work a shift at the local A&E department. However, armed with a date for dinner later in the week, she had levity in her step that she had not felt for a long time and an excitingly apprehensive flutter in her heart.

The following month was magical. Jonty was romantic and thoughtful. He did not ask her to sleep with him and Faith, who considered that she was very much of a novice in that department, appreciated the way he put no pressure on her while at the same time was worried that he had not. By the time they did spend their first night together, Faith was completely smitten with him and his confession that he had fallen madly in love with her were surely the most wonderful words she had ever heard. He was an exciting, but demanding lover and Faith felt self conscious of her inexperience. He took her to some amazing places, they rode together, he came with her to watch Glenda compete and he even rang her at work to enquire affectionately how she was.

Much to her surprise, Faith found that Glenda and Jonty got on famously. She had worried that her mother would not want her to get involved with anyone, find fault and be critical, perhaps even be rude to his face but on the contrary, Glenda was welcoming and magnanimous, always happy to put the kettle on and sit down with them for a cup of tea, usually to talk horses.

In the earliest days of their relationship, when days would pass without her seeing him, Faith, afraid that his silence was an indication of his ardour cooling, developed her own coping strategy, finding solace in, as usual, food. This was when she started to binge. Yearning to be slim and desirable for him, yet unable to stop herself from retreating into her time-honoured safety blanket of chocolate, biscuits and cakes, jam, ice cream and sugar, she had to find a way to prevent the weight from piling on. The first time that a whole two days passed with no contact from him, she stuffed and gorged herself to the point of gagging. Sitting on the edge of her bed, head in her hands, hair falling around her face, her shoulders heaved with sobs. Glenda, listening at the door as she happened to be passing, merely tutted and walked on, not wanting anything to spoil her own delight at having won the novice class at the Exelby three-day event.

Faith, oblivious to her mother, continued to weep, her sobs interspersed by hiccoughs and painful belches. So full, she knew that she had to vomit. She had read about patients with eating disorders. She had even done a case presentation when she was doing her student attachment in psychiatry about a young girl with anorexia. She knew how they made themselves sick and had always thought this incredible. Trembling, her heart pounding, she crept into her bathroom, drank a pint glass of water, leant over and put her fingers down her throat. It was horrible.
She loathed herself for doing it.

As time went by and it became clear that Jonty was quite content to be a constant in her life, she continued to vomit after meals and even though she repeatedly made mental promises that it would never happen again, to her horror, the whole process became sickeningly easy.

Chapter Three

Faith was up early the next morning, simultaneously anxious and excited about her interview. True to his word, Jonty had rung back in the early evening, working late again and promising to meet her later today. He'd sounded pleased for her about the potential job, making her promise to ring him as soon as she'd left the surgery to tell him how it had gone.

Stretching out under the bedcovers, Faith wondered what to wear that might make a good first impression. Outside, she could hear Glenda already shouting at one of the girls who came in on a daily basis to help with the horses and the dogs barking as they rushed about in search of early morning rabbits in the paddocks. She got up and wrapped her favourite dressing gown around her before padding downstairs to make a cup of tea, which she then stood with at the back door while she gazed across the fields outside. It was a glorious morning, fresh with the promise of a sunny, warm day. The air was pure and untainted as it hit her lungs; just magical. Had she not had a prior engagement, it would have been a perfect morning for a ride, but then she remembered Caspian and the tussle they had had the day before which she had only survived through the skin of her teeth.

Back upstairs, she threw open her wardrobe doors and surveyed the contents. She picked out the navy suit which she always wore for interviews, a pair of tailored beige trousers and a cream blouse, which she felt might be appropriate for a country practice and a long black skirt which was cosy and comfortable and went with a multitude of tops. Various trial runs ensued. The suit looked good, she decided, but she would have to keep the jacket on at all times so that no one was wise to the fact that the waistband did not meet and a button had to be left undone. Not happy, she tried on the trousers, which did at least fit nicely but was beige a good colour for someone of her size? Would they notice the very visible evidence of her pants underneath? But the blouse was smart and with a long jacket, which again would have to be kept on at all times, the overall effect was pleasing. Much happier, she removed her clothes, had a bath and washed her hair.

Finally ready, she went down to find Glenda to tell her she was off but there was no sign other than a handful of stubbed-out cigarettes in an old saucer on the table. She wandered down to the stable yard and was met by a barrage of muddy paws as the three dogs jumped up at her in ecstasy at her appearance, leaving their mark all over her clean trousers. Despairing, Faith ran back to the house and up to her bedroom. There was no way she would wear the suit so it would just have to be the black skirt with the same blouse. The effect was not as smart but she looked clean and tidy.

Leaving a note on the kitchen table for her mother, Faith drove off in her car, down the winding drive onto the equally narrow lane. Negotiating each bend with care she was not surprised to find herself face to face with Glenda, looking calm on top of a snorting Caspian, who took a sideways leap into the hedge at the sight of a vehicle. Glenda, nonplussed, dealt with the situation with skill.

'I'm off, Ma. I'll see you later. Jonty's coming round this evening. I expect we'll go down to the pub for something to eat.'

'Okay,' replied Glenda, Caspian reversing now across the lane. 'Good luck.'

Gently, she eased her car past the horse, whose eyes were out on stalks, sweat dripping down his shoulders, a testament to the rigours of his recent exercise. Driving along, she rehearsed in her mind how she might answer certain questions, if asked. It was vital she did well.

The first sign that she was approaching the small market town of Lambdale was the sight of the church spire, rising proudly up above the trees and a row of holiday cottages which backed onto the river. Crossing over the hump-backed bridge, narrowly avoiding a large on-coming tractor, she drove up the slight hill to the market square, keeping one eye open for the medical centre, which she had been informed was very close by. Fortunately, it was not market day, so there were plenty of parking spaces and she chose a convenient spot just opposite an attractive hotel, the name of which was completely obscured by the untamed jungle of red ivy that suffocated the walls. Around the perimeter of the square were a variety of different shops, with inviting names – a delicatessen called Delicious, an old-fashioned sweet shop, Goody Gumdrops and a gift and craft shop, Mumbo Jumbo. Exploration would have to wait until later, thought Faith, stopping the first person she saw to ask directions. Checking her appearance for a final time in the wing mirror of her car, not an easy task, Faith walked towards her destination, trying to control her breathing and, with five minutes to spare, walked in through the open doors.

To her surprise, she was welcomed by two receptionists, one of whom was male. He came round from behind the counter, introduced himself as Gary and escorted her up to the meeting room where he informed her the doctors were waiting. Faith could feel her heart thumping and her armpits sticky with sweat as Gary knocked on the door before opening it and ushering her in.

Thirty minutes later, Faith was waiting to have coffee with her new working colleagues, ecstatic that they had wasted no time in offering her the job and promising to start the following week. It was a four-partner practice. The senior partner, John Britton, was cheery and round faced, a feature only emphasised by the bow tie that he wore. His short-sleeved, checked shirt and corduroy trousers seemed to epitomise the traditional country GP and Faith suspected that he might well have a tweed sports jacket with leather patches on the elbows. He had been reading the *Yorkshire Post* when she'd walked in and his first question had been to ask her to solve one of the clues he was stuck with in the crossword, which had taken her aback but also taken away some of her nerves. Sitting next to him was Ellie Bonnington, who was simply gorgeous. With shoulder-length titian hair, faultless complexion and a figure to die for, she seemed unaware of the impact she created and came across as friendly and welcoming. The third partner was Ed Diamond, etiolated but wiry, a shock of black hair falling across his forehead. He'd asked Faith what her hobbies were away from medicine and expressed an interest in the fact that she rode, informing her that his greatest passion was rock- climbing. Immediately Faith could imagine him in black Lycra, scuttling up a rock face like a spider.

The interview had gone amazingly quickly. The questions had been straightforward. Faith's accomplishments were evident from her CV and the partners seemed more intent on establishing that she would fit in from a personality point of view than finding out about her medical knowledge.

Ellie handed her a mug of coffee and offered her a plate of biscuits, which Faith refused.

'We're so grateful that you can start immediately. Clare, the partner who's off sick, has left a huge gap to be filled and we're really struggling.'

'I'm really glad to help. I'm sorry to hear about Clare. What happened?'

Faith momentarily wondered whether she should have asked but Ellie carried on chatting quite happily.

'Unfortunately, she became very depressed and tried to take her own life...'

Faith gasped.

'...she's actually doing quite well now. There were a lot of underlying problems, which hopefully she's sorting out now, but you know how these things take time.'

'Yes, they do. I expect she'll be feeling guilty that she's not at work as well.'

Ellie nodded. 'Yes, she thinks she's let us all down and that we don't value her any more. That's just the negativity of her depression talking, really. I'm hopeful she'll be fine but when she'll be back at work, I haven't a clue. I suppose it's possible that she might not come back at all, or perhaps just part time.'

Faith wondered what to say and chose to change the subject. 'You mentioned that you were a training practice. Do you have a registrar at the moment?'

'Yes,' Ellie answered, pausing to take a sip of her coffee and a bite of a chocolate biscuit. Faith envied the natural way she ate it without giving it a second thought. 'He's called Rob Craven and it's his first year in general practice. He's a nice chap, very shy and unsure at the moment but I'm sure that Ed will soon bring him out of his shell. He's the trainer now – Clare used to do it but obviously...'

Faith gazed into her cup, hoping for inspiration. She could not help but notice that Ellie was upset and she felt gauche and clumsy.

'This is a lovely building you have here,' she managed finally. 'Some of the places where I've done locums before have had very poor premises, very old fashioned and not very practical.'

'I'll show you around before you go. You'll be using Clare's surgery but I'm sure she wouldn't mind if you wanted to put some of her things to one side and bring in some of your own – you know, photos, paintings.'

'That sounds lovely. It'll be great just knowing that I've got my own room. I'd be really careful with anything that belonged to Clare, of course.'

Ed and John joined them and they chatted amiably for some further time before Elliot Douglas came in, arms full of papers and files, to whisk Faith off to his office to complete some administrative details. Ellie waited for her to return and then obliged with the promised guided tour.

It was a triumphant Faith who left the building, shaking everyone's hand before she left and saying, quite genuinely, that she couldn't wait to start working with them. Outside once more in the by now hot sunshine, she virtually ran back to her car to find her mobile phone and ring first Jonty, who was just as pleased as she'd hoped and then Glenda, who, not surprisingly, was not in. She then walked around the square, peeping into all the shops one by one. She bought a rather lovely ornament of a Labrador, crafted by a local artist who clearly understood the breed and had captured the adoring look in the eyes perfectly. She thought it would look just right on her desk at work. She then browsed around Goody Gumdrops, feeling that she had stepped back in time as she gazed at row after row of jars containing brightly coloured sweets before buying pomfret cakes and pear drops, at the same time wishing that her father was with her to share in her delight. Suddenly hungry and discovering to her amazement that it was midday, Faith entered the delicatessen, which she noticed had a small café attached, ordered an iced coffee (with local home-made ice cream) and a generous wedge of coffee and walnut gateau, the size of which would probably have fed a family of four quite comfortably. But, she calculated, she deserved a treat. She'd acquitted herself well and now had a job, with a six-month contract in the first instance and the prospect of this being extended as necessary. Every mouthful was delicious. The sponge and cream filling slipped down orgasmically and the sweetness of her drink simply left her wanting more. She looked longingly at the array of other cakes and pastries, was tempted but today Faith was able to resist. She was too happy and content. Full of self-confidence from her recent success, she got up, smoothed down the black skirt, brushing off some stray crumbs and walked out, leaving a generous tip on the table.

Wanting to share her joy, she bought a bunch of flowers for Glenda and a little painting of the market square which she planned to give to Jonty when she saw him that evening. Before driving off, she tried ringing Dennis but he was unavailable, so she simply left a message on his voicemail and promised to try again later. He was currently working in Japan, but it should still have been early enough for him not to have gone to bed.

Back at home, she found Glenda in the garden, laid out on a smart sun lounger and sporting a candy pink swimsuit. She seemed quite touched with the flowers and Faith took them inside to arrange in a vase before changing into a T-shirt and baggy linen trousers and making two long, iced drinks which she took outside with her. Trying hard to keep cool in the shadow of the seats were the dogs, panting rather histrionically but refusing to be shut inside where they could take advantage of the cold, stone flags. Faith went and fetched their water bowl, filling it to the brim for them so that they could quench their thirst.

Glenda lit up a cigarette and took a long drag.

'It went well, I take it,' she commented.

'Brilliant,' agreed Faith. 'I start on Monday.'

'Good. Is it a big practice?'

Though not particularly interested in her daughter's career, Glenda had grasped enough information at an elementary level to know some apposite questions to ask.

Faith happily filled her mother in with all the details, chatting on, describing the building, the partners, the staff and the town, unaware that after the first five minutes or so, Glenda had fallen into a deep sleep and was snoring gently.

Jonty picked her up just after seven. He arrived with his father Hamish whose profile was a facsimile of his own and she showed them into the garden before running up to change. It was still so warm that Faith dared to wear a sundress with tiny spaghetti straps, which she felt was fairly flattering, plus her arms were quite toned from all the riding and tanned from the recent sunny weather. She breathed in his aftershave as he enveloped her in a bear hug when she joined them. He was looking as happy as she felt. They sat with Glenda, who, Faith was relieved to see, had covered the lower half of her body with a matching sarong and shared the best part of a bottle of wine. Hamish and Glenda had been friends for years and both were very much in favour of the blossoming romance between their children. Hamish, who owned a small stud that bred Cleveland Bays, was a wealthy widower, his wife having died almost a decade ago when she slid gracefully down her horse's neck when it refused to jump a fence, but landed at an angle and fractured her neck. Faith had often wondered if there was any possibility of her mother and Hamish becoming romantically involved. She felt that it might be the best thing that could happen to Glenda, that it might soften her prickly exterior and melt away the layers of bitterness and self-protection that had moulded around her since the divorce. But Glenda showed no sign whatsoever of a pending thaw in her armour.

Glancing at his watch, Jonty stood up and pulled Faith to her feet, insisting that it was time for them to make a move as he had booked a table. Hand in hand they took their leave, but not before Faith had taken out a second bottle of wine for their parents to start on.

It was only a few minutes stroll to the local pub, The Green Dragon, recently whitewashed so that it stood out from the other houses in the village and tastefully decorated with symmetrical hanging baskets full of multicoloured blooms. Though Faith thought it was rather a waste of such a beautiful summer's evening, Jonty led her inside and the two of them were shown to a tiny table in a dark corner of the lounge bar. Aromatic fragrances permeated out from the kitchen and Faith felt her stomach rumble in anticipation. As was often the case, their choices were identical, scallops to start with, rump steak for the main course, rare for Jonty and well done for Faith, with the traditional accompaniments of chips, onion rings and mushrooms.

Jonty listened attentively while Faith recounted the exciting details of her day and thought, not for the first time, how beautiful she could be when she was animated and full of happiness. The arrival of their starters silenced them both as they tucked in, only pausing to mutter their appreciation of each mouthful.

Replete after the main course and resting before dessert, they sat back and Jonty put his arm around Faith. She snuggled into his shoulder contentedly, feeling blissful and rested her hand on his thigh. He turned his head, kissed her softly on the side of her forehead and then rather destroyed the moment by jumping up saying that he was bursting to go to the toilet. Leaving her with the pudding menu, he disappeared. Faith surveyed the choices before her, unable to decide between jam roly-poly and custard or kiwi fruit pavlova, which she knew from previous dining experiences would be heaped up with not just with cream but also ice cream and topped generously with chocolate sauce. Musing to herself, weighing up the pros and cons of each one, she was startled by Jonty's voice.

'Faith, darling?'

She looked round and saw that he was on bended knee before her. In his outstretched hand was a small jeweller's box. From the corner of her eye she could see the other people in the pub turning to watch them and even Guy, the landlord, had frozen mid pint-pulling to see what happened next.

'Jonty!' she gasped, incredulous.

'Faith, will you do me the honour of becoming my wife?'

'Jonty!' she repeated, unable to say anything else.

She looked deep into his eyes, unable to see anything other than his love.

'Please?' he prompted.

As if to help her make up her mind, he opened the box to reveal a large, diamond solitaire, which sparkled richly in the dimmed light of the pub.

'Oh, Jonty, I'd love to.'

Barely had she time to finish her affirmative reply before her fiancé had bounced up, dragged her to her feet and was kissing her passionately on the lips whilst all around them clapped and cheered.

Guy, primed earlier by Jonty who was confident of being accepted, approached them bearing chilled champagne, which he opened with a flourish, causing Faith to recoil as the cork flew across the room. Jonty insisted on buying a drink for everyone and Faith, heady with her new-found status, kissed neighbours and strangers on the cheek as they came up to congratulate her.

When the excitement had finally died down and the regulars had gone back to their usual seats and resumed their conversations about the weather, politics and the impossible questions in the pub quiz earlier in the week, they took their desserts, Faith had gone for the pavlova, which Guy had decorated for her with a sparkler, into the garden and sat, hand in hand, eating and feeding each other, whispering and laughing as the sun set over the trees and the dusk came down. Faith alternately had her left arm stretched out in front of her, so that she could admire Jonty's choice of ring from afar, or bent up close to her face so that she could marvel at the brilliance of the gem. She was reluctant to bring the evening to a close but Guy called time, scooping up their glasses in a rather final way and so she and Jonty started off on the short stroll home.

But Jonty had another surprise in store for Faith. Steering her towards a five-bar gate, he opened it and led her into the field. Unable to believe what she guessed was about to happen, Faith was erotically appalled. As he kissed her almost ferociously, she felt her knees buckle beneath her and they fell onto the grass where he proceeded to make rather rough love to her, thinking of his own needs and desire for rapid relief than hers for tenderness and affection. He fell off her, having climaxed alone, and they lay side by side gazing up at the sky, which was as clear as it can be only in the countryside, unspoilt by the exudates of mankind.

Faith, drunk and unsatisfied, felt slightly sick from too much food and drink but still her over-riding emotion was how thrilling the evening had been.

Brushing the grass from her dress, Faith laughed half-heartedly, watching Jonty pull up his trousers and tuck his shirt in. She hoped that there were no telltale stains on her dress. If there were then Glenda would be sure to spot them. Jonty made her jog back to the house, eager to make an announcement, unwilling to take into account the high heeled mules that Faith was wearing that more or less forbade any pace other than a controlled walk.

Hamish and Glenda were still in the garden. Some tin-foil dishes were all that remained of an Indian takeaway, the lion's share of which would have been downed by Hamish who frequently admitted to gluttony as one of his hobbies. Glenda was smoking and drinking what looked like another gin and tonic; Hamish was puffing on a cigar, bottle of beer in his hand, obviously in the middle of some long story about a horse. The two of them looked up expectantly at the arrival of their offspring, both of them having been privy to the purpose of the evening for some time.

Faith thrust her left hand under her mother's nose. 'Jonty's asked me to marry him and I've said yes.'

Hamish applauded loudly and raised his beer bottle to the two of them.

'Congratulations, darling,' Glenda boomed, turning her cheek so that she could be kissed by both her daughter and her prospective son- in-law. She then proceeded to study Faith's ring in minute detail.

'When's the wedding?' asked Hamish.

Faith and Jonty looked at each other.

'We thought at the end of this year,' Faith informed them, suddenly feeling rather shy.

'Late November probably,' Jonty added.

'Perfect,' agreed Hamish. 'Plenty of time to make preparations. You'll be busy from now on, eh, Glenda? Flowers, dresses, receptions – all that sort of thing.'

'Oh, I expect Faith will do most of it, she's far more organised than I am. She'll have her work cut out though to have it all sorted by then. Although of course, if there is anything I can do to help, I'll be there for her.'

'I must tell Pa,' added Faith, ignoring the bilious look that appeared on her mother's face as soon as she uttered these words. 'I'll have to work out what time it is over there. Shall we go and look at dresses tomorrow, Ma?'

Glenda inhaled deeply and let the smoke from her cigarette loiter in her respiratory system before she breathed out, thus allowing time for composure.

She turned and smiled sweetly.

'Darling, as Hamish says, there's plenty of time for preparations. No need to look at dresses yet as I'm sure you'll want to lose a stone or more before your big day. Let's leave that for a few months.'

Faith, acutely embarrassed, looked down at the ground, grateful for the appearance of Otis who wanted his ears scratched.

'Yes, of course, I expect you're right. But I think Jonty loves me for who I am, not what I look like.'

Her fiancé came and stood by her.

'Of course I do, Faith. I adore you as you are. But, don't you think your ma's got a point? You really are carrying a bit too much flesh and all brides like to be slim, don't they? So this really would be the perfect incentive to get some weight off and I'd love you even more for doing it.'

Chapter Four

After Jonty had gone, Faith headed for her bedroom to consider the enormity of his comment. She tried hard to be positive and recapture the exhilaration she had felt earlier, but was persistently haunted by his words. Though she was used to the constant carping from her mother, she'd never experienced criticism of her size from Jonty; indeed he had repeatedly admired and complimented her on her looks, so this most recent revelation came as something of a bombshell.

She wept for a while, clutching the ring in her hands before putting it carefully on the bedside table when she went to shower, fearing that if it got wet then it would lose some of its sparkle. Only a couple of hours ago they had been in the pub garden, chatting intimately, lost in their own tiny world, untouchable, invincible.

Snuggling down under the duvet in the dark she heard Hamish slamming his car door and driving off and then the reassuring sounds of her mother's final ritual of the day, letting the dogs out for a final pee, locking all the doors and switching off the lights. She heard Glenda and the dogs stomping upstairs and the bedroom door shutting firmly behind them – Glenda was a great believer in the dogs sleeping with her.

For Faith, sleep was elusive. She let what she hoped was a decent interval elapse before creeping stealthily down to the kitchen in search of comfort. There was little to be had. As usual, shopping had been right at the bottom of Glenda's list of priorities. After a degree of frantic searching finally, to her relief, Faith found a packet of biscuits at the back of a cupboard and ignoring the fact that they were well past their sell-by date, crunched on them, one after another, ripping off the wrappers, forcing the wayward crumbs into her mouth, paying little if any attention to their taste. Before she had finished, she was already wondering what she could have next. Struck by a brainwave she looked in the bread bin, where to her delight there was a whole loaf of cheap, sliced white bread, which

Glenda had bought to hide medication in when worming the horses. Starting off with toast and jam, Faith soon ran out of patience and abandoned this for the quicker option of soft pasty bread which felt so good as she bit into it, jam oozing from the sides, thick margarine greasing up her fingers as she did so. Half a loaf later, discarded crusts around her, she was hungry for something different and found ice cream in the freezer. Adding drinking chocolate powder and cream to this, she ate straight from the tub, sitting on the kitchen floor, too lazy to look for a bowl and past the point of caring, having been overtaken by her compulsion. It was as though she was being controlled by an outside force; much as she wanted to stop, there was simply no way that she could.

Finally, when she was bloated, belching and ashamed, her feast came to an end and she leant back against the cupboards trying not to look at the debris of wrappers, dollops of luridly red jam and cardboard tubs around her. Suddenly she was frightened by a noise above, possibly someone moving about and she rapidly gathered up the mess to dispose of the evidence as best she could. Tiptoeing back up to her bed, she made the obligatory detour to her bathroom, to relieve herself as quietly as she could – not easy, but certainly possible for one as skilled in the art of inducing emesis as she was.

The following morning, Faith slept in. On rising, she dressed, carefully checked that there were no signs in the bathroom to incriminate her and ran downstairs, surprised to find that she felt a lot better than anticipated. Usually after a bad binge, she could wake with what felt like a bad hangover, tongue coated, mouth parched, bile rising in her throat, heady and shaky. So maybe it was a combination of her newly acquired status – that of having a fiancé – the glorious sunny day that met her when she stepped out of the open back door and the effusive welcome from the dogs, paws all wet from scavenging in the early morning grass, that made Faith uncharacteristically optimistic. Singing a little, she poured a glass of chilled pineapple juice and made a cup of coffee. Guiltily spotting a jam stain, she hurriedly wiped it up, preferring there to be no visible reminders of her indiscretions of the previous evening.

Jonty and Glenda were right. Of course she wanted to be slender for her wedding. What girl didn't? How wonderful would it be to feel fantastic, turn heads as she walked down the aisle and have photos that she could cherish for life? She would show them that she could lose weight. She had done it before and she could do it again, but this time, it would be different. The weight would stay off because she would be happy. Her new-found svelte and willowy figure would ensure that Jonty always adored her and he would be the envy of all his friends.

Checking the clock, she dialled her father's number, not expecting him to answer but he did. Bubbling, she told him her news. He was thrilled for her. He and Hamish had, some years before, been regular golf partners and so Jonty was someone he knew and remembered. They chatted for several minutes, both tactfully avoiding mention of Glenda's name, Dennis promising to take his daughter and her fiancé out for a celebratory meal the next time he was in the country. As they talked, Faith pondered over raising the question of whether he would come to the wedding or not, suspecting the latter as he would not want to risk ruining her day by appearing with his new wife, an event that would surely send Glenda spiralling out of control with vehemence. She decided against for the moment and had just put the phone down when Glenda appeared in the doorway.
Faith uttered a silent prayer of thanks that she had not been caught out mid- conversation.

'Jonty called in on his way to work,' Glenda announced, switching on the kettle. 'He didn't want to disturb you so asked me to tell you that he'll be back at lunchtime with a friend of his father's who is going to take your photo.'

'Photo?' queried Faith.

'Your engagement photo. Hamish has arranged for one of his chums to take some snaps. It's a momentous occasion, you know, and I'm determined that we acknowledge it appropriately. It'll only happen once in your life.' Glenda sniffed loudly and cynically. 'If you're lucky,' she added spitefully.

Faith knew better than to argue.

'So, the two of them will come here at lunchtime. That should give you plenty of time to get ready. Use the drawing room but you might have to tidy up a bit first. Hamish and I were drinking in there after you'd gone to bed last night.'

It was a close thing but somehow Faith, perhaps driven by the thrilling sensation that was coursing through her veins, managed to get both the drawing room and herself looking respectable by the time Jonty arrived, closely followed by Hamish and a small, stubby man with an accent that would have cut glass, who was introduced as Gilbert Swaffingham.

Pleasantries exchanged, Glenda and Hamish made their excuses and retreated to the garden for a drink, but not before inviting the others to join them when they were ready. Faith and Jonty, not really knowing what to do next, positioned themselves rather traditionally in front of the mantelpiece, he with his arm draped protectively around her. But Gilbert, for all his rather unassuming appearance, was not a lover of the formal photograph and before they knew it, he had them in a variety of far more natural and easy poses. Faith found that she was, for once, enjoying the experience of being photographed, something that she would usually try to avoid at all costs. Gilbert had the knack of being able to put them both at ease and thus any smiles or laughter that he captured on camera were genuine rather than forced.

They were both thrilled when they looked at the images on the computer once Gilbert felt that he had enough for them to choose from. It was hard to select which one they liked the most and they debated amiably for so long that Gilbert left them to it and went out to join the others. Faith's choice was one of the two of them face to face, half smiles on their faces, eyes for no one apart from each other. She thought it was wonderfully romantic and perfect for an engagement memento. Jonty, on the other hand, favoured one in which he was facing the camera, smiling broadly, with Faith curled at his feet looking up at him. Faith could not argue that he did not look extremely handsome in this photo and as their discussion started to become rather more heated, particularly from Jonty's end, she acquiesced and let him have his way, not wanting to risk any form of argument that might result if she did not.

If Gilbert was surprised by their choice, he had enough tact not to show it and promised that the photo would be ready in a couple of days and he would drop it off for them, sure of the fact that he would be passing nearby.

An impromptu party was developing in the garden as a bunch of Glenda's horse-riding friends had arrived, wanting her advice about an upcoming event, wondering if she would have the time to fit in some tuition so by the time Faith and Jonty joined them, the wine was flowing freely, Hamish had taken on the

34

mantle of host and Glenda was chattering in an animated fashion, glass and cigarette in one hand, the other gesticulating towards the stables, all the while taking care to toast her back in the baking sun. An additional surprise arrived in the form of champagne and the biggest bouquet of flowers from Dennis, which Faith managed to escape into the house with but not before Glenda had time to assume a contemptuous look.

Having had her offer to make some sandwiches accepted eagerly by all those present, Faith rushed off in her car to the nearest shops, grabbed various items off the shelves, including a loaf of sliced white bread to replace the one she had eaten most of the night before and returned to the house where everyone seemed significantly more tiddly than when she had left. She also noticed with considerable chagrin that Glenda had opened the bottle of champagne sent by Dennis and that its contents had been well and truly drained.

She made hearty sandwiches of granary bread, tuna and cheese and served these with cherry tomatoes, sticks of celery and carrots together with a bowl of hummus. On a plate she cut halved strawberries, sliced peaches and arranged these around a centrepiece of cherries and kiwi wedges. Calling Jonty to come and help, they carried out the food which was demolished in a moment by Glenda's friends who had undiscriminating appetites like locusts.

Jonty kissed Faith affectionately before leaving for work and she wandered back to join the others having waved him off and had some lunch – a carefully chosen bowl of fruits that she had saved and secreted in the fridge, away from the hungry guests. This she took outside, not wishing to appear unfriendly, and sat under one of the green umbrellas, eating while she listened to a discussion about a particularly promising youngster that Hamish was bringing on and hoped to compete with next year at some novice events.

Chapter Five

Ellie, with that sixth sense that is only bestowed on women, spotted the scintillating engagement ring within minutes of Faith arriving in the staff room on her first morning.

'Wow!' she exclaimed. 'Is that new? You weren't wearing it last week.'

Faith coloured a little. 'Yes. Isn't it fantastic? Jonty – that's my boyfriend – proposed to me last week. On the same day that you offered me this job in fact! What a wonderful day that was.'

'Let me have a closer look,' Ellie asked and Faith obliged by extending her hand.

'It's beautiful,' Ellie agreed. 'Congratulations. Look, John, Faith's got engaged.'

John Britton, entering the room with a rather heavy heart as it was another Monday morning and his weekend had, as usual, passed far too quickly for his liking, switched on a smile.

'My, that's wonderful. All the best to both of you.'

He was shortly followed by Ed, bursting in through the door with much more enthusiasm, making a beeline for the kettle but instructed by Ellie to make a detour to come and view the ring. He shook Faith's hand warmly and sounded genuinely pleased for her.

But Faith, embarrassed at being the centre of attention, sought to change the subject as soon as she could.

'I'm looking forward to my first day,' she announced.

'That's good,' agreed John. 'We've been looking forward to you joining us. Mondays are usually fairly busy, I'm afraid, but we all share the work amongst us, so we'll get through it. Ah, here's Rob. I don't think you've met him, have you?'

Faith turned to see a young man coming into the room. Ginger haired and freckled, with the pallid complexion that often goes with this colouring, Rob Craven, the current registrar, was working at the practice for a year as part of his training to become a general practitioner. He had a pile of journals under one arm and a traditional Gladstone bag, which looked not only very new but very heavy, in his other hand.

'Rob,' called Ed, summoning him over. 'Meet Faith Faber. She's come to do a long-term locum for us.'

'Hello,' began Faith, 'it's lovely to meet you.'

'You too,' replied Rob, shyly.

'Have you much more of your training to do?'

'Another two years. I've just done an obstetrics and gynaecology job before coming here.'

'Are you enjoying it?' Faith gratefully accepted a cup of tea from Ellie, who was walking round with a tray of mugs.

Rob nodded enthusiastically. 'It's great here. I'm sure you'll love it. The partners are brilliant.'

'What are you after, Rob?' laughed Ed, who, despite sitting down with his feet up on the coffee table, had been listening in.

'Nothing. Just telling it how it is. How was your weekend, Ed?'

'Good. Camping and lots of climbing in Scotland. Hope to go back again on Friday, if the weather holds up. Now, let's you and I go and have a quick ten minutes before we start surgery and then we'll have a review of who you've seen when we're done, before visits.'

'See you later,' Faith called as they left.

Ellie rinsed her mug under the tap and put it on the draining board. Drying her hands she called to Faith. 'If you're about ready, I'll go down with you, just to see you settle in.'

Faith thanked her and followed her down the stairs, all the while envying her gloriously lissom body which looked terrific in some well-tailored, low-waisted trousers and a light linen blouse.

Opening the door, they went into the surgery.

'It's weird,' commented Ellie, 'but it almost feels cold in here. Nobody's used it since Clare went off sick.'

She picked up a photo that was on top of the small bookcase, which housed a variety of textbooks and files.

'That's Clare with my daughters, Lydia and Virginia. She's their godmother.'

Faith smiled a little as she looked at two identical girls, sitting on their ponies with a small, happy-looking woman between them.

'This one's Clare and her husband David.'

They were standing close together, obviously at a posh function, Clare in a long dress, David in a bow tie and dinner jacket.

'And this is a fantastic shot of David.'

Feeling increasingly like a voyeur, Faith looked at the last photo. David was smiling broadly, the corners of his eyes crinkled in an attractive way, his hair blowing all around on what must have been a stormy day.

'They look so happy,' murmured Faith. 'It's hard to believe what happened.'

Ellie agreed with a nod, lost for a moment in her thoughts.

'She had such a terrible time. Anyway, she's getting better slowly, so,' she shook herself mentally, 'let's make sure you've got all you need. There's a list of useful phone numbers on the desk and lots of information, guidelines, which consultant does which speciality – things like that, on the intranet. If you've any questions then either ring through to reception, as they know the answer to most things, or one of us. Don't worry about disturbing us as we can all remember what it was like when we started and you'll get the hang of it in next to no time. Okay?'

Faith nodded and thanked her, not wanting to keep Ellie any longer, and anxious not to keep patients waiting. She unpacked her bag, putting her stethoscope on the desk and making a mental note to bring in a photo of Jonty, perhaps one of the engagement photos if they turned out to be as good as she hoped. She'd not forgotten to bring the Labrador ornament, which she placed carefully next to the computer, glad that she had something to make it feel more like her own surgery. In time, she might well take up the suggestion of changing some of the paintings, though they were perfectly pleasant, soothing watercolours which seemed to blend in well with the atmosphere.

Mrs Tonbridge, who liked to visit the practice at least twice a week, was delighted to be the first patient to see the new locum. A large woman, who walked badly with the aid of a curiously coloured enamelled walking stick, she wore ill-fitting clothes, which included, despite the fact that the start to the day held the promise of more hot sunshine, a heavy tweed overcoat and an old trilby with a feather in it. She had thick support stockings on and some specially made orthopaedic shoes, which she had polished to perfection. She managed a brief grimace, which could have been interpreted as a smile by any optimist, before she sat down heavily and arranged her bags around her.

39

Faith introduced herself. 'My name's Dr Faber. How can I help you today?'

'It's my knees and my hands. Then there's my skin – that itch is no better at all. My angina's been bad over the weekend and I need a repeat prescription for all my tablets except the little yellow ones that I take for my bowels. And I think we better talk about them too. I haven't been for a number two for nearly a week and I know I need to go as I can feel it all sitting there waiting to come out. I tried putting my finger in to help...'

'Let's start at the beginning,' suggested Faith tactfully. 'We could make a list of your problems. There seem to be quite a few things. Perhaps we could discuss a couple of them today and then meet again soon to carry on where we left off.'

'Dr Jennings always lets me talk about everything,' Mrs Tonbridge sniffed.

'I know you're used to Dr Jennings but I'm determined to be just as much help if I can. You'll have to forgive me if it takes me a little time to get to know all about your medical history. I promise I'll try to catch up as quickly as I can.'

More sniffing ensued to let Faith know that her patient did not approve of this approach.

Slowly, they compiled a list, determined which were the most pressing problems of the day and Faith worked her way towards what she felt was a satisfactory conclusion to the consultation, a belief that, sadly, was not shared by Mrs Tonbridge. She hirpled out, one fist clutching her nylon shopping bags, the other, her prescription and Faith, having thankfully closed the door behind her, went back to the desk and sat back in the chair. She'd only seen one patient and was already running over thirty minutes late.

The phone rang. It was Joan, one of the receptionists. 'Are you all right, Dr Faber? We noticed how long you took with Mrs Tonbridge. Don't worry, she's always like that if she can be. We're booking patients in every fifteen minutes for you today, just to get you started, so there's only one waiting at the moment. Shall we bring you a coffee?'

Faith, touched by the concern, breathed her thanks but declined the coffee and girded her loins for the next patient. A double buggy managed to get into the room on the fourth attempt, pushed in an unwieldy fashion by a tiny blond girl, who in turn was followed by two toddlers, each dipping into giant packets of crisps. Ignoring them, with long-established practice, the girl extracted one of the babies from the buggy and sat with him perched on her bony knees. He sneezed, as if on cue, and trails of green snot bubbled from his nostrils. It was hard to take a history and ignore the clamour that was going on in the background as a fight broke out over the crisps. The packets burst, the other baby screeched and both toddlers burst into tears. The pervading smell of someone having just filled their nappy reached Faith's nostrils. Somehow, she managed to assess and treat what turned out to be a chest infection, all the while wondering how anyone, let alone a young girl like their mother, could cope with four children under the age of three. They left, leaving in their wake a legacy of crisp crumbs all over the carpet.

But this was general practice and Faith loved it. She was fascinated by the variety of problems that she was faced with and now she felt she was getting into her stride. Perhaps her surroundings were new but the vagaries of human life that she had to deal with were the same wherever she worked. She was, however, very grateful that the rest of her surgery was made up of more straightforward problems – an acute back pain, emergency contraception, gout and sinusitis.

Finally finished, she was just tidying up when Joan appeared at the door.

'I'm so sorry, Dr Faber, but a young woman's just come to the desk. She's quite upset and we've no appointments left. Is there any chance you could see her?'

'Of course I will. Send her in.'

She sat back behind the desk and logged back on to the computer. In came Pollyanna Smith. In her late teens, she was morbidly obese, thighs chafing together as she walked, her gait cumbersome and onerous, as evidenced by her breathlessness. Her face, which seemed to merge seamlessly into her neck and body, was red, blotchy from crying, maybe even bloated but it was hard to tell. Faith allowed her time to settle on the chair and offered tissues. Pollyanna blew her nose with force.

'Hello, I'm Dr Faber. You're Pollyanna Smith?'

'Yes.'

'That's a pretty name. Unusual though.'

'It was my mum's favourite film.'

'I'm sorry to see you so upset. Is there something I can help with?'

Pollyanna cleared her throat and wiped her eyes on the sleeve of her blouse.

'I've just had enough.'

'What do you mean by that?'

'This...' Pollyanna prodded her stomach, then her arms and thighs. 'Just look at me! I'm just sick to death of being this size. Everyone laughs at me. I can't find nice clothes that fit. In fact it's hard to find any clothes at all. I have to wear hideous sacks like this. Diets don't work 'cos I'm hungry all the time and exercise is a non-starter as I can't jog and there's no way anyone is going to see me in a swimsuit. I bought an exercise bike thinking that I could use it while I was watching TV or something but the first time I sat on it, it collapsed because I was so heavy. How humiliating is that? This morning I stood on the scales and my weight had gone up yet again and that was just the final straw.'

'Oh dear,' Faith murmured, hoping that she sounded empathic.

'Do you know, I can't even wipe my own bloody bottom after I've been to the loo.'

'That's truly awful,' agreed Faith with feeling.

'It's all right for people like you. You'll never know what it's like.'

'That doesn't mean I don't want to help. Tell me what diets you've tried.'

'You name it, I've tried it. Low calorie, high fibre, liquid, vegetable... If I see something on the front of a magazine, I buy it and try it. But they never work, probably because I haven't the willpower to keep going. I've read something about stomach operations and I think I'd like to have that done. It's got to work, nothing else has done and I can't go on like this.'

'Okay, well let's weigh and measure you now, shall we? Then that gives us somewhere to start from. Mmmm, seventeen stone and five pounds, five foot three. Okay, sit yourself down again and tell me about your general health. Any problems?'

Pollyanna mopped some perspiration from her brow. 'Only that my knees and hips ache, I get breathless easily and when the nurse last took my blood pressure, she said it was up a bit but nothing to worry about.'

'Do you have a job?'

'I'm a secretary of sorts at an estate agents. They're not very keen on me dealing with the public though. I can't blame them for that,' she added cynically.

'Any family history of diabetes or thyroid problems?'

'My mum's got diabetes. She's fat too but looks slim beside me. I know that I'm heading that way too if I don't get some weight off, which is something that really scares me.'

'Do you live at home with her?'

'Yes, and my dad, who of course is as thin as the proverbial rake and eats like a horse.'

'How unfair is that?' asked Faith. 'Look, of course I'll help you all I can. But I do think it would be wrong to rush into any sort of operation. There'd be risks with the anaesthetic as well. I think we should start off with me giving you a diet sheet and then you come back to see me on a regular basis to be weighed. Maybe knowing that you have to report here to me for that might boost your determination. If you manage to lose a few pounds then we could think about some medication that might help.'

'I've read about them. I'd like to try them. Do they work?'

Faith felt her heart melt as she saw the look of hope on Pollyanna's chubby face.

'Yes, they can be really helpful. Well, first we ought to check a couple of blood tests. I'd like to be sure that they're fine, so while we're waiting for the results, which will only be a few days, I want you to try really hard with the diet. Then, I promise, we can try tablets.'

'Oh thank you. I'll really try my hardest I promise.'

Smiling, Faith gave her a note to take to the practice nurse and told her to re-book an appointment for the end of the week.

Pollyanna wobbled out of the room, a decidedly happier person than when she had come in.

Faith made her way up to the coffee room, feeling that she had done a good morning's work. The room was empty, the others having either gone on their visits or back to surgery. They had left her a couple of fairly easy-looking visits at a nursing home nearby, so she felt it reasonable to have a drink before she went. She had brought a low-calorie can of pop with her and some slices of melon, determined to keep going with her own diet, which she had now been on for several days and stuck to assiduously. She had even brought her lunch, a salad of loads of different chopped-up ingredients, topped with some tuna that had been canned in brine, hoping that this would be enough to dissuade her from heading back to the delicatessen to try out another of their home-made delicacies. Already she felt that her belly did not protrude quite as much and her waistband was less strained. Meeting someone with a problem like Pollyanna had been quite an eye opener and had even helped get the concerns she had with her own weight into perspective. The least she could do for Pollyanna was to stick to her own diet, even if she was totally unaware of what her doctor was doing.

She tried ringing Jonty, simply wanting to hear his voice and tell him about her first surgery, but he was unavailable, doubtless in a meeting, so, leaving a message and feeling incredibly virtuous about ignoring the rumbling in her stomach which the melon had done nothing to assuage, Faith made her way to the nursing home and swiftly dealt with an old lady who had incipient gangrene of two toes and with an even older man with a scaly scalp.

By the afternoon's surgery, she was beginning to feel much more at home. A steady stream of patients came and went, some with acute problems, in and out in minutes, some with more chronic illnesses, necessitating time to be spent and some merely curious to see who the new locum was and put her to the initiation test of solving their plethora of concerns that had been baffling doctors consistently for many decades.

Ed and Ellie asked her to join them for a drink at the pub opposite and whilst longing for a glass of wine, Faith opted for a slim-line bitter lemon with lots of ice which if nothing else was refreshing and free from calories. Rob joined them, excited by and eager to talk about his last patient of the day, who had had an obstructed hernia, necessitating immediate admission to hospital. His enthusiasm was infectious and the others started to contribute their most interesting cases of the day. Thanks to the fact that Ed had had two pints of a particularly strong local brew, this rapidly spiralled out of control as he made up the most ludicrous and unlikely scenarios, which had them all holding their sides which were aching from laughing and Faith bursting with happiness to have found such good colleagues to work and be friends with.

Chapter Six

The week passed in what seemed like moments. Faith, still full of excitement, enjoyed every minute, from the challenges of surgery consultations to the often more relaxed home visits, which frequently encompassed a drive out into the beautiful countryside. Even the less desirable aspects of the job, the monotonous paperwork and two return visits from Mrs Tonbridge, could not even put the tiniest dent in her bubble of contentment.

Even returning home each evening, her perfect life continued. Waiting for her, looking ruggedly attractive, was Jonty. Her heart faltered for a second as she caught the first glimpse of his car, lying low by the side of the house. She would find him ensconced in the garden or kitchen with Glenda, relaxed and happy, deep in conversation when Faith arrived but breaking off to give her their full attention as soon as they saw her. Faith, not for the first time, marvelled at how well they got on together. Jonty always seemed to bring out the nicer side of Glenda, a skill that was not shared by many. Glenda had proved to be impermeable to the most civil of advances from her daughter's friends in the past. Perhaps it was their shared love of horses and Faith that proved to be the common denominator for them.

Faith was moved by Jonty's concern for her, the very fact that he wanted to be there for her, squeeze her tightly while he enquired tenderly how her day had been and listen receptively to the stories she had to tell. On fine evenings he often rode out with Glenda, Faith content to stay at home and cook the supper.

Relishing her role of housewife she conjured up simple dishes such as fish or steak and salad with baked potatoes rather than roast or chips. Hungry after his outdoor activity, Jonty would be ravenous. He was an appreciative recipient of Faith's home cooking and would help Glenda polish off a bottle of wine, while Faith stuck to mineral water. The three of them then passed the evening, Jonty and Glenda swapping yarns and arguing politics while Faith washed up, caught up with some medical journals before brewing strong coffee to sober up her rather drunk fiancé who then, after a rather emotional goodbye pinning her against his car, drove a little unsteadily back home.

It was rare that he actually stayed overnight. Glenda had neither vetoed this behaviour nor encouraged it and Faith had no wish to risk rocking the boat that seemed to be bobbing along very satisfactorily on calm waters. Occasionally, at the weekend, Faith spent the night at Jonty's if they had been out somewhere special. Hamish was either away or had friends round and showed absolutely no compunction whatsoever about what his son got up to under the roof of the family home. Despite this, Faith felt inhibited when Hamish was at home, afraid that their love making was audible to him, sometimes wondering if he ever listened on purpose. So when he was away and Faith stayed over, it was only then that she could truly relax and enjoy the intimacy of their relationship. Faith longed for the time when they had their own home and could be together every night.

Jonty was an energetic and accomplished lover. Faith chose not to think how many women it had taken him to acquire these skills, preferring to be grateful that he had picked her to perfect them with. He was romantic and unpredictable, surprising her with flowers and gifts, or just as he had in the field, on the way back from the pub, by ravishing her in the back of his or her car, in a lift and even in the women's toilets at a local restaurant and though the good girl in Faith was horrified by his audacity, the bad girl found his behaviour thrillingly addictive.

The engagement photograph had been delivered, ostentatiously mounted in a heavy gold frame, and was now hanging in pride of place in the drawing room. Glenda had been a little less than enthusiastic with her reaction, suggesting that it made Faith look too servile but at least had the grace to praise the professionalism of the camera work. Faith, bothered by her mother's words, printed out one of the other images, of them both smiling directly at the camera, put it into a little wooden frame she already had and took it with her to work, where she placed it on her desk. It was comforting to think that Jonty was there with her all the time. She also sent this same photo by email to Dennis, knowing that his preference would match her own.

Visitors to the house were steered into the drawing room to admire it and Faith was quite taken aback by the number of congratulatory cards and presents that arrived for her and Jonty.

Back at the surgery, Pollyanna returned, true to her word and Faith made much of the fact that she had lost two pounds in weight, something that could well have been natural day to day variation. Her positivism seemed to appease Pollyanna, who was still wary of putting any of her trust in this new doctor, who appeared to be interested in her but who might well let her down like so many others before her.

'Right then,' started Faith. 'You've made an excellent start.'

'I suppose you're not going to let me have the tablets then,' she replied, truculently.

'Not a bit of it. I like to keep my promises.'

Pollyanna relaxed.

'Let me tell you a bit about them. You ought to know about possible side effects to start with.'

'I don't care about those, so long as they work.'

Faith laughed gently.

'I still have to tell you. There shouldn't be many, if any. Sometimes people feel nauseous and a little headachy. Usually that passes within the first week or so. The other common side effect is that they can cause some bowel upset – diarrhoea, some urgency to get to the toilet. Do you think you could cope with that?'

Pollyanna, determined that nothing would interrupt her mission, nodded her head vigorously.

'You take one, twice a day, before you eat. They act by stopping you absorbing the fatty part of your meal mainly but they also help you to feel full up more quickly, so that overall you eat less.'

'That would be amazing,' Pollyanna said, adding with some scepticism, 'they sound a bit too good to be true.'

'I'll need to see you every two weeks to start with as I have to keep an eye on your blood pressure and do a blood test but that should be just a formality. Any questions?'

'Only when can I start?'

Faith giggled with Pollyanna.

'I like patients who are eager to take advice. Just one word of warning. These tablets are not a substitute for a diet. While you're on them, you have to eat sensibly and stick to a low-fat, high-fibre diet. They're not an excuse to go out and eat as much as you can.'

'There's always a drawback. Only joking, Dr Faber.'

Faith wrote the prescription, signing it in her neat handwriting with the fountain pen that Dennis had sent her one year for a birthday present. Though no expert, Faith could tell that it had been hugely expensive and she was glad that she had managed to stash it away in her handbag before her mother had had yet another opportunity to pour scorn on his generosity.

She passed the prescription to Pollyanna and uttered a silent prayer for the success of the tablets as she could not fail to see the look of hope and expectation in her patient's eyes.

'I'll see you in two weeks then. Good luck.'

'Thank you, Dr Faber, I'm so grateful to you for listening to me. I'll try really had not to let you down.'

'I'm here to help. Go and make your appointment now, so that's all fixed.'

'I will. I can hardly wait until I see you next to see how well I've done. It won't be long until I'm as slim as you.'

Faith watched Pollyanna wend her way to the reception desk and saw how the heads of those waiting turned to follow her out, agog at her bulk. She was wearing baggy trousers and a long smock, black from head to toe, apart from the tropically coloured flip-flops on her feet, her only acknowledgement of the fact that it was early summer and the temperature was rising.

Returning into her room, Faith stood tentatively on the scales, having first taken off her shoes. She was gratified to find that she had lost nearly half a stone since her own diet had started.

Up in the coffee room, Ellie was dealing with some post, having finished the ante-natal clinic early, there having been an unusually small number of patients booked in. She looked up as Faith entered and smiled.

'The kettle's just boiled,' she told her.

Faith made herself a coffee with semi-skimmed milk and with Herculean effort managed not to take a piece of the freshly made, gooey chocolate cake that was tempting her from a plate on the small worktop.

'No cake?' asked Ellie, who had just demolished a generously sized portion. 'It's Elliott's birthday. He always brings us in a cake.

He's an amazing cook on the sly, though he'd never admit it. This,' she added, waving the fork she had been using, 'just melts in the mouth. Help yourself.'

'No thanks,' answered Faith, 'I'm trying to lose a little weight before I get my wedding dress.'

'You don't need to do that,' Ellie retorted,' you'll look great just as you are.'

Faith smiled at her. 'You're very kind. I still feel I need to lose a few pounds. It's going quite well so far. Since I started I've lost nearly half a stone. So I must keep it up for a bit longer.'

'Well, I admire your resolve. By the way, that reminds me, who was that really big girl waiting outside your surgery as I came through?'

Ellie cut another smallish portion of cake.

'Pollyanna Smith,' Faith informed her. 'I've just prescribed some of those new pills, Obesigon, for her. She's desperate to lose weight.'

'I hope they work for her. I've tried those tablets with one or two patients. One did really well but the other had to stop them as she couldn't tolerate the bowel upset.'

'I'm afraid that might happen with Pollyanna but I'm heartened to hear you've had one success story. Is there a local surgeon who does gastric bypass surgery or banding? She was asking about that but I don't know who I'd send her to.'

'The nearest would be either Mr Smollett or Mr Parkin in Leeds. I'm not sure that she'd get the op done on the NHS though at the moment, with funding being what it is. They've really cut back on what they consider to be non-essential procedures.'

'I hadn't thought of that. She'd be devastated to be turned down. That's even more reason for me to hope that the tablets help. It might buy me some time to find out more about possible surgery.'

Ellie looked at her watch and quickly forked up the last crumbs of her cake.

'Time I was off on my visits. If I crack on, I'll have time to fit the shopping in before I come back this afternoon. I'll see you later.'

Faith watched her leave, wondering if she could ever hope to achieve such an attractively slim physique and suspecting not. The telephone rang, summoning her back down to surgery. She was in charge of the morning's emergency surgery, an open-ended entity that was for those patients who perceived that their problems were urgent and needed to be addressed that same day. The spectrum of conditions that actually ended up in this surgery was vast, from the very genuine left-sided chest pain, which could be a heart attack, requiring prompt assessment and treatment, to the heart-sinking and plaintive cry of fatigue for months, possibly years.

She deftly dealt with a little boy with a florid tonsillitis and a bricklayer with muscle spasm in his back. Wondering whether to go back upstairs and read or stay in surgery, she heard her mobile phone trill, signifying a voice mail. This proved to be Jonty so Faith, eager not to miss him, rang back immediately.

'Hi,' she greeted him.

'Darling! Thanks for getting back to me. How's your day going?'

She loved the sound of his voice. 'Fine. How's yours? I can't wait to see you tonight. Is your father still away? Shall I stay over at yours? I'm so pleased it's Friday. We can spend the whole weekend together.'

There was a pause on the other end of the line that spoke volumes and Faith felt her heart plummet.

'That's why I needed to talk to you, darling.'

'What do you mean?'

'I'm afraid this weekend's going to have to be put on hold. Simon's asked me to work away, go and see some thoroughbreds down in Hampshire with him and we reckon we won't be back until late Sunday.'

'Oh, Jonty. I'd been so looking forward to us having the house to ourselves.'

'I know, I know,' he tried to sound soothing. 'And so had I. But it's just not going to be possible. We're setting off in the next hour. I'll ring as often as I can and I'll be missing you desperately.'

'I'll miss you too, Jonty. Drive carefully, won't you? Don't let Simon lead you astray,' she added, trying to lighten the atmosphere.

She heard him guffaw.

'No chance of that. Anyway, there's only one girl for me and that's you. You have a good weekend and I'll see you soon.'

She heard more noises which she correctly interpreted as kisses and sadly switched off her phone. The weekend, which had been so full of promise, now stretched ahead like a gaping chasm and she felt quite lost. She had planned special meals for the two of them, adhering to the rules of her diet, bought some of Jonty's favourite wine and had even, though she found the whole process acutely embarrassing, bought some rather naughty but glamorous underwear which she anticipated would surprise and titillate him. She had found it quite excruciating in the shop, sifting through the diaphanous garments on their hangers, all the while aware of the waif-like assistant's beady glare boring a hole into her back. At one point tempted just to rush out and buy nothing, she had somehow plucked up enough courage to select some items and pay for them, without batting an eyelid at the extortionate price, hoping that the sizes would be correct when she got home, not having the temerity to ask to try them on in the shop. When she did try them on, in the privacy of her own bathroom with the door firmly locked, she had been erotically excited by not just the feel of the material but also the way she looked. She could not wait to see Jonty's reaction.

But now that would have to wait, until who knew when. Probably until Hamish went away again and it would be just her luck for him to announce that he was going to spend a few months at home, concentrating on the stud. The sooner they got married and got their own place, the better.

Mind only half on her job, it was a miserable Faith who failed to establish any meaningful rapport with a sullen-looking man who had an ingrowing toenail and a giggly fourteen year old, accompanied by her equally giggly friend, who wanted to start taking the contraceptive pill. Her consultations were adequate but no more as she worried about the prospect of her fiancé and his somewhat hedonistic boss and friend speeding down to the other end of the country, ostensibly to work but doubtless hell-bent on having a good time as well.

Cross for doubting him, the voice of reason arguing in her own mind that she had no cause to be worried, as there had never been the merest hint of Jonty looking at another woman, Faith went and walked round the market square, in need of some fresh air and to escape from the medical centre. The clouds were scudding across the sky bringing a dismal grey to the day, threatening rain or even thunder, as it felt humid rather than refreshing. Faith moved briskly, barely stopping to look in shop windows, which would have been her normal routine. But just at this moment, her desire was to clear her head, to calm down and rationalise what had happened, aware that she was letting it get out of all proportion. She hoped that repeated references to the still sparkling engagement ring on her finger would exert a tranquillising effect but nothing was forthcoming. Her thoughts would not cease from contorting the situation into a spectre most vile.

By the time she got back to the surgery, the rain was starting to fall in large, heavy droplets, a promise of worse to come. In the distance, a soft rumble of thunder could be heard. One solitary receptionist was reading a paperback novel behind the counter and the waiting areas looked uncharacteristically empty. Faith shook her head to remove the wet as she ran upstairs to the staff room, which was also deserted. She went to the fridge to extract her little plastic box of chopped salad, today with some chicken pieces and a few strips of lean ham. As she pulled it out, together with the can of lurid green pop, calorie free but rich in additives and chemicals with unpronounceable names, she could not help but spot the chocolate birthday cake, which someone had thoughtfully put on the top shelf to keep cool.

Shutting the fridge door firmly, Faith took her healthy lunch and went and sat down, choosing from a selection of magazines and newspapers one that she could flick through while she was eating. The salad tasted dull, the same as the day before and the one before that, in fact every day for the last ten days since she had started on this diet. She was bored with it and pushed it to one side after but the fewest of mouthfuls. The magazine article was a waste of time as well.

On edge, she rang Jonty, wondering if he had set off yet, about to dare to ask if she could go with him but she was too late. He was in the car and she could hear Simon laughing uproariously and loud music in the background. The line was bad and kept breaking up, making meaningful, let alone reassuring conversation unachievable so that when she was cut off (in reality or on purpose, she wondered), Faith did not bother to try again.

She drained the last of her drink and went to dispose of the can, plus the discarded contents of her lunchbox. It was still early, far too soon to consider going back down to look at her afternoon's surgery. She did have one or two letters to write but perhaps a cup of tea would be nice first. Kettle boiling, tea bag in mug, Faith looked for the milk and her eyes rested yet again on the cake. She had been very good about her diet and not wavered even once from her proscriptive daily intake. The weight loss was proof of her strong will. A small piece of cake would be more like a reward for doing well and it would inspire her to keep going for a further ten days. That was a good idea, a treat every now and then as an incentive to persevere. Hadn't she read somewhere that total deprivation of the foods you loved was just asking for trouble? A slice now and she could easily make up for it over the weekend. With Jonty away, she could do lots of exercise, perhaps ride Caspian and cut back food wise, so that by the time he returned she would be back on track and possibly even another pound or two lighter.

Mind convinced, Faith cut a sliver of cake and went and sat down. There was thick chocolate ganache between the layers and the most sinful topping that tasted sublime. As Ellie had commented, the sponge was feather light and seemed to melt to nothing the moment it hit her tongue.

Not surprisingly, despite the fact that she was eating as slowly as she could, Faith found that she was wiping up the remaining stains of chocolate from the plate with her fork before she knew it. It had been a very conservative slice; another similar would do no harm. Not even equal to a normal portion in fact. Hadn't Ellie had two slices? And it was Friday after all...

Faith helped herself to a much more generous wedge, this time standing up to wolf it down. Another followed and another. The fork abandoned, she was cramming cake into her mouth with her hands, part of her terrified that someone would come in and find her but powerless to stop. Fingers sticky, face smeared, she clawed at the remains of the cake, as desperate as anyone with an addiction. Only when there was just the smallest portion left did Faith manage to stop eating and hurl the remains in the bin. Surveying the scene around her, there was chocolate everywhere – on the fridge and cupboard doors, the worktop and the draining board. Frantically, Faith turned on the taps, mopped up as best she could with the dishcloth, washed and dried the plate before putting it back in the cupboard and then used the tea towel to dry up the watery mess she had made. Unsure what to do with this, she rammed it in the bin too. Racing all the time against the clock of her own invention, she made one final check then tore downstairs, scared witless at the prospect of meeting anyone on the way, and into her surgery where, locking the door behind her, she made a bee-line for the sink and proceeded to make herself vomit.

Nothing could have prepared her for the enormity of guilt and shame that she swept through her. It was bad enough bingeing on food that she had bought in preparation, it was dire to raid the kitchen at home, but to abuse the trust and friendship that she had come to appreciate in such a short space of time and steal was a new horror. Faith sat in her chair, shaking from head to foot, heart threatening to leap out of her ribcage, tears running down her cheeks. The indignant bloated feeling in her stomach had gone but only to be replaced by a burning in her throat and a foul taste in her mouth, of chocolate-flavoured vomitus.

She wept, as silently as she could, then fought to regain some semblance of composure, seeing on the clock that it was close to the time for surgery to commence. Checking in the mirror, she saw that her face looked a mess and even a liberal application of foundation and powder only gave her the appearance of a caricature of her normal self. Hoping that the patients would not notice and if they did, she could plead bad hay fever, she opened the door to call in her first patient. John Britton was crossing over the waiting area, walking with Ed. As Faith opened her mouth to call in Eleanor Driver, it was impossible not to hear what he said.

'I thought Elliot said he'd bought in a birthday cake. I couldn't see any sign of it just now when I went up for some. I'd especially not had any pudding at home, knowing how much I was looking forward to it.'

Faith was surprised how quickly she worked her way through the afternoon. She found it helpful to have something on which she had to concentrate, fearing that if she did not apply her concentration one hundred percent then she might make a mistake. Nobody questioned the way she looked, much to her relief and by the mid-way point, when she had a quick look at her image in the mirror, she did think that she looked considerably better. Even though there was a lull at one point and Gary rang through to tell her that she would have time to go up for a cup of tea if she wished, Faith stayed firmly put in the safety of her surgery, fearful of having to face the others and look them in the eye.

The only slight hiccough was when she was completely bewildered about the diagnosis of a rash, widespread all over a woman's body, violaceous and intensely pruritic, the irresistible desire to scratch keeping her awake most of the night. Faith knew that the sensible thing to do would be to call in John, Ellie or Ed to ask their opinion but the prospect of seeing them appalled her. So she bluffed her way through the consultation, issuing a prescription for emollients and topical steroids, and asking the patient to come back after the weekend for review.

Finishing with a sigh of relief, Faith packed up her bag and realised with a groan that she had left her handbag up in the staff room. She checked her watch. Perhaps the others would have gone. They did tend to be much more proficient than her at running to time. As she came out of her room, it did seem promisingly quiet. All the chairs were empty apart from one, the magazines which had started the day arranged neatly on the small tables were now in complete disarray and one of the cleaners was starting to tidy up over near the nurses' room.

Hoping these were good omens, Faith trotted upstairs and went into the staff room, only to be greeted by a babble of chatter and a sea of people. Before she knew it, she felt an arm around her shoulders guiding her into the crowd and a glass of fizzy wine being thrust into one of her hands.

'Faith,' cried John, 'you're just in time. We're having a celebratory drink for Elliot before we go home. Help yourself to nuts and crisps, if you'd like.'

'Oh, thank you,' she stuttered, feeling an obvious blush creeping up her face.

Awkwardly Faith moved across the room, looking to reclaim her handbag and mentally planning an escape at the earliest possible moment. Having retrieved it, she spotted Rob, pouring himself another glass of wine. He saw her edging in his direction and waved the bottle at her, offering to refill her glass too. Faith put her hand over it and shook her head.

'No thanks. I really can't stay long.'

'How's your week been? You seem to be settling in well. They're a great bunch of people, aren't they? Look at the way they just put on a bit of a do like this.'

Faith nodded and made a big show of having a sip of wine.

'Yes, they're all really nice.'

She couldn't bring her eyes to meet his. There was a palpable lull before Rob spoke again. 'Ed told me you've just got engaged. Congratulations! Sorry I didn't say something sooner but I've hardly seen you this week.'

'I think I've been quite busy, settling in, trying to get to know the patients. It's been quite hard at times as a lot of them are so used to Dr Jennings. She was clearly a very skilled and clever GP.'

'Yes, from what I've heard, she's a hard act to follow. It's a bit different being a registrar.'

'I'm sorry, I think I ought to be going,' Faith started, not in the mood for conversation.

'Oh, okay. Have you a busy weekend ahead? Don't let me keep you. It was nice having a bit of a chat.'

Faith glimpsed the crestfallen look on Rob's face and felt awful. She swallowed hard. 'You're right, it has been nice. I'd like to stay but unfortunately I've made plans. I had no idea that anything like this was going to happen.'

'Tell you what,' blurted Rob, just as Faith was turning to elbow her way to the door, 'why don't we have lunch one day next week? You don't go home for lunch and neither do I, so why don't we get together for a bite to eat?'

'Yes of course, that'd be lovely.' Faith was champing at the bit to leave. She would have agreed to anything if it meant that she could get away.

'I'll look forward to it,' beamed Rob and Faith was momentarily touched by his sincerity.

'So will I,' she answered and found that she meant it.

Chapter Seven

The rain cleared away overnight and on Saturday morning, Glenda and Faith awoke to iridescent blue skies with no sign of cloud. Faith had been surprised to sleep well; a slushy call from a very drunk Jonty as she was preparing for bed helped her to think rosy and romantic thoughts as she settled down under her duvet. He rang again as they were having breakfast, such that it was – fruit for Faith, whose stomach was growling with a longing for a bacon sandwich, and four cigarettes and innumerable cups of strong coffee for her mother. Glenda answered the phone and talked horse-related matters before handing over to Faith who was almost hopping from one foot to the other, longing to speak to him. His voice was croaky and hungover but his words were sentimental and just what she wanted to hear. She was in such a good mood after the call, in which he made just as many protestations of love as he had done when under the influence of alcohol, that she readily acquiesced to her mother's suggestion of a ride and went up to put on her jodhpurs which were, if she wasn't mistaken, considerably looser than last time she had had them on. She wondered whether Glenda would notice but felt that there was only the slimmest of chances of that happening.

Caspian was already pounding on his stable door but when he saw them coming down the path towards him, the ferocity in his hooves doubled. The dogs ran ahead deliriously, noses up in the air, sniffing for the first rabbits of the day. Glenda, Faith was deeply relieved to see, went to put a head collar on Breeze, a sensible, intelligent mare, unflappable in most circumstances and who would surely exert a stabilising influence on Caspian. They chatted in a companionable way while grooming their horses and tacking up. The dogs barked with excitement, sensing a run through the woods and Glenda barked instructions at Dawn, who came in at the weekends to earn some pocket money and the occasional ride in return for mucking out, cleaning tack and generally tidying up. She was a slim, tall girl who insisted on being fully made up no matter what she was doing. This morning was no exception, Faith noted, amazed at the layer of foundation that had been applied, together with stark, black mascara and eyeliner, not to mention the luscious pearl-effect red lips. Glenda, though she would never have admitted it, was very fond of Dawn, who had proved to be a reliable and thorough worker and also a gifted rider.

'Right, let's go,' Glenda announced, swinging her leg with ease over the saddle and managing to locate her stirrups without as much as a look.

Faith failed to manage such a dignified mount onto Caspian, who refused to stand still, preferring to prance around in tight circles. She dropped the reins but scooped them up just in time to get some sort of control. Breeze, with the air of one who has experienced many things in life, ambled off to the gate while her girth was being tightened and then stood patiently as Glenda leant down to open it. Faith and Caspian followed, moving sideways like an ataxic crab.

'Shorten your reins and lean back,' shouted Glenda acerbically.

'Yes, Ma, I'm trying to.'

It was not long before Faith wished that she had not agreed to come. The alternative of sitting in the garden reading seemed far more attractive, she thought, as she hung on for dear life following Glenda, who had set off at a spanking trot, causing Caspian to bounce about eccentrically. But Faith was not her mother's daughter for nothing and although she felt exceedingly uncomfortable, heart in her mouth, she tried her hardest to hide her nerves from the perceptive Caspian and take control. By the time they had traversed the field and were entering the woods, Faith had succeeded in putting on a fairly convincing display of horsemanship and, much to her delight, saw a nod of approval from her mother.

'Much better,' came the praise.

In a more confined space, Caspian settled, content to walk beside Breeze as they made their way down the leafy dark corridors of the wood, inhaling the smell of coniferous trees. Random shafts of sunlight found their way between the branches creating sudden blasts of brightness from which they had to shield their eyes. The only sounds were those of crackling twigs under the horses' hooves and the occasional pheasant being sent up by the dogs who were far ahead, scavenging in the undergrowth. It was quite magical, thought

Faith, until Glenda lit up a cigarette and smoked it as they hacked along, rather spoiling the ambience before taking care to extinguish the stub which she then tossed to the ground. The pathway widened and they trotted briskly to the next gate.

Knowing what was coming next, Faith tensed up and tightened her reins, in doing so alerting Caspian, who had been quite content to walk along beside Breeze in an affable way, to the fact that there was some excitement pending. As the woods cleared and they felt the full force of the sun hit their backs, Glenda led them into a large pasture of several acres and with the merest of backwards glances at her daughter, set off at a gallop. Caspian snorted and followed, wanting to race, intermittently bucking and Faith clung on not sure if what she was experiencing was terror or exhilaration. Mud splashed up from his hooves and splattered on her face. Sweating and puffing, the horses pulled up, Caspian only condescending to slow down because Breeze was doing so.

Glenda looked elated. 'Let's swap,' she suggested, crossing her leg over Breeze's neck and slipping gracefully to the ground. Faith agreed with alacrity.

'Jumps?' asked Glenda, seemingly oblivious to Caspian's irrational behaviour.

Without waiting for an answer, she led the way back into the woods, further up from where they had been before, where there was a line of small cross country jumps spread out between the trees. Expertly, she set Caspian at the first and he cleared it with ease, just as he did the others, taking them all at a gallop. Breeze and Faith, content to take things at their own rather slower pace, performed creditably, the surefootedness of the mare instilling confidence in her rider.

Glenda was waiting impatiently for them to catch up. 'Let's go back the road way and let them cool off a bit,' she called, heading off again. 'He's going really well, isn't he?'

'He looks marvellous with you, Ma,' Faith shouted back, trying to make herself heard above the clatter of the hooves on the lane.

Back at home, they handed their horses to Dawn and headed back to the garden. Faith went to fetch cool drinks. She was longing to change out of her sticky riding clothes into a skirt and T-shirt. By the time she returned, Glenda was resplendent on the sun lounger in her swimsuit, this time turquoise, riding clothes in a pile on the lawn. Faith was pleased to see her applying some sun block for once.

'Here you are, Ma.'

'Thanks.'

Taking her drink she eyed Faith carefully. 'So,' she began, searching for her cigarette packet, 'what are you thoughts about this wedding?'

'Well, we're talking about November, as you know. We'd like to get married in church, hopefully St Beowolf's in the village. Hamish knows the vicar quite well and Jonty was christened there.'

'That's a nice idea,' Glenda took a long, slow drag. 'What about afterwards?'

'We're not sure about that. We had discussed having the reception here. How would you feel about that?'

'What on earth do you want to have it here for?' Glenda was astounded.

'I thought it might be nice to be at home,' argued Faith, taken aback at her mother's instant disapproval. 'We'd thought we could hire a marquee…'

'In the middle of bloody November?' Glenda coughed gutturally.

'Well, you can have heating of course. We could decorate it just the way we wanted, get in some caterers, hire a bar…'

'Don't go any further,' Glenda interrupted. 'That really is the most ridiculous suggestion I've ever heard. This is your wedding, Faith. It's got to be special. It's supposed to be the best day of your life so make the most of it. Who knows what's in store for the two of you.'

Faith chose to ignore her mother's last statement.

'So what do you suggest?'

'The Swindlehurst Castle Hotel, naturally. We had the hunt ball there last year. It was top notch. Glorious setting – that'd be perfect for the photographs –providing that it isn't raining or foggy, which it probably will be if you insist on doing this at such a ridiculous time of year, splendid interior, excellent cuisine.'

'But the cost,' started Faith. 'It would be prohibitive. We were thinking of about eighty guests. That would be a small fortune.'

'Yes it will but so what? You and I won't be paying. Faith, that man who purports to be your father will be footing the bill, so why not make it as expensive as you can. That's what he's supposed to do. You're his only daughter, so bleed him dry.'

'Ma, that's so unfair.'

Glenda sniffed. 'I suppose he'll be wanting to come and give you away. Well, he'll be good at that; he's had a lot of practice. He gave away our marriage without a second thought. Just so long as he doesn't think that he can bring that trollop with him. There's no way that I can tolerate her presence at your wedding.'

'But he'll want her to come. And I think I want her to come. They're happy together – I can't expect him to come on his own.'

'Huh,' snarled Glenda. 'That'll be just great, won't it. Him and his floozy prancing about together, but me on my own. What will people think?'

Faith tried to appease her. 'People won't think anything. Ma. The people there will either be family or friends, so everyone will understand. I've an idea! Why don't you go with Hamish? I'm sure he'd be delighted to escort you,' Faith added as an afterthought.

The noise that emanated from Glenda defied description. 'I'm not after the sympathy vote either,' she snapped.

Faith was exasperated. 'I really don't know what to say to make things better for you. Going with Hamish would be the perfect solution. I know you'd prefer me to say I don't want Pa there, but I do. I want him to walk with me down the aisle. I can't imagine anyone else doing that and I won't even try to.'

'It'll make the seating plan at the reception a nightmare,' huffed Glenda, determined to be obstreperous.

'That's nothing. I can sort that. Obviously I would like him at the top table with us but if you find that impossible to contemplate then I shall come up with the best I can and we'll just have to make do. It's only one day, Ma. Surely you could manage to be polite to him for that long?'

'Huh. Just make sure that his trollop doesn't get any ideas about upstaging me as mother of the bride...'

'I'm sure she won't. I doubt something like that would ever occur to her. She'll probably feel quite nervous about being there, so perhaps you could be nice.'

Glenda glared. 'I shall not be saying one word to her.'

With a grunt, Glenda lay back on her lounger and closed her eyes, to emphasise the finality of her comment.

Faith shook her head sadly and sipped on her drink. She found it tragic that Glenda had made no progress at all in moving forward and away from the venom she felt for her ex-husband. She appeared to be trapped in a maelstrom of odium for no reason whatsoever. She had what seemed like a perfect life – her animals, her riding and this fabulous house. She had no financial worries, completely the opposite in fact as she was a very wealthy woman. Thinking back, Faith could not recall ever witnessing any affection between her parents. There had been no touching of hands, no welcoming or goodbye kisses, not even the gentlest stroke of a cheek or whisper of a comforting word. Rarely when she had been a child, had they done anything as a family. For sure, she had been to many, many events with her mother and spent as much time as she could with her father, when he was not away, but what had happened to all those times when they should have been a threesome, a happy family? At home they never sat down together to eat or talk, or even to watch television. On birthdays and Christmases the house would be overflowing with guests, arranged deliberately to dilute out the intensity of Glenda and Dennis being under the same roof. They had never seemed happy in each other's presence, which was why Faith found it all the more incongruous that her mother continued to act in this way, affecting a grief of pathological proportions.

On more than one occasion, Faith had plucked up the courage to tackle her mother on this issue. She had picked her moments, she believed, tactfully. Once, on going into the kitchen, she had found Glenda crying quietly to a melancholy piece of music on the radio, an emotion she rarely displayed. Another time, Glenda had become uncharacteristically loquacious, after a significant quantity of alcohol. The third time, trying a completely different tack, they had been driving home from a one-day event, in which Glenda had won the open competition and was understandably cock a hoop. The responses had been fairly predictable each time. As soon as his name was mentioned, Faith could see the metaphorical shutters snap into place as her mother's eyes became cold and tinged with revulsion. There then followed a tirade of abuse which included an itemised description of Dennis's inadequacies and then a soliloquy about how Faith, just because she had gone to medical school, need not think that she could practise any psychobabble or elementary counselling skills on her that she might possess.

Not in the mood for a fight, Faith said no more and retrieved the novel that she was halfway through from under the table and tried to find some shade so that she could read, or at least pretend to be reading. It was difficult to concentrate. Her mind was full of the wedding and the prospect of the hotel her mother had suggested. It was a fantastic place and looked, from the outside at least, as if it should be perfect. She remembered an email she had had from Dennis, allowing her carte blanche with regard to the arrangements, promising to pay for everything and, more importantly, promising to be there to give his daughter away.

Excited at the prospect, Faith planned a drive out for her and Jonty, one evening next week for a recce and then, if the reality lived up to the promise, it might be wise to book, always assuming that the date they had in mind was available. Inspired, she rushed indoors and tried ringing Jonty but his phone went straight to voicemail, probably for the best as he would not have been able to discuss wedding matters if he was in a meeting.

Faith made some lunch. She felt she needed something with some substance after the morning's exertions and the allure of lettuce and tomato was non-existent. Cheese, however, whilst full of fat on one hand was also high in protein and calcium, so concluding that the positives outweighed the negatives she placed liberal helpings of Stilton and Gouda onto her plate, nibbling on more as she did so. In an attempt to avoid more confrontation, she concocted a small salad for Glenda, decoratively arranging the ingredients and topping them with a far smaller portion of cheese and quartered a slice of buttered bread. Armed with this and a fresh, cold drink, she was on the verge of returning to the garden when Glenda entered the room, fanning her face and professing a need for the coolness of the house for a while. She poured herself a large gin and tonic and Faith, anticipating her next move, took ice cubes from the freezer for her, a gesture that Glenda at least had the decency to acknowledge with a monosyllable of gratitude.

Chapter Eight

It was turning into something of an impasse. Faith was sitting studying the surly teenager opposite her. Barely dressed in the shortest of mini skirts, a skimpy, grubby top which made no attempt to conceal the orange bra beneath, Alison Sloper slunk lower in her chair wishing she was somewhere else, anywhere except the doctor's surgery. Unbeknown to her, the doctor was having very similar feelings too.

Summoning up a smile and what she hoped was a friendly and engaging tone, Faith tried a different angle.

'So, you need the morning-after pill?'

'Yeah, I said, didn't I?'

Faith nodded. 'That's fine but we do need to talk a little more first. When did you last sleep with your boyfriend?'

'I haven't got a boyfriend.'

'Then, why…?'

'It was just some fit bloke I met at my mate's party the night before last. I don't even know what his name was.'

'Oh.' Faith was taken aback but tried to be understanding. She made a mental note to make an attempt to raise the thorny issue of sexually transmitted disease. 'Did you use any form of contraception? I mean, did he use a condom?'

'Nah.'

There was a longish pause. Faith could sense that some further comment was on the tip of Alison's tongue and resisted the urge to speak first.

'I wasn't going to come, but my mate, Cheryl, told me I should.'

'She's absolutely right,' agreed Faith. 'Why on earth did you think that there was no need to come?'

'Well, they say you can't get pregnant the first time, don't they?' Alison retorted with the wisdom of one who knows.

Incredulous, Faith glanced at the medical record in front of her. 'But, Alison, you've been in here for the morning-after pill five times already this year. How could this possibly have been the first time?'

Pouting, Alison permitted the briefest of eye contact. 'Well, it was the first time for quite a long time,' she shrugged.

Faith sighed internally and tried to explain her concerns carefully.

Suggestions of some reliable, regular contraception fell on deaf ears and she was left to capitulate and concentrate on doing the best she could, ensuring that Alison's immediate needs were met, whilst trying to educate her for the future. A glazed look floated across Alison's face when the subject of infection was raised; she was confident that the invincibility of her youth would protect her from any unwanted disease. That sort of thing happened to others, but not to her. She left, bundle of leaflets in her hand, only because she knew she was expected to take them. Reaching the other side of the waiting area, she tossed them on to a table and made for the door, delighted that her ordeal was over and her prescription secured.

Faith was worn out. Not only had her surgery seemed more challenging than usual but she had slept badly the previous night, tossing one way then the other, punching and pummelling her pillow to find comfort.

Jonty had not returned as promised. She had been on tenterhooks the whole afternoon, waiting in so as not to miss the sound of his car followed by the warmth of his arms enveloping her. All that she knew from one hurried call in the middle of the evening was that he and Simon had been delayed. More information was not forthcoming as his signal was lost and the line went dead. Frustrated, she had spent what was left of the time before bed hoping that he was either playing one of his practical jokes and would suddenly bound into the house or, failing that, he would ring back from an area where he could talk at length. The telephone had remained stubbornly silent, save for one call for Glenda that had at least been mercifully brief.

So she had gone to bed depressed, smuggling into her room two large packets of biscuits and a box of little apple pies which she had bought from the village shop while fetching the Sunday papers. She then munched her way through the food in a robotic fashion, dismissive of her diet and wallowing in her unhappiness.

Her surgery was running late, because the patients had been difficult. At least that was her excuse. In reality, only the smallest fraction of blame lay with them, the true reason being her incomplete concentration on her job as she had one ear permanently cocked for the bleep of her mobile phone. The voice of common sense, which she allowed to speak occasionally, reassured her that, knowing Jonty, his phone by now would need recharging and that he was probably driving back that very morning. More invasive, though, was the voice of irrationality which cruelly presented her with a choice of unsavoury scenarios ranging from death in a road traffic accident to emergency admissions to hospital with life-threatening illness, to say nothing of the voluptuous harpy that he had allowed to lead him astray.

She finally saw the last patient to the door and was left with the uncomfortable feeling that, whilst her competence would probably pass muster, she could have performed a lot better. Up in the coffee room, she made a drink and took a handful of biscuits from the tin. She read letters and wrote some, dealing with referrals and forms for life insurance requests, all the while affecting a cheerful countenance, not wanting either Ellie or John, who were sitting with her, to have any idea of her inner turmoil.

Margaret, one of the receptionists, appeared. At least they presumed it was Margaret, for the legs looked familiar but the top half of her body was completely hidden from view by the enormous bouquet of flowers that she was carrying.

'Dr Faber! Somebody loves you!'

'Wow!' exclaimed Ellie. 'Just look at those.'

Faith rummaged for the attached card, which had slipped down between the stalks, anxious, hoping, all thumbs as she tried to open the fiddly envelope. Then she felt her heart soaring with joy as she read the loving message and apology from Jonty. She blushed pinker than some of the blooms as she realised that all eyes were on her.

'They're from Jonty, my fiancé,' she explained. 'He's been away for the weekend.'

Ellie's mouth dropped open.

'You get something like that when he's just been away for two days?' she asked, amazed. 'Lucky you.'

'It was a bit more complicated than that,' Faith mumbled, burying her nose in the bouquet.

The others turned their attention back to their own work and Faith, relieved not to be the centre of attention any longer, got up and gently rested her flowers in the corner of the room in a bowl of water. The list of jobs that still needed to be done, whilst huge, was no longer the unassailable mountain that it had been and she attacked each task in turn with a vigour and willingness that had been turned on as though by a switch.

Ed entered in a rush, looking fraught.

'Can anyone keep an eye on Rob for me for the rest of the morning? He's doing the duty surgery – it's not busy, but he likes to have one of us in the building in case he needs advice.'

'I'll do it,' offered Faith, aware that her paperwork and telephone calls would keep her occupied for a good length of time.

'That'd be great, Faith. Thanks. I'm just dashing off to the postgrad centre. I'd forgotten all about this lecture and I mustn't miss it. I'll be back this afternoon.'

'Off you go. Just tell Rob that I'm up here if he wants me.'

'You're a star. I'll pop my head round his door as I go. See you all later.'

John and Ellie divided up what few visits there were, leaving just one for Faith and then also left. Faith, who had been trying hard not to beam with happiness too much, stretched out in her chair, put her work to one side and tried to phone Jonty. His phone was switched off. Obviously driving, she decided and settled for re-reading the card that had come with the flowers.

She had more or less got up to date by the time Rob finished his surgery. He had coped well with the variety of conditions that had been presented to him and even in the short time that she had worked at the practice, Faith could see that his confidence was improving by the day.

'Any problems?' she asked as he folded his body down on the chair beside her.

'None at all. A bit of hay fever but there must also be some sort of sickness bug going around at the moment as the majority of patients were complaining of either nausea, vomiting or diarrhoea. Any way, it was all quite straightforward but thank you for being on stand by. Have you many visits?'

'Just one.'

'What is it?'

'Funnily enough, an elderly lady with nausea and diarrhoea. She lives about five miles from here, right on the edge of the practice area.'

'Tell you what,' started Rob,' why don't I come with you? I've nothing now until afternoon surgery and we could have a bit of lunch somewhere, on the way back perhaps.'

'I don't know,' began Faith doubtfully, who had been planning a shopping trip to buy ingredients for a romantic supper for her and Jonty, who would surely be home that evening.

Rob looked at her expectantly. 'It would be very useful for me,' he added persuasively. 'I'm sure I'd learn a lot and it is very educational for me to watch other people's consulting techniques. It's been advised that I see as many as I can to help me fine tune my own. I know it would be a positive and beneficial experience for me.'

Faith looked at him, wondering if he was serious but spotted the glint of humour in his eye and burst out laughing. 'I've never heard so much rubbish in my life. Go on then. I'll be setting off in about five minutes. Be ready or I'll go without you and then the aspects of my consulting that are unique to me will remain for ever secret.'

'See you in the car park! I'll go and get my stethoscope. Don't you dare leave me behind. I'd never forgive myself for missing an opportunity like this.'

Faith could not help but smile as she bundled up her paperwork into piles to be distributed either to the receptionists, secretaries or taken back to her surgery, and checked that she had everything that she might need in her bag. She had a last try at phoning Jonty and was delighted when he replied. Effusive with thanks for her flowers, she invited him for supper and promised to make all his favourites. She then wondered whether she dare ring her mother and suggest that she went out for the evening but decided against this plan, preferring to trust that Glenda would intuitively make her presence scarce, which she had been known to do rarely in the past.

Rob was waiting by Faith's car, leaning against it nonchalantly while he watched her walking towards him. He climbed into the passenger seat as she opened the door and started fiddling with the radio and CD player, admiring the make and the power of the speakers but not her choice of music.

Faith was a careful driver, who, owing to the fact that she had been brought up to expect a horse coming round every bend, drove even more slowly when out of the town than when in it. But unlike Jonty, who would show his exasperation at her caution, Rob seemed content to wind down the window and enjoy the beauty of the countryside, pointing out attractive cottages, rabbits on the grass verge and the sun glinting on the river whilst acting as chief navigator. Fearing for her tyres, Faith parked the car at the end of an unmade track, full of ominously sized potholes and the two of them picked their way up the hundred metres to the small cottage. A ginger cat was sunning itself on the doorstep but scooted away as they approached, leaving a lethargic sheepdog to greet them, the fur around his muzzle white with age, his eyes dulled by cataracts but his tail still able to wag happily.

'Hello,' they called, knocking on the open door and walking in.

A feeble voice replied from upstairs and they picked their way up the threadbare carpet, taking care to avoid the rail of the stair lift, and followed the sound to the front bedroom.

It was a large room which felt small and pokey. Most of the light from the large window was blocked by the mirrors of the kidney-shaped dressing table and a large, ugly and cumbersome wardrobe dominated the remaining space.

Miss Stanhope was like a tiny ghost. Pale, almost to the point of being transparent, with wisps of feathery white hair dancing from her scalp, she was lying in a huge double bed covered by an old-fashioned quilted eiderdown and patchwork bedspread. She seemed to merge in with the pallor of the pillowcases. A commode stood by the door, emitting a noxious stench and a toilet roll had unravelled its way across the floor before disappearing under the bedside table.

Faith introduced herself and Rob and began to ask questions. Miss Stanhope did her best to reply and even attempted a weak smile, revealing a solitary yellow tooth. She produced a small skeletal hand for Faith to check her pulse which was rapid and thready. Her blood pressure was very low.

Rob raised the lid of the commode gingerly. 'Faith?'

She turned and looked. The pan was full of black tarry faeces, incontrovertible evidence of bleeding from the gut.

'Phone for an ambulance, would you please? Let's get Miss Stanhope into hospital as soon as possible.'

Turning back to her patient, Faith explained her concerns and the need for immediate admission. She enquired if there was anyone she could contact for her. Miss Stanhope, exhausted, nodded. 'Could you ring my nephew? His number's by the phone. He'll come and look after the animals.'

Rob popped his head round the door, having retreated to the landing to make his calls. 'The ambulance is on its way. I've rung A&E as well, so that's all sorted.'

'Thank you,' smiled Faith. 'Now, Miss Stanhope, can I put some clothes in a bag for you?'

'I packed a suitcase in case I needed to go into hospital. It's in there.' She raised her head with an effort and pointed a bony finger at the wardrobe.

'How very sensible of you,' commented Faith, easing her way around the end of the bed and opening the door. Right at the back was a small, battered leather case, with an old brown paper label and a thick layer of dust on it.

'Is this it?' she asked.

'Yes, that's it.'

Faith pulled it out, laid it on the bed and opened it, coughing as the disturbed dust exploded into the atmosphere. The contents seemed well preserved and all that Faith had to add was a small wash bag that Miss Stanhope directed her to.

'I think you must have packed this some time ago.'

'Yes, I did. About ten years ago. It pays to be ready for these events you know. I'm very fortunate that I haven't needed it before. Oh, I do feel sick. I think I might be— '

Rob instinctively reached out for the first object he could see, which was the waste-paper bin and somehow managed to get it to Miss Stanhope just in time. Ominous black fluid spurted from her mouth, making him gag as he watched. She fell back on the pillows, gasping. Thankfully, he could hear the sound of an ambulance approaching as Faith deftly inserted a cannula into Miss Stanhope's forearm, securing intravenous access while she was still able to and keeping up a steady stream of reassuring conversation.

They heard the dog barking and the ambulance crunching up the last bit of the drive. Rob ran down to greet them and outline the problem so that by the time he and the two paramedics reached the bedroom, all that needed to be done was to transfer Miss Stanhope gently onto a stretcher and then set off with as much haste as possible to the hospital.

'What about the nephew?' Faith turned to Rob as they stood in front of the house watching the ambulance lurch through the potholes.

'He's on his way to the hospital to meet them there. He told me just to drop the latch and his wife will be over as soon as she can. The dog will be fine just sitting outside apparently.'

'Right-o. Let's go, shall we?

Rob patted the dog and left a bowl of water for it, which Faith found a thoughtful touch and hoped that it would not be on its own for too long.

Driving along they discussed the case and agreed how what sounded like a straightforward problem could unexpectedly prove to be very serious.

'Do you think she'll live?' wondered Rob.

'I think the outlook is a bit grim, quite honestly, but you never know. Let's hope we got there in time to make a difference. Why don't you ring the hospital later and find out what happened?'

'I will do and I'll let you know.'

They journeyed on for a little before Faith realised that she had taken a wrong turning.

'Oh, damn,' she mumbled. 'I think I'm lost. We didn't come this way, did we?'

'I don't think so. It's not looking familiar to me. Hang on though – look! There's a sign there to a hotel. Let's go and grab some lunch.'

Faith followed his gaze and was curious to see a smart sign directing her to the Swindlehurst Castle hotel, some half a mile away.

'We can't go there!' she exclaimed.

'Why not?'

'Well, it's where I'm hoping to have my wedding reception and it's dreadfully expensive.'

'What? Even a bar snack?'

'I'm not sure, but I would imagine so. I've never actually been there. Jonty and I were going to have a look round one evening this week.'

'That's perfect! Let's you and I go and case the joint first.'

Faith was still hesitant, feeling that it was something special to be shared by her and Jonty only, but Rob, insisting, persuaded her to follow the sign.

First impressions were, as she had hoped, quite stunning. Set in its own grounds, the perimeter of which was marked by a high stone wall, the castle stood proud amidst the precisely tended gardens where neatly and symmetrically arranged flowerbeds edged with box hedging spread out magnificently between some of the finest examples of topiary she had ever seen.

She parked the car and got out, transfixed by the view, immediately able to imagine herself and Jonty strolling on the manicured lawns hand in hand, refusing even to consider the fact that in November it would be cold and might well be raining. Perhaps they could stay here for their wedding night and then leave for the honeymoon the next day. That would be so romantic. If only Jonty was here now. She couldn't wait for his reaction when he saw this place. It was perfect.

'Come on, Faith, we've got to keep an eye on the time.' Rob's voice brought her back to reality. 'Let's go through to the bar and see what's on offer. My treat!'

Looking at the menu, Rob rather wished that he hadn't made that statement as the prices were certainly way beyond those he had expected. Faith, still far too occupied taking in the ambience and trying to commit as much as possible to memory so that she could tell Jonty that evening, told Rob that she would have the same as him. He ordered two Ploughman's lunches and two fresh orange juices before managing to steer Faith to a table by the window, so that she could not only soak up the beauty of inside but also that of the grounds.

The lunch when it arrived looked exquisite, almost too good to eat. Both expecting the traditional generous wedge of cheese, crusty fresh bread with pickles and perhaps a side salad, they gazed at their plates with a mixture of disappointment and at the same time appreciation for the artwork that lay before them. Tiny cubes, each one a testament to the perfect symmetry of cheese, were arranged in a pyramid beside some curls of melba toast and a teaspoonful of colourful tomato and pepper salsa.

It was impossible to eat slowly, as to create a worthwhile mouthful resulted in a large portion of the meal disappearing. Rob caught Faith's eye as he tried to balance a piece of cheese precariously on the toast and then anoint it with the salsa. She giggled quietly, not wanting to draw attention from the handful of other people who were in the room.

'If all their meals are like this, I think your wedding guests are going to be very hungry,' he whispered.

'But it's delicious, what there is of it,' Faith insisted, refusing to let anything dispel her perfect wedding vision. 'Mind you,' she acknowledged a little ruefully, 'you're right, it doesn't really fill even the smallest corner, does it?'

'Come on, let's finish up and go back to Lambdale. We can have cake and coffee at Delicious. No, don't look at me like that – there's plenty of time and we need something to sustain us before afternoon surgery. I'll just go and settle up.'

Faith picked up some extremely glossy brochures as she walked through the hall, describing details of the wedding services they offered, including some sample menus, which was more information to share with Jonty that evening.

As they drove back, she rehearsed in her mind the excuses that she would give to Rob to get out of going for coffee. She reckoned that the meagre lunch she had just eaten would only have contained minimal calories, so if she ate nothing more, then she would be able to share a dessert with Jonty. Her stomach rumbled, disagreeing with her plans. She was very hungry.

No sooner had she parked than Rob was out of the car and across the street, gesticulating wildly to her.

'Quick, there's a table free.'

He disappeared inside before Faith could open her mouth to speak, so she followed him over, deciding that a coffee would do no harm, preferably black.

'Which cake would you like? I'm going to try the cherry and almond, or perhaps the lemon meringue pie, or the date flapjack. Oh help, it's so hard to choose.'

Faith surveyed the choice before her. A cursory look would be polite then she would demur. Her will power evaporated in a moment.

'Oh, go on then. I'll have a slice of the orange and chocolate. Just a tiny bit. At the back there,' she pointed.

'I'd not seen that one. Good choice. I wonder… No, cherry and almond. I'll try the others another day. We ought to make this a weekly visit, don't you think, then we could try them all! Cappuccino?'

He turned to the attractive middle-aged woman with towering black hair and a flawless complexion who was behind the counter and ordered for the two of them before Faith could get a word in edgeways. If she had been hoping for a sliver, she was to be disappointed, as the slices they were presented with were, in keeping with the owner's usual generosity, vast.

'We should just have had one slice and two forks,' Faith commented, all the while thinking that she would just have a taste and then ask to take the rest home. Jonty would love it.

'Rubbish, we deserve it after the morning we've had.' He took a large forkful. 'Mmmmmm.' An ecstatic expression appeared on his face. 'It's gorgeous. Try some. Here, I'll swap you a bit.'

He held out a forkful to her. She took it in her mouth, agreed with his opinion and then settled down to consume her own piece in its entirety, each sinful swallow making her feel torn between guilt and hedonistic delight.

Chapter Nine

A week later, Pollyanna came back to see Faith. She was wearing a pair of enormous tracksuit bottoms in cerise velour and a man's large T-shirt in black. Her fine hair was drawn back into a pony tail and her podgy feet this time were wedged into some yellow flip-flops. Someone had painted each of her toenails in plum.

'Hello, Pollyanna, how are you?'

'Hi, Doctor. I'm not so good, I'm afraid.'

'What's wrong?'

She shifted her bulk to one buttock while she wrestled to remove a small box from her pocket, which she then placed on the corner of Faith's desk.

'I had to stop these tablets. I'm sorry.'

'There's no need to apologise. Why? Did they give you side effects?'

Pollyanna scratched the back of her neck and nodded. 'They made me sick. Not just feel sick but be sick. I couldn't bear it.'

'Of course you couldn't,' agreed Faith. 'That's horrible. You did the right thing to stop them. Have you stopped vomiting now?'

'More or less. I just feel sick now. I haven't actually been sick for two days now, thank goodness.' She looked more cheerful for an instant. 'But at least I'll have lost weight. I must have – I haven't eaten for days.'

'It might have just been a stomach bug – we have been seeing a lot of patients with similar symptoms.'

Pollyanna shook her head, a soft lock of hair escaping from its hold and falling over her face. 'I don't think so. It did come on just after I'd started the tablets and I do feel quite a lot better for stopping them. I'd rather not try them again.'

'No, no of course not. As I said, you were right to stop them. There's no point in taking anything that might be helpful in one way but that gives you intolerable side effects. Do you want to step on the scales today?'

Pollyanna thought for a while and then assumed a look of optimism. 'Yes please.'

Faith pulled out the scales from under her examination couch and placed them in the centre of the floor, taking care to see that they were set at zero. Sitting back up, she saw Pollyanna steadily removing her hair clip, her bracelets, necklace, watch, earrings and finally her shoes.

'Every little helps!' she quipped, cheerfully. 'Here goes!' She stood on the scales warily, keeping one hand on the side of the desk before standing up straight, closing her eyes and letting go. 'I can't bear to look.'

Faith peered down. 'It's good news! You've lost half a stone. Well done – even if it wasn't in quite the way we'd intended.'

'That's so fantastic.'

Faith smiled at Pollyanna's animated features, happy for her. 'It's a great start. Does that change your mind about the Obesigon? Do you want to give it another try?'

'I can't really make my mind up now, Dr Faber. Something seems to have worked. I've never lost this much weight in so little time before.'

Pollyanna sat down again, deep in contemplation as she rearranged all her jewellery and squeezed her feet back into the flip-flops.

'It's obviously hard for you to make a decision,' started Faith. 'How about if I give you another prescription and then you can get it if you want to? Just imagine – if you did carry on, then next time I see you, you might have lost over a stone. How wonderful would that be?'

Pollyanna nodded in agreement but continued to look unsure, biting her bottom lip. Sensing that she was going to agree with her in the end, Faith typed the details of her prescription in to the computer, hesitated for the briefest of moments before pressing the print button. She reached over for the slip of paper, signed it and held it out for her patient.

'Okay,' was the resigned reply. 'I might start them again tomorrow as I do feel quite a bit better today and I've had some toast for breakfast. Thanks, Dr Faber. Thanks for being patient and encouraging.'

'Just remember – half a stone already,' reiterated Faith, trying to instil a subliminal message into Pollyanna. She felt sure that, with perseverance, the side effects might wear off – at least that's what the drug information suggested.

Pollyanna heaved herself up again, took the prescription and made her way to the door.

'I do feel thinner,' were her parting words over her shoulder and Faith grinned back at her delighted face.

Faith felt full of confidence and in control. Her professional life, as usual, was running in tandem with her private life, where things were definitely hunky dory. Jonty had been round at the house every evening since his weekend away, waiting in the kitchen for her, having a drink with Glenda. Faith loved to hear the sound of them laughing as she came in through the door. It made the house feel so much brighter and livelier. Even the dogs looked happier. When there was just she and her mother alone together, it was as though the ghost of Dennis was ever-present, coursing through the rooms like a noxious gas, following them wherever they went, casting a permanent spell of depression and gloom.

Jonty had, however, been very enthusiastic about the idea of having the reception at The Swindlehurst Castle Hotel. Faith omitted to mention that she had already had quite a close look, merely saying that she had popped in briefly one day to pick up the brochures. So they had had a fact-finding mission there one evening which had proved to be successful in all respects, particularly when they discovered that larger portions were available as desired. Best of all, the hotel was free the weekend they wanted, so they had booked, there and then, including the bridal suite for their first night together, too excited to risk the prospect of anyone else beating them to it, a decision that left Faith feeling just a tad worried that she had not passed on more information in the last email to her father, particularly about the cost.

There had followed several evenings when they passed the time putting together a tentative guest list and poring over the sample menus, wondering whether the chef's idea of fish and chips would be the same as theirs and whether passion fruit cheesecake would please everyone as a dessert.

Faith felt that she had never been so happy or close to Jonty as they planned their future together. She loved sitting near to him on the settee, leaning into his shoulder, feeling his lips brush against her hair as they made plans or watched television and the way he kissed her good night never failed to leave her in any doubt about the strength of his love for her. The only slight fly in the ointment was that they had not slept together for some weeks and she longed to feel his body touching hers and the joy of waking next to him. Had he not been so attentive and loving in all other ways, she would have been growing anxious lest his desire for her was waning, as usually he managed to come up with some plan for them to make love, even if it did turn out to be in rather uncomfortable and unconventional surroundings.

Today, though, Glenda had gone away. That morning, she had loaded not only her best horse, Prospero, into the horse box, but also Caspian and had set off for a two-day show in the New Forest, where she had some good friends who could put all three of them up for the requisite amount of nights. This meant that for the next three days Faith and Jonty would have the house to themselves, and Faith could barely contain her excitement. Everything seemed perfect. Her period had finished, the diet for the last week had been a breeze and the scales that morning (which she had used prior to surgery starting) had verified the weight loss she had been hoping for. She had dressed in smart trousers for work; they had fitted like a dream, even with pants underneath and with a neatly tailored summer jacket and a camisole top, there was no doubting that she looked good, maybe not quite up to the standard set by the delectable Ellie but none the less, a more than satisfactory result.

From the moment that she waved Glenda off, she knew that it was one of those days, few and far between so as not to encourage complacency but rewardingly sublime when they occur, when life would treat her kindly. True enough, nature smiled down upon her as she drove to work, the sun shimmering in between the trees, glinting on the windscreen, which for once was free of squashed flies. The traffic had been light and all the tractors that she usually got held up behind were today going in the opposite direction and the local radio station played some of her favourite tunes.

With so much to look forward to, including the fact that it was her half day, she finished surgery on time, had a quick drink with her colleagues and then offered to do the three visits at the local nursing home, calculating that this would leave her plenty of time to shop at lunchtime and then get home with more than enough time to prepare. She noticed with interest that Rob was going to visit Miss Stanhope, who, with a fortitude that curiously often goes with such a slight frame, had not succumbed to the gastro-intestinal bleed she had had secondary to her arthritis tablets and had been able to be discharged the previous day.

The nursing home did not keep her long. One urinary infection, one annoying wart and a repeat prescription review later, she was headed back into the centre of Lambdale, shopping bags on either arm to survey the delicacies on offer in the local butcher and Delicious. Smoked salmon mousse to start with, then fillet steak with chips and vegetables and finally a gooey lemon tart, all of which she knew would appeal to Jonty. She packed her purchases in the car and then, at the last minute, decided to nip into the surgery to see if there were any messages for her that could be dealt with easily. Joan, Margaret and Gary were chatting behind the reception desk, making the most of the calm and quiet before the bedlam of the afternoon's patients arrived. Gary was immersed in filling his colleagues in on the details of his pending holiday in Menorca.

Faith leant across the desk. 'There's just one thing for you, Dr Faber.' Gary moved some papers to one side. 'That girl, Pollyanna, handed this in for you.'

Faith accepted the bulky but light envelope that was passed to her, opening it curiously. Inside were two boxes of Obesigon and a short note explaining that, whilst she had been to the pharmacy and acquired the next month's treatment, on reflection Pollyanna had come to the conclusion that she did not want to carry on with the medication. It was signed with gratitude, plus a promise to keep going with the low-fat diet and keep her appointment for a couple of weeks' time.

'Oh, that's a shame,' Faith mumbled to herself. She saw Joan looking at her quizzically. 'It's nothing to worry about – she's just returning some tablets. I'll see you both tomorrow.'

'Not me, Dr Faber,' Gary was quick to point out. 'This time tomorrow I'll be at the airport waiting for my flight. I can't wait. Sunshine here I come.'

'Well, have a great time. You deserve it. You all work so hard for us.'

She turned and walked out, hearing Gary comment as she left, 'Isn't she lovely?'

Still a little disappointed with Pollyanna, Faith threw the envelope on the passenger seat and set off on the drive home. The traffic was decidedly busier, there were some temporary traffic lights that held her up for nearly twenty minutes and some grey clouds were starting to beetle across the sky, blotting out the sun for increasingly long periods of time.

Otis and Sam were delighted to see her. Miffed as Rex had been allowed to go with their mistress, they had ambled down to the stable yard where Dawn was working away, leaving everything spotless as usual and looking equally perfect simultaneously, found a shady patch where they could still keep an eye on all that was happening and settled down to snooze. The sound of Faith's car had them up in an instant, bouncing and barking up the path, falling over each other in their attempts to reach her first and bury their heads in her bags, ever hopeful that there might be something in there for them. They went with her into the house, refusing to move from her side, in case she was to leave them. Faith noticed how still it felt without Glenda's overbearing presence. She busied herself, opening windows to let in the bursts of sunshine, filling the dogs' empty water bowls and spoiling them with some chewy treats, which they took to worry under the kitchen table.

Unpacking her shopping, she stowed perishables away in the fridge before switching on the kettle to make a cup of diet soup, which was to serve as her lunch, unappetising though it may be.

By mid afternoon, the lemon tart was finished. Perhaps it had taken her two attempts to get the pastry case absolutely correct, with no defects for the filling to leak through, but that was a minor detail now that something approaching perfection was cooling near the window. Most of the meal was all ready bar the cooking. She was optimistic that the salmon mousse would relinquish its grip on the sides of the greased ramekin dishes and slide out onto the plates without losing its shape and that the home-made mayonnaise would tingle every taste bud on Jonty's palate and leave him wowed by her prowess as a cook.

Remarkably, she had nibbled nothing while she had been creating their dinner. Mindful of the fact that the scales had been more than encouraging that morning, she was able to rise above the temptation to lick out the bowl of creamy lemon filling or make a quick sandwich with the leftover prawns which she had bought to garnish the starter. Even the salted peanuts, which tumbled noisily into a wooden bowl, to be served with the pre-prandial drinks, did not have their usual allure. It was ever thus –

82

when Faith felt in control of her own destiny, food assumed a role of lesser importance. Only when she started to teeter and wobble on the tightrope of life did her literally all-consuming relationship with all things sweet and fattening assume bulbous proportions that took control of her.

Counting the hours, she changed the sheets on her bed, tidied the already pristine room and re-checked everything in the kitchen before spending a giddy twenty minutes in an empty paddock with the dogs who untiringly retrieved sticks and balls with constantly wagging tails. Glancing at her watch, she had just got time to shower, do her hair and make-up and put on the new dress that maybe would have incited rude comments from her mother about the fact that it revealed quite an alarming amount of her cleavage but tonight that was of no concern as Glenda was not there to see it. She knew Jonty would love it. Half of her hoped that he would just steer her up to the bedroom as soon as he saw her. It might make the meal a little later than she had planned but there was nothing that could not be postponed.

There were several different species of butterfly dancing a wild tango in her stomach as she returned downstairs, looking quite stunning in a calf-length indigo dress, her hair shining and held back with some diamante clips. Otis sneezed at her arrival and she panicked, wondering if her perfume was overpowering. Jonty would be arriving any minute. Should she wait, or would it look better if she was busy preparing the meal? She chose the latter option, preferring to have something to distract her as much as possible and while waiting for the pan of water to boil for the vegetables, prescribed herself a large glass of wine which should eschew the nerves effectively. She thought she heard his car and leant over the sink to peer through the garden but all she saw was Dawn, running past, waving and shouting goodbye as she did so. Faith noted, with chagrin, that it had taken her the best part of an hour to get ready whilst Dawn had somehow managed to go home after a hard day's manual work, looking as flawless as when she arrived. Faith waved back, then turned her attention to the table details, checking that all was in place. Again, she thought she heard the sexy throb of Jonty's car engine but assumed that she must have imagined it when the door did not open soon after.

The phone rang. It was Glenda, announcing her safe arrival in Hampshire, checking that there were no problems with the animals or the house and wanting Faith to fix up an appointment for the farrier for when she returned.

The phone rang again. This time it was Dennis, aware from a recent email that Glenda was away and taking the opportunity to speak to his daughter without the background accompaniments of loud and disparaging comments from his ex-wife. Faith, delighted to hear from him, tried to make conversation but all the while was leaning on the dresser watching the hands of the kitchen clock march steadfastly onwards and there was still no sign of Jonty. She wound the telephone cord around her hand as she listened, noticing with dismay that it was now pouring with rain outside.

Dennis at least sounded delighted with the venue for the reception. He reiterated that cost was no problem and that Faith should just continue to go ahead and book or buy whatever she desired and he would settle all the bills. Sure of his attendance at her wedding, he broke it to her gently that it was unlikely that he would be back in the country beforehand. He rang off, promising to ring again while Glenda was away and instantly the phone rang for a third time.

Hungrily, Faith snatched up the receiver.

'Hi, honey!' sang the unmistakable tones of Jonty.

'Where are you? I'm getting dinner ready. Will you be long?'

'Five minutes! Sorry I'm late but work dragged on. But I've finished now and just out of the shower. Pour me a drink and I'll be with you before you know it. What's for dinner? I'm ravenous. I've barely eaten all day.'

'Oh, that's wonderful. I was so afraid that something was going to go wrong and you'd not be coming.'

'Nothing would stop me. You know that.'

'I've got all your favourites,' Faith told him.

'Great. I've picked up a few things too. See you in a mo!'

He rang off and Faith sighed with relief. She hardly dared think how she would have coped if he had cancelled their arrangement again. A few deep breaths, a couple of swallows of wine and she was ready for action, ordering Otis and Sam to their beds so that she could concentrate on slicing potatoes into chips and putting plates to warm.

Suddenly the house was filled with noise and Jonty's presence. His hair still wet in places, he burst into the kitchen, handing flowers to Faith, patting the dogs and removing his jacket

84

simultaneously. Overjoyed, Faith threw herself into his arms and luxuriated in the ensuing embrace and kiss.

'Mmm, something smells good and somebody smells good too,' Jonty commented, gently extracting himself from her arms and reaching for the bottle of wine. 'Are you doing chips? Do plenty, won't you?'

He sat down at the table and took a handful of nuts, tossing them into his mouth with frightening speed. He emptied his glass without pausing for breath and refilled it to the brim before, as something of an afterthought, topping up Faith's.

Faith, accepting rather sadly the fact that she was not about to be whisked up to her room and ravished, turned back to the worktop where she had been preparing the vegetables.

'That's better,' breathed Jonty. 'What a day I've had. Non stop since breakfast.'

'Well, you can relax now,' Faith reassured him. 'Dinner's well on the way, so it won't be long. There's another bottle of wine in the fridge, or some red if you'd prefer. Tell me all about your day, while I cook.'

It's going to be like this for ever, thought Faith devotedly as the evening progressed. Jonty, normally loquacious but his tongue loosened even more than usual by the amount of alcohol he was consuming, kept up a steady commentary while Faith listened attentively, adoring each minute she spent watching his animated face as he recounted all the tales he had to tell. As the skies darkened, heralding the approach of night, they sat together at the table and savoured each mouthful of the food. Faith's good intentions to avoid the chips and mayonnaise evaporated after her third glass of wine and she knew that the next morning she would be horrified to think that between them they had eaten the entire lemon tart, which the recipe book had promised would serve six to eight, with thick, whipped cream and fresh raspberries.

Finally replete, Jonty belched loudly. He got up and put his arms around Faith's waist as she stood at the sink, waiting for hot water from the tap so that she could start the washing up.

'Leave that, my darling. Let's go to bed. I can't wait any longer.'

Faith giggled and offered no resistance, allowing him to lead her up the stairs and then into her bedroom. She excused herself, ostensibly to go and brush her teeth but also to have a moment alone so that she could change into the wisps of expensive lingerie she had bought before. Daringly, she completed her ensemble with a further generous helping of his favourite scent and then ventured back to the bedroom, only to find that he was tucked up under her duvet, snoring loudly, his mouth wide open, a little trickle of saliva leaking from the corner of his mouth in a far from attractive fashion.

Exasperated, Faith thought briefly of waking him up but decided against it. Slipping in beside him, she cuddled up to the curves of his body, which he acknowledged with some deep grunts but no return to consciousness. She lay there, enjoying his warmth and his smell, until, on the verge of joining him in sleep, she remembered that Otis and Sam needed to be let out and reluctantly traipsed back down to let them have a last run before locking up finally for the night.

Chapter Ten

The following morning, they woke later than intended and were jolted into reality by the uncomfortable feeling that they needed to rush – well, at least Faith did. Jonty seemed quite content to doze fitfully, whilst his fiancée cursed and swore, oblivious of her vestigial underwear, as she crashed around the bedroom, trying to pull herself together. It was certainly not the start to the day that Faith had envisaged in her master plan for their three days together alone. Had things gone accordingly, then they would have been woken early by the sun streaming in through the open window, made sleepy, ecstatic love, following which there would have been plenty of time for her to serve warm croissants and coffee in bed for them both. But she had forgotten to set the alarm clock as a back-up and so the idyll was doomed from the moment she opened her eyes and saw what time it was.

Jonty finally rolled over and opened his eyes. 'Wow, just look at you,' he mumbled, mouth fuzzy and dry from too much alcohol-induced stupor. 'Where did you get that little outfit? Come here and let me have a closer look.'

He made a grab for her but she was too quick.

'I can't, Jonty. Just look at the time. I've to be at the surgery in forty minutes and there's so much to do here before I go.'

He collapsed sideways onto his back and rubbed his eyes. 'Phone in sick, then we can spend the whole day together in bed.'

Faith gave him a withering look. 'You know I can't possibly do that.'

'Then just tell me what needs doing and I'll do it. I don't have anything planned for this morning apart from trying out a new horse. I'll even check that Dawn's okay. The washing-up can wait until tonight, surely. We'll have a takeaway – it'll save you cooking and won't create any washing-up if we don't use plates.'

But Faith was already in the shower, emerging after a matter of minutes, wrapped in a towel but still dripping as she ran downstairs to open the door for the dogs and put on the kettle.

She drove off with uncharacteristic haste, leaving Jonty still in bed with a meagre mug of coffee, the croissants still in their bag on the worktop. She had grabbed one to eat on the way which exploded at the first mouthful, showering her with crumbs that she tried to brush off, veering perilously near the grass verge as she did so. Angrily, she steered the car in the direction of Lambdale, upset because her plans for the morning had not come to fruition but equally anxious at the thought that she would most probably be late for her first patient, which was not an auspicious start to the day and one which also might be frowned upon by the partners. But arriving at the practice with seconds to spare and the first patient, who burst into floods of tears before either of them had even sat down, meant that she had no time for further deliberation of how things should have been.

It was a frantic morning at the surgery. Rob had telephoned in sick, suffering from a high fever and raging sore throat, doubtless contracted from one of his patients. He had assured his trainer that he had tried to get up and dressed but just felt too ill to do so. His appointments had to be divided up amongst the others, the result of this being that fully booked surgeries became unpleasantly tight with extras, to say nothing to the emergencies that rang in and had to be dealt with, without delay. Faith was more than happy to help out. It made her feel as though she was one of the partners and she hoped that her alacrity to agree to see additional patients had not gone unnoticed.

She telephoned Jonty as soon as she had ushered out her last patient, a troubled middle-aged woman with fibromyalgia. He was still at the house and assured her that everything was under control. Dawn had arrived to see to the horses and had offered to walk the dogs when she had finished mucking out. He even promised that he had done the washing up and tidied the kitchen and whilst Faith suspected that this really meant that he had crammed everything into the dishwasher so that everything was out of sight, she was at least grateful that he had gone to that amount of trouble.

With promises to see her after work and provide the takeaway, thereby excusing Faith from the additional pressure of having to fit shopping in with her busy schedule, he rang off, terminating the conversation with the usual utterance of his undying love for her.

True to his word, when Faith arrived home, tired from a hectic day, he was waiting for her, glass of wine in each hand. He led her into the garden, where, on a small table, he had arranged an assortment of dips and crisps for them to nibble on as a relaxing prelude for the evening. The ambience was helped by the knowledge that it was Friday, with no work to get up for the following morning and no prospect of Glenda until at least teatime on the Sunday. A bottle of wine later – Faith was quite appalled at the amount of alcohol they were getting through but at the same time did not want Jonty to think that she could not keep up with him – they were forced inside by the arrival of heavy, ponderous clouds and threatening spots of rain. Jonty's takeaway duly arrived and they ate, picnic style in the drawing room, enjoying huge slices of pepperoni and mushroom pizza, strings of melted cheese drooping like elastic and sticking to their chins and fingers, with accompanying garlic bread, wickedly dripping with butter but so irresistible. He had ordered far more than was necessary but between them they still managed to eat everything, washing it down with great gulps of wine, laughing as they wiped their mouths and reached for more, their appetites, both for food and each other, insatiable.

Drunk, full to bursting, they made love on the carpet, Faith bubbling over with desire and wanting to please Jonty however she could as he peeled off her clothes in a tantalisingly slow fashion, wishing that she hadn't opted for plain white and serviceable, rather than exciting, bra and pants. It can only be imagined what Glenda's reaction would have been if she could have witnessed the coupling in her best room, but this was a fact that thrilled Faith all the more. As opposed to last night when alcohol had exerted a soporific effect on Jonty, this evening it seemed to fuel him with extraordinary stamina and energy and Faith was amazed and delighted, if not a little shocked at times, by the ideas he had and expected her to join in with. Finally worn out, they rolled apart, sticky with sweat and expended emotion, mutually satisfied and happy. Faith was on the verge of suggesting that they make their way upstairs to bed when Jonty, as if granted by some supernatural force a second wind, jumped up and disappeared from the room only to return with yet another bottle of wine and a box, which he opened, revealing a raspberry gateau, decorated with thick, whipped cream.

They ate large wedges with their fingers, Jonty starting a new game by anointing different parts of Faith's body with the cream and then going to an inordinate amount of trouble to lick it off. Faith found that she was ravenous again and rationalised her indulgence by reassuring herself that the energy she had just burned off must surely equate to a portion of cake.

That night they slept well, arms and legs intertwined, bedclothes all over the place, Otis and Sam at the foot of the bed, having crept upstairs when they found the kitchen door had been left open by mistake.

Faith got her wish in the morning when they woke and she was able to serve Jonty his breakfast in bed on a tray complete with a small vase of roses. The effect was spoilt somewhat by his spilling the orange juice on the pillow, but Faith, determined that nothing was going to faze her, merely laughed and handed him her glass instead. Her rosy glow of how married life would be continued, as they showered together, made more coffee and then wandered down with the dogs to the stables, hand in hand.

For Faith, it was one of those magical days that she wished would never end. She kept willing time to slow down so that she and Jonty could be captured in this bubble of perfection where they were immune to the world. She wanted to savour every second and commit it to memory, so that it would be with her for ever more. Faith was sure that Jonty would suggest they went for a ride but, uncommonly for him, today he seemed content just to look. The horses checked, which really did not need to be done as the ever-reliable Dawn was already at work, looking jaw-droppingly chic in skin-tight jeans and a sleeveless top, they strolled across the fields with Otis and Sam, until Jonty announced that they were going on a surprise day out and ordered Faith to get her coat and then get into his car. He drove too fast, keeping one hand on her knee the whole time, swerving round the sharp bends on the country lanes, making Faith clutch the sides of her seat, until he reached a major road which afforded him the opportunity to go even faster but at least in straighter lines. He had insisted on having the soft top down and their faces were battered by the noisy wind. Faith tried to speak to him but, even shouting, could not make herself heard above the growl of the engine and the perpetual roar of the pounding air. She gave up and concentrated on trying to keep her hair under some semblance of control until they slowed down to join the long, crawling stream of traffic that was stopping and starting as it made for York.

Miraculously, they found a space in the first car park they tried. Arms around each other, they tried to weave their way into the centre of the city. The pavements and pedestrian precincts were thronged with hordes of shoppers, each of whom seemed to be carrying a minimum of four carrier bags, and tourists from all over the world, cameras around their necks, guide books in their hands, chattering in incomprehensible languages. It was impossible to make any progress walking as if in a three-legged race, so reluctantly they let go of each other, settling for occasional hand holding when space permitted.

After coffee and cream cakes, sitting outside a small café and watching the world go by, they visited the Minster and the Shambles, Jonty ever patient while Faith paused to admire the architecture, peered into mullioned bay windows or dived inside tiny shops to make purchases. They ambled round the market, Faith wanting to buy fresh ingredients for supper but Jonty pulling her away from the stalls, insisting that they would be eating out. She was to have a complete break this weekend – that was his intention.

Feet throbbing from all their walking, Faith was relieved when Jonty led her into a dark but friendly bistro for lunch. Conscious of how much she had been eating over the last couple of days, she tried to ask for a simple salad, with tuna, plus mineral water to drink but Jonty countermanded her order and requested lasagne and chips for them both, well aware that she would never be able to resist, and a bottle of red wine. It arrived in bowls, the cheese topping surrounded by orange oily bubbles. If the aesthetic appearance left a little to be desired, the taste made up for it. There was no denying it – dipping the fat, golden and crispy chips into the bolognaise sauce and biting into them was a satisfying sensation.

The dessert menu arrived. Faith steeled herself to refuse and was intensely grateful when Jonty checked his watch, waved away the waitress, asking for the bill. He settled up, leaving a generous tip, and pulled Faith to her feet. Outside it was duller and cooler but regardless, he led her to the river just in time to board one of the small boats for an afternoon cruise. The temperature continued to drop as they chugged upstream, giving them an excellent reason to huddle together, excitedly pointing out things to each other, laughing at their own private observations and jokes.

By the end of the two-hour trip, Faith was glad to get back to the car. Inappropriately dressed with only a blouse and thin coat, she felt quite chilled to the bones and the cup of tepid tea that she had bought had done little to warm her up. Obligingly, Jonty turned on the heater and unearthed an old picnic rug from the tiny boot, wrapping it around her, tucking her in and making her feel like an invalid. He drove back at a similarly hectic pace and wasted no time on their arrival at the house to run her the hottest of baths and make her a really piping hot cup of coffee.

Feeling the life regenerate through her body, courtesy of the heat, Faith submerged herself as far as she could under the water. As she warmed up, she felt suddenly weary, unaccustomed to so much physical activity and mental excitement, so after a cursory drying, she slipped under the duvet and curled up in a ball, nodding off almost immediately.

She was woken by Jonty kissing her. She briefly thought how romantic that was, truly like something out of a fairy tale. Stretching out, she was about to reach out for him, but he was raring to go.

'Come on, Faith. Get up! Look at the time. The table's booked for half seven, so you'll need to get ready. Dress smartly, we're going somewhere special.'

'Oooh, where?' Faith was curious.

'Ah ha. Wait and see. I've fed the dogs. Your ma rang. She's fine and having a great time. The horses went well, though Caspian apparently threw her off into a lake.'

'Is she all right?' Faith asked anxiously. 'I never even heard the phone.'

'You know Glenda, she's made of strong stuff. Yes, she's fine. So's Caspian. They went on to finish the course without any more problems apparently.'

'I wish she'd be more careful,' commented Faith, head in her wardrobe, looking for something suitable to wear. 'She's not as young as she used to be.'

Jonty laughed. 'I wouldn't advise that you let her hear you say things like that.'

Faith turned and grinned at him.

'Hurry up, Faith. Oh, you're hopeless! Let me choose for you.'

So she did, trusting his judgement as she did everything else about him. When she put on his choice of dress and stood back to be admired, she felt sure that she had guessed where their destination was to be. She hugged him tight.

He took her to The Green Dragon.

'I thought you said we were going somewhere special?' Faith asked as they headed for the door, feeling embarrassingly overdressed in her sequin- bespattered evening gown of peacock blue.

Jonty turned to her. 'This is special. It's where you agreed to marry me.'

'Oh Jonty, how wonderful. I do love you.'

The fact that she would have looked more at home at the Swindlehurst Castle Hotel, which was in fact where she had secretly hoped he was taking her and thus been dressed accordingly, no longer mattered. Who cared if everyone else in the pub was wearing the same jeans that they had had on all day? Did it matter one jot that all eyes were upon them as they walked to the bar? Let them titter to each other, hiding behind their pint glasses. All that she cared about was Jonty. He had requested they have the same table and there was a single red rose waiting on her side plate. Again he ordered for her, knowing so well what she preferred most of all, well aware that if she just had a taste then she would carry on until she had a clean plate.

In stark contrast to their hurried lunch, they ate at a leisurely pace, spinning out their meal so that it lasted until nearly closing time. A lot of their conversation centred around Glenda, Faith expressing yet more reservations about her mother's potentially dangerous pastime, Jonty gently contradicting her and pointing out that she would never change. It was a difficult debate for Faith to win, for she knew that Jonty experienced the same thrill from riding as Glenda did, feeling high from the element of danger and thriving on taking risks. Faith preferred feelings of control, predictability and reliability, traits which bored her mother and fiancé to distraction.

Driving the short distance back, Jonty's blood alcohol way over the legal level, Faith succeeded in turning the topic away from her mother, whom she felt had managed to monopolise the evening almost as much as if she had been present, and onto the wedding. Considerable progress had been made and arrangements seemed to be coming together smoothly.

'What about your dress?' asked Jonty, pulling off his tie and slumping down on the sofa, patting the cushion beside him as an invitation that Faith should join him.

'No, I've not got that yet. I've looked at a few but not seen anything that I even fancy trying on.'

She ignored the fact that she was still hoping to be at least two sizes smaller before she even entered a shop that sold bridal wear. But Jonty seemed to have the skill of mindreading to add to his many other virtues.

'How's the diet going? When are you going to start that?'

Faith, who had, with uncustomary directness, begun to undo Jonty's shirt buttons, froze just as she was about to tackle his belt as well. She felt hurt that he had not noticed that she had lost over half a stone. About to speak, she was unable to get any words out before he carried on.

'I mean, don't get me wrong. That dress you have on this evening looks amazing but it is a tiny bit tight, isn't it? You know, around your waist and hips.'

He must have seen her face fall and rushed to make amends. 'You look voluptuous, my darling. You always do. You know I love having some flesh to get hold of.'

Any desire that Faith might have felt drained away like water down a plug hole. Jonty was in full flow. He continued to dig himself into an ever deeper hole.

'I'll always love you, you know that. Whatever you look like. But losing a stone or so just might make all the difference. You'd look gorgeous, even more than you do now,' he hurried to correct his faux pas, 'and you'd feel better – yes, think of the health benefits. You doctors are always telling patients to lose weight. Surely you have to practise what you preach.'

'I have actually lost some weight already, Jonty,' Faith muttered, trying to contain herself, feeling a lump in her throat and wanting desperately to avoid tears.

'Good for you, my love. But you've a way to go still. I'm with you every step, you know. I'll back you on this one.'

'Thanks.'

'Tell you what, I'll help even more. I know a guy who's a personal trainer. I'll have a chat with him and get you an exercise programme and a diet, then I'll take you through it. I might even do the exercises with you but I am going to be very busy for the next couple of weeks, so it might be hard for me.'

'Of course, Jonty. Whatever you say.'

'That's my girl. I'll ring him in the morning. No time like the present to get started. Plus, time's running out – not long to go now!'

He must have spotted the tears welling in her eyes. 'And I'm crossing off every second.'

Faith managed a watery smile.

'Now, I don't know about you, but I'm bushed. Let's go to bed.' He made his way to the door and turned, realised that Faith wasn't following him in the expected fashion.

'You go on up. I'll just see to the dogs,' she said.

He yawned, shrugged his shoulders and left. She listened to him climbing the stairs. Her bubble had been punctured. The belief that Jonty loved her unconditionally had been shot to smithereens. He wanted her slim. She knew that. She could read the real thoughts behind his words and see through the blundering comments that came out of his drunken mouth.

Sam and Otis, instinctively aware that she was sad, shuffled up beside her, onto the sofa and lay their heads on her knee. She stroked them distractedly, fighting back her tears, sitting there morosely, wondering what to do, how to change and be what he wanted her to be.

The first step was inevitable. Waiting until she was sure that she could hear the indubitable sound of his snores, Faith crept into the downstairs cloakroom and put her fingers down her throat. Perhaps, if she were to do this after every meal, distasteful though this prospect was, then the pounds would drop off speedily and some form of control over her weight might ensue. This could be the answer that she was looking for but it would involve so much clandestine behaviour that the utmost care would be required so as not to arouse any suspicions. But on this occasion, she felt only minimally better afterwards; for once she had not managed to bring up as much as she thought equated to the meal she had devoured. This had happened before and only resulted in frustration and despair. Clearly, it was not going to be the entire solution to her weight loss.

Later, lying in bed, unable to sleep, her mind too full of madcap ideas on how to lose weight, Faith stared up at the ceiling of her bedroom, wanting to reach out and cuddle Jonty, but he had rolled over onto one side, his back towards her and she felt that he had created a barrier between them that she dare not cross. The minutes clicked past on the digital clock. Faith thought of her skinny mother, the perfection of Dawn's body and the svelte elegance of Ellie's. Then she thought of Pollyanna, supermorbidly obese, with little realistic hope of ever achieving a normal healthy weight, regardless of how many tablets she took or what operations she underwent.

That was when the idea first occurred to her. Sitting in her car, thrown onto the front seat, were the anti-obesity tablets that she had prescribed for Pollyanna but she had declined to take. Initially, Faith dismissed the idea. It would be foolish to take them. They had been prescribed for a patient, not for her. To self medicate was wrong and took advantage of her position. Arguably, she was sure all doctors did so at some point or other, presumably just pain killers or perhaps antibiotics for a chest infection or cystitis. There was nothing wrong with that. Why was this different? She knew what the drug was, what the potential side effects were and how to take it. Trying it would do no harm, in fact it might give her the kick start in the right direction she so desperately needed. There was no reason for anyone to find out and she knew that there was about six weeks' supply which surely would produce some dramatic effect and would negate the need to vomit after meals. Anything that did that would be more than welcome. It was hardly equable to taking dangerous drugs like opiates or anything with an addictive risk.

As the idea took shape in her mind, the temptation grew out of all proportions. Unable to wait until the morning, she slipped out from under the covers, tiptoed needlessly, for Jonty was deeply asleep, across the room, shushing the dogs who raised sleepy heads and yawned as she passed. Slipperless, she cut a painful path across the gravel drive and retrieved the tablets from the car. The dose, she reminded herself, was one, twice a day. Trembling very slightly, she popped out a capsule from the blister pack and swallowed it with some water.

'This must work,' she insisted, out loud. 'It must.'

About to put the tablets safely into her bag, she hesitated, cogitated briefly and then quickly extracted two more and slipped them into her mouth before she could change her mind.

She jumped as she heard someone at the door, zipping her bag closed, almost caught in the act. Her heart was thumping in her chest as she saw Jonty was standing there, sleepy and tousled, rubbing his eyes and face.

'What on earth are you doing?'

'I've just got a bit of a headache. It was stopping me from sleeping, so I came down for a paracetamol,' she answered, grateful that she had not put the light on, so that he could not see the guilt that was written all over her.

'Well, come back to bed now. I was missing your curves to curl up to.'

'I'm coming. I'll just get another glass of water. I feel a bit dehydrated. It must be all that wine.'

'Bring me one, would you?' Jonty called, already halfway up the stairs and more than half asleep.

Chapter Eleven

A month later and the effects of the tablets had been amazing. Faith had lost over a stone, was proudly wearing new clothes that flattered her new physique and was exuding a level of confidence that she had not been privileged to feel before. She positively loved the Faith that she saw when she looked in the mirror, still possessed of curves but only those in the right places. Gone was the roll of fat that had thickened her waist, gone were the wedges of fat wobbling on her hips that Jonty laughingly referred to as her love handles and virtually gone were the flabby thighs. What a joy it was to open the wardrobe each morning, turn a blind eye to the shapeless garments that she used to rely on and instead opt for pencil skirts and fitted dresses. How she now loved to go clothes shopping; suddenly all sorts of fashions were flattering and she no longer felt that all eyes were upon her in the communal changing rooms. Better still, she had not felt the need to vomit once and, best of all, her appetite had shrunk to a minimum.

But her achievements had not come without a downside. Despite sticking to the prescribed dose of medication, apart from the odd day when she felt that she had overindulged a little and so took a double dose, she was still a victim of the incontrovertible side effects. The loose stools were just about manageable, though they came with a certain degree of urgency that necessitated a close proximity to a toilet at all times. There had been an acutely embarrassing incident when she was out riding with Glenda and had suddenly had to leap off Breeze, toss the reins to her mother and dive behind some bushes, blaming some seafood she had eaten the day before. Harder to bear was the sticky, oily discharge from her bottom, which oozed out with no warning whatsoever, staining her underwear and possessed of a nose-curling odour. But this too was bearable with forward planning – that of never going anywhere without a couple of pairs of clean pants in her bag, pushed right down to the bottom and covered by her cheque-book holder, purse and umbrella.

It had taken some time to get used to the dizziness, which rocked her world when she stood up too quickly, bad enough to make her reach out for something to grab onto until her equilibrium adjusted to her new position. Similarly, rotating her head too quickly to the right or left resulted in similar disquiet, which made driving particularly hazardous as she learned to adjust. She had only just avoided scraping the side of John Britton's new car last week when she was reversing out to go on her house calls. The tremor in her hands was harder to conceal, though with practice this too became a skilled art and she felt sure that nobody had noticed.

Bad as the side effects were, they were far outweighed by the benefits. So many people had noticed and commented favourably. At home, Glenda had come as close as she ever would to giving her a compliment.

'You've lost weight at last, Faith. Better start looking for that dress now before you start putting it back on,' she'd sniffed only a couple of evenings ago, as she watched her daughter push away a plate that was still half full.

Jonty had been more gracious with his praise. He had bought her flowers and a pair of earrings and, best of all, cancelled the personal trainer. He kept telling her how proud he was of her and seemed even more tactile than he had ever been, as if unable to keep his hands off her new body.

'Put her down, Jonty,' Glenda had snapped, blowing cigarette smoke at the two of them. She had come into the kitchen irate after an unfulfilling schooling session with Caspian to find her daughter and prospective son- in-law cuddling.

At work too, remarks had been passed, even patients had noticed. Faith had been most eager to hear from Ellie, desperate for her seal of approval.

'You look great, Faith,' she'd nodded. 'How have you done that so quickly?'

'Just diet and exercise,' lied Faith, aware of her cheeks reddening.

'I wouldn't lose any more, if I were you,' Ellie had warned her. 'Sometimes if you lose too much too soon, you can end up looking a bit gaunt.'

And Faith had thanked her for her advice, assuring her that she had almost reached her target weight, when in reality she was hoping to lose at least another half a stone.

Rob had said very little, something that Faith had attributed to his being male and therefore he probably had not even noticed. But he had and one day, when they were sitting in the staff room together, ostensibly busy with paperwork he looked up at her and caught her eye.

'You've lost a lot of weight, Faith,' he started.

'Yes, I know,' she replied, trying not to sound smug.

'You're not ill, are you?' He sounded anxious.

Faith laughed. 'No, not at all. I just want to be slim for my wedding. Jonty and my mother suggested it and they were right.'

Rob was silent, the thought processes of women mostly a mystery to him.

'There was no need, you know, to go as far as you have done. I thought you looked very nice before.'

'That's kind of you, thanks. I feel much better though for having lost the weight. You know, more energetic, fitter generally.'

'Mmmm. You could probably have achieved that just by doing more exercise. You'd be welcome to come out running or cycling with me any time, if you'd like.'

'Thanks,' repeated Faith, with a rather wry laugh, 'I'm not sure I feel that energetic!'

Façade intact, secretly Faith was beginning to fret. The problem looming was that she was about to run out of tablets. She dared not stop taking them, fearful that the weight would pile back on and her efforts would be wasted. The question was how to acquire some more. An option that was dismissible immediately was to ask one of the partners to sign a prescription for her. Obesigon was only licensed for those with a body mass index of over thirty and as Faith's had never been more than twenty-seven, she should never had have the tablets in the first place, let alone be allowed to continue them now.

Her panic was mounting until she spotted a potential solution when reviewing her list of patients for the day. There, at the end of the morning surgery, was Pollyanna Smith. Faith felt a frisson of trepidation run through her veins. It would mean taking a considerable risk but then again, there was no reason why anyone should find out. She was not jeopardising anyone's life, certainly not that of her patient and it would be an easy and convenient way of procuring the tablets and covering her tracks at the same time.

The relief that she felt made the surgery run smoothly which was just as well as Mrs Tonbridge was back as her penultimate patient, having somehow managed to concoct yet another list of complaints, regardless of the fact that she had only been seen a few days earlier, when she had taken over twenty minutes of Faith's time.

Mrs Tonbridge's body language screamed challenge before she even opened her mouth. She fixed Dr Faber with her gimlet eye and when confident of her undivided attention commenced to read her list out loud. She worked her way steadily from head to toe, from stuffy nose and burning scalp to indignant bunions and murderous corns. Before she finally came to a halt, she begrudgingly confessed that her bowels were quite a lot better with the new capsules prescribed last time.

Faith rushed through the problems, barely giving Mrs Tonbridge the opportunity to enlarge on her symptoms, firing closed questions at her in the hopes that she would simply answer yes or no and be prevented from the usual diatribe that she was capable of. But Mrs Tonbridge was not to be hurried. She was far too experienced in the art of taking up the doctor's time to be affected by such a facile ploy as this. She wanted her usual amount of time and nothing was going to stop her.

Having exhausted all the techniques that she knew to bring a consultation to an end, Faith sat back in her chair, admitting defeat. She was anxious least Pollyanna felt she could not wait, aware that her surgery was running late.

Pollyanna, however, was perfectly happy waiting. She was deeply immersed in an old and battered copy of a magazine about celebrity life and had earmarked several others of a similar ilk that she would like to read, if possible, before she left. It was one of the best things about coming to the surgery as these glossy publications oozed with intrigue and gossip but were too expensive for her to consider buying on a regular basis. She was just in the middle of an article about a well-known English starlet with a penchant for illegal substances, no dress sense and a staggering number of lovers, when Faith called her in. Pollyanna stood up, glanced around the waiting area which was largely empty save for an elderly gentleman who appeared to be asleep and covertly stashed the other magazines into her voluminous bag.

'Hi, Pollyanna! How are you? I've not seen you for a while.'

'I'm okay. I'm sorry I didn't come back sooner, as I promised but as I wasn't taking the tablets, there didn't seem to be much point. I left them at the surgery for you. Did you get them?'

Faith managed somehow to remain expressionless. 'Yes, thank you, I did. So, how can I help you today?'

'I'm still hoping that you can help me with my weight. I've been trying to diet. I've been really good. I've got fruit coming out of my ears. My mum can't believe it. She says she's never known me refuse a pudding before, so I've surely lost some.'

Pollyanna looked pleadingly at Faith as if the latter had control of the weighing scales.

Faith gave her a sympathetic smile. 'Let's see then.' She reached and pulled out the scales.

Pollyanna performed her ritual of removing anything she thought might have a deleterious effect on the outcome before gingerly lifting her first foot off the ground. It took her a few seconds before she stood fully upright and let go of the edge of the desk. She shut her eyes tight.

'Oh, I can't bear it. I don't know why I've closed my eyes, I can't see the scales for my tummy. That doesn't seem to be getting any smaller yet.'

Faith studied the wobbling needle. 'Okay, off you get.'

Pollyanna sat down heavily and started replacing her jewellery. 'Well?' she asked warily, a tinge of hope in her voice.

'I'm sorry.' Faith shook her head, 'You haven't lost anything.'

'Nothing? Not even a pound?' Pollyanna was distraught.

The truth of the matter was that she had actually gained almost 3 pounds but Faith could not bring herself to break news of this magnitude.

'I'm so sorry,' she repeated.

'What am I going to do now?' Pollyanna wailed.

Faith patted her hand, hoping this gesture would be empathic.

'Let's talk about what we can do next to help.' Her voice hesitated slightly. 'What about the tablets? Would you like to try them again?'

Pollyanna had no problem answering immediately. She shook her head vehemently. 'No way. I felt so terrible with them. It took ages for the sickness to wear off once I'd stopped them.'

'There are others we could try. I've never prescribed them before but I've heard about them.'

'I don't really want tablets, Dr Faber. I was wondering about surgery.'

Faith pulled an apologetic face. 'There are lots of downsides to that. It's a big operation and not without risk. To start with the anaesthetic would be risky for you, then you might get an infection—'

'I don't mind about that,' Pollyanna was quick to interrupt. 'I had my wisdom teeth out and had to be put to sleep for that... and my appendix. I was fine.'

'This isn't just surgery, you know. It's major surgery.'

'So?' Pollyanna was not to be put off. 'Can you refer me? Please?'

'The trouble is,' began Faith, 'that there is an even bigger hurdle for us to get over. I have been asking questions and I've been told that it's unlikely that this would be possible on the NHS.'

Pollyanna's mouth dropped open. 'But my aunt's next door neighbour had the operation last year and she had it done on the NHS.'

'It all comes down to the money that's available at the end of the day,' Faith was quick to tell her. 'There have had to be a lot of cutbacks in our referrals and I'm afraid that this sort of surgery is one of them.'

'That's so disappointing and unfair. I've tried everything. I've starved myself, I took those horrible, horrible tablets and this is my only hope. I'd really believed that you could arrange it for me. I've read all about it in magazines, too, people have had amazing results.'

'I'm so sorry,' Faith said softly, feeling personally responsible for letting Pollyanna down. 'We all feel as frustrated by the cutbacks as the patients do. Only yesterday I had to turn down someone's request to have their varicose veins operated on.'

'Varicose veins? That's nothing. My problem is far more important. I could become diabetic, have heart problems, arthritis. Yes, I've read all about what can happen and I want to do something to prevent it – now, while I'm still young enough to do so.'

Faith felt uncomfortable as she sat on the receiving end of Pollyanna's wrath. She chose to stay silent.

'It's not your fault,' sniffed Pollyanna, looking as though she was about to sob. Faith passed the box of tissues.

'You could have it done privately,' Faith suggested, eager to provide a solution. She could hardly have said anything worse.

'And how would I pay for it?' Pollyanna was really crying now. 'It would cost thousands of pounds and I haven't any money anyway. I earn hardly anything and have to give most of it to my mum for my keep.'

'Yes, it would be a lot. Perhaps you could save up?'

Pollyanna shot a withering look at her, which Faith appreciated was about as much as she deserved for such a tactless suggestion.

'There's always the tablets…'

Pollyanna was on her feet, heading for the door, using the sleeve of her shirt to wipe her nose. 'No thanks. Good bye.' The door did not exactly slam shut but there was a distinct degree of finality about the way it closed.

Faith was left feeling completely impotent. It was rare that she had a patient walk out on her and it was a distinctly unwelcome feeling to be left with. She could have handled things far better which would have resulted in a much more satisfactory conclusion, plus a patient who was likely to come back and see her again. She shook her head sadly and made a mental note to drop a line to Pollyanna in the next few days, offering her the chance to come back and talk. Sighing, she turned to the computer to make an entry in the notes. Her hands were shaking as she typed: 'Weight up 3lbs, asking about bariatric surgery. Difficulties with this option discussed. Offered medication again.'

She clicked on the prescription and waited while it was printed out. After all, that was more or less what had happened. Hurriedly altering it by hand so that it was for two month's supply rather than one and then signing it, she shoved it in her pocket and finished her paperwork without another thought.

At lunchtime, she ventured into the local pharmacy, hoping that it would be quiet. For once, luck was on her side and, uncharacteristically, the old-fashioned shop was empty. Though devoid of human form it was stuffed from corner to corner with merchandise. Shelves filled the entire available wall space and were crammed with everything imaginable, from loofahs and pumice stones to hot-water bottles and bejewelled pill boxes. A multitude of over-the-counter remedies were packed in neat, tight rows in alphabetical order, many of them preparations that had

104

stood the test of time, thanks to their faithful disciples, rather than their medically proven prowess.

Faith wound her way amongst rotating displays of toothbrushes, flannels and sponge bags, trying not to knock any off. Each step that she took on the wooden floor echoed around the room, announcing her presence. She was of half a mind to leave and go further afield but any bid to escape was thwarted.

'Good afternoon, Dr Faber,' came a call from the back of the dispensing area. 'Can I help you?'

'Hello?' Faith's heart was thumping ferociously as she glanced about to see where the voice has come from

Alan Gough, white haired, ruddy cheeked with half-moon glasses that were balanced on the top of his head, made his appearance behind the counter and beamed at her.

'We've got some very good offers on this week in soaps and shampoos. Nit combs are two for the price of one. There seems to be a bit of a problem at the local primary school.'

He pointed vaguely to one corner of the shop and then tidied a box of emery boards that were next to the till along with a jar of sugar-free lollipops. Faith wondered how he remembered where everything was.

'Or do you need something for your doctor's bag?'

Faith shook her head. 'No, it's nothing like that. One of my patients left her prescription behind this morning by mistake. She's a bit forgetful! We'd been talking about all sorts of things. I've tried ringing her but there's no answer. I've got a house call out near where she lives, so I thought I would drop it in for her.' She knew that she was gabbling.

'That's very kind of you. Hang on, I'll not be a moment with this. You've picked a good moment to come in. The lunch lull, I call it. A welcome respite after a busy morning. I was just about to have my sandwiches, but I'll do this first.'

He disappeared again, returning after what seemed like an age. 'Here you are. You've not been here long but I hear a lot of complimentary words about you from patients as they come in here for their medication.'

'Oh,' Faith was taken aback. 'That's nice to hear. Anyway, thank you so much. Sorry to interrupt your lunch.'

She took the bag from him quickly, hoping that he would not see how she shook and said goodbye, trying not to rush too obviously as she made her way to the door.

Relieved to be outside, her mission successfully accomplished, Faith made her way back across the square. Out of sheer habit, she stopped to look into the window of Delicious, marvelling at the customary array of irresistible delicacies and wondering whether to buy something to take home for Jonty.

'Faith!'

She whipped round before thinking what she was doing and just had time to see Rob crossing the road towards her, before she was engulfed in a vertiginous wave which made her knees turn to water. She only just managed to steady herself by leaning back on the window and taking some deep breaths, willing her in-coordination to calm down.

Rob was running now, alert to her need for help. He grasped both of her shoulders with his hands, a surprisingly strong grip for one with such a slight frame.

'Faith, are you all right? You look terrible.'

'I'm fine,' she stammered. 'I just felt a little faint. I'm fine now.' She hoped she sounded more convincing than she felt.

'Come into the café. You can sit down and I'll get you a drink and something to eat. I bet you haven't had any lunch, have you?'

Faith wanted to remonstrate with him but hadn't the energy, so allowed him to lead her inside and thankfully sank onto a seat. Rob watched her for a moment, then as happy as he could be that she was not about to pass out, went and ordered quickly before returning to his patient.

'I'm fine now,' Faith repeated, actually feeling rather better.

'You're still very pale. Here, drink this.'

A foaming cappuccino delicately dusted with chocolate was pushed across the table.

'I've put some sugar in it. And don't argue,' he could see Faith on the verge of protesting, 'just get it down you.'

Faith sipped at the sweet, hot drink, ending up with little in her mouth but a fine creamy moustache. She managed to laugh.

Rob was pleased to see her relax a bit. He broke up his shortbread biscuit, which was the size of a saucer, and offered her a piece. 'Go on, it'll do you good.'

In the manner of an incredibly shy mouse, Faith nibbled at one corner. She noticed Rob giving her a stern look and took a larger bite. He waited until she had finished and then made her take a second piece and a third, watching her while she ate every crumb.

Slowly but surely, she did genuinely feel better as her blood sugar rose to a more healthy level. She had forgone breakfast, partly because there was no cereal left but largely because she had lately been trying to eat only one meal a day, that of supper with her mother and more often than not, Jonty. In her blinkered desire to maximise the weight loss, she had been far too ready to attribute all her symptoms to side effects of the Obesigon, never considering for a moment that perhaps simple starvation was also playing a role.

Pinker in the cheeks, the world around her finally staying still, her head and the nausea subsided, Faith thanked Rob for his concern and help. She assured him that she felt completely back to normal, which was more or less the truth and blamed a non-stop morning with no time for a mid-morning coffee for the interlude he had just witnessed.

Rob was relieved to see the rapid improvement and accepted her explanation without question. He did not tell her that in reality he did not believe that such a scenario would result from a mere missed coffee, nor did he comment on the fact that he had noticed how her hands shook, even after her recovery.

Chapter Twelve

Horrified, Faith noticed that the weight loss was plateauing out, regardless of her having decreased her intake even further. For several consecutive weigh-ins, done behind the closed door of her surgery, with the door locked, so that she could strip down to the minimum of clothing, there had been no change. She had tried standing on the balls of her feet, the sides of her feet and her heels but nothing made any difference to the result on the scales. Her target weight seemed so close yet equally unattainable. She was desperate to reach it, mindful that her goal was almost palpable. Dennis, or more likely his wife, had emailed her some photos of simply stunning and unique wedding dresses, conjured up by a local, Yorkshire designer who happened to be a friend of theirs and – joy of joys – there was a shop in Harrogate that might stock them. There was one dress in particular that Faith adored on sight and lusted after, but in order to do it justice, she felt she needed to be just that little bit slimmer.

She started to cut her evening meal down to such a negligible amount that even Glenda started to notice.

'For God's sake, Faith, eat something,' she'd barked one evening when Faith had barely touched a meal.

Excuses such as that they had had a working lunch around a practice meeting or that she had eaten out with colleagues soon dried up and so, instead, she started to arrive home later and later, hoping that supper would have been and gone by the time she turned up.

After an infuriating fortnight at a static weight, Faith was so depressed that she put her head on her desk and burst into tears. All that effort and agony for nothing. She had put up with dizziness, nausea and tremor, to say nothing of the gastro-intestinal effects and the overwhelming lethargy that had set in as her metabolism slowed down to adapt to the modicum of calories it was being forced to function on. Surely she deserved to lose some weight just as a reward for the hell she had subjected herself to.

She could well understand why Pollyanna had thrown the tablets into touch after just a few days. No one could be expected to tolerate feeling like this. Faith concluded, with reluctance that she would just have to stop taking the tablets and hope that she could control her eating to, at the very least, maintain the weight she had stuck at.

But quite the final straw had been yesterday evening, when, after a day of self-denial, missing breakfast, lunch and then making do with a mug of strawberry and mango tea for supper, she had been so ravenous that she had driven to the nearest supermarket, ignoring the fact that the local village shop would be open, for fear of seeing someone who might recognise her. Hoping that she merged in with all the other shoppers, she had bought junk food – a family-sized bag of cheese and onion crisps, some doughnuts, a large Swiss roll and several large bars of chocolate. Feeling compelled to explain her purchases to the vacuous blonde sitting at the checkout, whose mind, in reality, was far removed from her customers and what items they had in their baskets, Faith had assumed a nonchalant smile and informed her they were having a children's party. She had hurried to the car, ripping off the first of the wrappers as soon as she closed the door behind her, frantic to get the first taste of the food she had resisted for so long. She had eaten as she drove, throwing paper onto the car floor, paying scant attention to the road. Not far from the house, she had stopped and finished her feast, stuffed to the point of serious discomfort, her stomach having shrunk with the exertions of stringent dieting. An owl had hooted mysteriously as she rolled herself out of the car and disappeared behind a hedge to gag, heave and retch, refusing to stop until she felt that she had ejected all that she had eaten and hopefully a bit more.

Hating the reminiscences that haunted her mind, she blew her nose and washed her face at the small sink in the corner of the room. It gave her yet another opportunity to admire her new profile in the mirror above. Ignoring the blatant fact that her face looked haggard and considerably more than its chronological age, if she stood on tiptoe then she was able to focus her attention on her neat figure, today clad in a short-sleeved, well-tailored navy dress, nipped in at the waist by a narrow red belt and ending just above her knees. Even Faith had to concede that she looked good. Last night's binge had apparently not been detrimental. She had never been so slim and despite her achievement having been so hard to come by, it was definitely worth it.

The image of that amazing wedding gown flashed before her. She had to have it. It was a major component of her dream day which she had planned down to the very last detail. The idea of accepting the slightly larger size was not one that was even worthy of consideration. There was nothing else for it – she would have to continue with the Obesigon, just for a couple more weeks. Looking at the positives, it had stood her in good stead apart from recently. She wished that she had had more experience with patients taking the same drug; perhaps they too stopped losing weight temporarily. She pondered on how, with some drugs, people developed tolerance, needing to increase the dose at intervals to maintain the same benefits. Though there was nothing in the prescribing information to suggest that Obesigon was such a drug, it might just be worth a try. The side effects could hardly get worse and if it just restarted the weight loss again, then the desired aim would be achieved. It was only for a short time, she reassured herself. Once that dress was secured, she could safely stop taking any drugs as the resultant euphoria would be more than enough to control her eating habits.

Plan settled, Faith felt somewhat happier, though at the same time apprehensive about the prospect of feeling so unwell, and possibly worse, for a longer period of time. So, before she had the chance to change her mind, she quickly swallowed two tablets together with a gulp of the fizzy, diet drink that she had brought with her, never thinking that the caffeine and chemicals in this might only exacerbate her symptoms.

She worked her way methodically, but half-heartedly, through a fully booked surgery composed mostly of elderly ladies. Faith studied them each in turn as they regaled her with their problems. There was some sort of uniformity between them which initially she could not put her finger on but then realised that the common denominator seemed to be their clothes. Faith wondered at what age women stopped wearing brightly coloured things, settling instead for the anonymity of beiges and wishy-washy shades of mauve and green which did nothing to complement their complexions and only served to make them blend in with the background to the point of insignificance. Somehow, try as she might, she couldn't imagine Glenda embracing old age with the same quiet acceptance. When not in her jodhpurs, she favoured colours that announced her presence with a statement, leaving no one in any doubt that she was there. No, Glenda would never allow her hair to be permed into a neat round helmet, she would never be seen with a shopping basket with wheels and she would most certainly sooner slit her wrists than settle for sensible flat shoes unless of course they were riding boots.

There was one sprightly patient amongst them, Cheryl Liddle, happily overweight, confident in her curvaceous femininity, dressed outrageously in a pair of cut-off linen trousers and a patriotic shirt of red, white and blue, who bounced into the room, booming with self-assurance. Faith liked her immediately. She was one of those women who simply radiated a welcome to all she met. Faith perked up a little as they chatted, unable to resist the infectious cheerfulness and was almost sad when it transpired that all she had come for was to discuss some holiday vaccinations which meant that she simply had to be directed to the practice nurse for further advice. It was with more than a degree of envy that Faith watched her leave.

Rob and Ellie were up in the coffee room by the time that Faith arrived, their surgeries completed in reasonable time. She tried to avoid Rob's eyes as she entered, as both looked up to greet her.

'Kettle's just boiled,' Ellie told her. 'I love your dress. Is it new?'

'Yes.' Faith executed a twirl, delighted that Ellie had given her seal of approval. This was a foolish if involuntary movement as the room span round at an alarming speed. 'Am I interrupting?' she asked, half hoping that they would answer in the affirmative and that would give her a reason to leave the room.

'No, not a bit of it,' Ellie assured her. 'We were just chatting. Talking about good places to eat around here. I was giving Rob some suggestions. Can you think of anywhere?'

Faith laughed a little too loudly to be convincing and reached the sink, which she leant against, while putting instant coffee into a mug. The spoon rattled against the china as she shook.

'We're spoilt for choice, quite honestly. There are good restaurants and a multitude of pubs that do excellent meals. Was it for something special?'

'My parents are coming up to visit for a weekend. My cooking's not up to much apart from the real basics, so I thought I'd take them out for a meal.'

'There's the Black Duck at Mallington,' Ellie suggested. 'Ian took me there for our last anniversary. It was delicious. Have you been there, Faith?'

Faith shook her head.

'Where's Mallington?' asked Rob.

'It's a tiny village just north of Bedale,' Ellie explained, reaching for a pen and starting to draw on an unused prescription. 'Here, I'll do you a map. They source all their ingredients locally. You can really taste the difference.'

With their heads bowed over the table, Faith was delighted to have an opportunity to cross the room and sit down with neither of her colleagues watching her. She was very concerned that they would notice how her hands shook as she held her mug, which she quickly placed on the floor beside her chair.

'Sounds good!' concluded Rob. 'Thanks, Ellie. I'll give them a ring and book a table.'

Faith tried to busy herself with some paperwork, not feeling up to much conversation.

'There was only one house call request today,' Ellie told her. 'How amazing is that?'

'I'll do it,' Faith offered rapidly, glad to be provided with an escape route.

Ellie was shaking her head. 'No need. John's already on his way. Not that it was urgent, but he finished in good time and it's his half day. Ed's on holiday, so Rob and I were wondering about going back to my house for lunch. We're due to do a tutorial, so thought we'd combine it with a snack and some time away from the practice. You'd be very welcome to join us – I'm sure your input would be helpful. Would you like to come with us?'

Faith willed her brain to come up with a tangible excuse, immediately.

'I'm sorry, I can't. I've promised to do a follow-up visit on a patient. Terminal care, not long to live, so really needs me to go in every day.'

'All right – that's a shame. Another time perhaps.'

'Yes, that would be lovely. I'd better get a move on.' Faith glanced at her watch. 'It's later than I thought.'

She stood up deliberately and grabbed her bag.

'What about your coffee? You've not touched it,' Rob pointed out.

'How silly of me!' Faith pretended to have forgotten. 'Not to worry, I'll get one later. See you soon.'

She sped out of the room before they could call her back about anything, heart racing, mouth parched and longing for the drink she had left behind.

Half an hour later, Rob was sitting in Ellie's kitchen, smiling as a tiny ginger kitten with white, soft paws but claws like glass fought a losing battle with his shoelaces. Ellie was buttering fresh baguettes that they had stopped to buy on the way and filling them with ham and salad.

'Mayonnaise or mustard?' she asked, not looking up, concentrating on slicing some cucumber wafer thin.

'Both please,' was the reply.

Ellie raised her eyebrows at the unusual request but complied with the order without saying anything. Slicing each sandwich into two, she arranged them on a couple of plates and pushed one towards Rob, paying particular care to which one was his.

'That's great, thanks, Ellie.'

They munched in silence for a while. Ellie tore off a square of kitchen towel and mopped up a blob of mayonnaise that had found its way onto her chin.

'That's better. I was really hungry. We did say that this was going to be a tutorial, you know, Rob. What would you like to talk about? Any glaring gaps in your knowledge that you think I might be able to fill?'

Rob laughed. 'Plenty. Ed and I are working through a fairly comprehensive timetable of pre-planned topics on a weekly basis. Otherwise we tend to concentrate on things that have cropped up in surgery day to day.'

'Fine. I'll not disrupt the timetable then. Tell me something interesting you've seen in this morning's surgery.'

Rob thought, ate some more sandwich, chewing slowly.

'Come on, there must be something…' Ellie sounded impatient.

He swallowed. 'There is,' he began hesitantly. He looked down at the kitten, upside down, rolling around, innocent of all life's dangers.

Ellie waited. He seemed to be struggling to find the right words.

'Go on,' she was more encouraging now, alert to the fact that he was clearly troubled. She watched him inhale sharply.

'What would you do... if... you were worried about someone at the practice?'

Ellie looked bemused. 'A patient? Well, I think you know the answer to that already. We discuss worries like that amongst ourselves most of the time, occasionally we involve hospital colleagues. Which patient is it that's worrying you?'

Rob ate the last of his sandwich with great deliberation. He wiped his mouth. 'No, not a patient. A doctor.'

'Ah,' Ellie said quietly. 'That's slightly different, I guess. I suppose the first thing to do would be to share your worries in confidence with someone else who knows that doctor and then perhaps speak to the person it is that you're worried about. That's what happened when Clare was ill. It can be very difficult. Especially if they're friends outside of work as well.'

She could see that Rob was digesting this and got up from the table, returning seconds later with a cake tin, prising the lid off as she sat down.

'Help yourself. Lydia made them and they're really good.'

Rob peeped inside and took out a butterfly bun with lurid blue icing under the soft sponge wings, scattered with a scandalous amount of hundreds and thousands and silver balls. He peeled the paper case off carefully.

'Want to tell me any more?' suggested Ellie.

'It's Faith,' he blurted out.

'Go on.' Ellie sat still.

'I'm really worried about her. Oh, I don't know. I can't put my finger on anything in particular. It's just that she doesn't seem the same these days. She's lost so much weight, have you seen her hands shaking? And the other day she almost collapsed in the market place.'

He described the incident in more detail, Ellie listening carefully throughout.

'Well, there's no doubting the weight loss,' she agreed. 'But she's just been doing that because of the wedding, or so she says. Although it's extreme to say the least. She's really looking as though she's taken it too far now.'

'The wedding is three months away, Ellie. If she goes on at this rate, you'll not be able to see her if she stands sideways – that is if she can stand up at all. Why did she refuse to come and have lunch with us today?'

'She said she was off to see someone who's terminal. That's easily answered.'

'Sure it is, if it's true. Can you think of anyone at the practice that's dying at home at the moment?'

Ellie thought and shrugged. 'No and usually we all know so that we can cover for each other. I had noticed the shaking as well. I'd put that down to nerves. She's quite an anxious girl, anxious to please. The fainting episode sounds scary. Perhaps, like you suggested, she just skipped breakfast that day and her blood glucose was low. Perhaps she's got an overactive thyroid. That would account for the dramatic weight loss and the shaking.'

'Maybe, but usually thyrotoxic patients are famished and can't get enough to eat. When did you last see Faith eat? Plus there's more.' Rob was getting into his stride now. 'Yesterday I saw one of Faith's patients. A really obese woman called Pollyanna Smith. She just had a sore throat, but that's not the point. I noticed in her notes that she was on Obesigon and asked her how she was getting on with it. I know that one of the rare side effects can be that it drops your white cell count down and thought that maybe that was why she had the throat problem. She says she hasn't had a prescription for weeks yet there was one, clear as day, issued recently. You don't think Faith has been taking that, do you?'

'Surely not,' gasped Ellie, 'that would be appalling.'

'But it all makes sense, doesn't it?' Rob continued, urgency in his voice. 'For whatever reason, there's the question mark hanging over that script, she's lost loads of weight, impossibly quickly and that drug can make you shaky and dizzy – I looked it up last night. The list of side effects was vast, most of them revolting. I can't imagine anyone wanting to subject themselves to them.'

Ellie was dubious, not wanting to contemplate that Faith would use a patient's prescription fraudulently.

'No, there's got to be some simple solution here, Rob. Some women get obsessed with dieting. Maybe she's one of them. I think she's just taken it to an extreme. I'd love to meet her fiancé though. What must he be like to let her do that to herself? You'd have thought he'd noticed.'

'She told me that he'd suggested it. Well, him and her mother.'

Ellie shook her head. 'I don't particularly like the sound of either of them.'

The door to the kitchen opened and Ian, Ellie's husband, came in. Tall, tidy and good looking with smiling eyes behind spectacles with designer frames, he leant over to kiss his wife on the lips.

'Hello, Ellie, hi, Rob.'

'Ian!' Ellie was delighted to see him. 'Sit down. We need your advice.'

Dutifully obeying, he sat down and gently removed the kitten who had clamped its claws into his trouser leg. He raised his eyebrows at Ellie, who, understanding instantly, passed him the tin of buns.

'Tell him what we've been discussing,' Ellie urged Rob.

Ian ate three buns before he spoke his verdict. Ellie moved the tin out of his reach.

'She sounds a sorry soul, if you ask me. Rob's theory about the tablets, whatever they were called, has some substance you know, Ellie. Sometimes you can be a tad naïve – you know you only like to see the good in people.'

Ellie ignored his last comment. 'So what do we do? Tackle her at work? Tell John, as senior partner?'

'No,' Ian answered. 'I think that's a bit extreme. Firstly, do you have any concerns about her clinical practice? No? Then let's find out a bit more. Why don't you invite Faith and her fiancé, what's he called again?'

'Jonty.'

'Right. Invite Faith and Jonty to dinner and then we can meet him and get to know her better.'

Rob and Ellie exchanged glances.

'He's a genius, Rob. He always knows exactly the right thing to say or do. I think it should just be the four of us. Not that I don't want you to come for dinner –you're welcome anytime, but I don't want her to be suspicious.'

'It sounds like a plan to me,' Rob concurred, 'and I agree with you that I shouldn't be there. She really admires you, Ellie, so I'm sure she'll want to come.'

'Right, that's settled. I'll ask her this afternoon. Talking of which, we'd better get back. Are you picking up the girls, Ian?'

He nodded.

'You are truly amazing.' Ellie gave her husband a big hug. 'I shouldn't be late. Can you make sure they go out and groom those ponies? They're covered with grass stains after rolling this morning.'

Chapter Fourteen

Ecstasy hardly does justice to the feeling Faith experienced when Ellie asked if she and Jonty would like to go round for dinner at the weekend. Quick to reply in the affirmative, she then had to endure an onslaught of mental ramblings while she decided on the best plan to accommodate her host's beneficence – for Ellie had a reputation as being a tremendous cook – and her own personal diet arrangements. Not an easy task to sort through the various permutations of possibilities and come up with one that satisfied her obsessive mind. It was not just the dilemma of what she might be expected to eat but also that of making sure that the evening was not marred by her tremor and dizziness. After reflection, Faith decided that she would have to forgo the Obesigon for a minimum of twenty- four hours beforehand and just hope that she had sufficient will power to control her appetite in the meantime. That ought to mean that she could eat a normal dinner at Ellie's, be an appropriately enthusiastic guest and then restart the tablets before she went to bed. Perfect! She reminded herself that Ellie knew she was on a diet and was the sort of person who would take this into account, wanting to please as a hostess, so she would be unlikely to produce overly fattening and indulgent foods and hopefully would opt for light but tasty courses which all would enjoy.

Happy with her solution, the next problem was Jonty. His reaction to the invitation was a far cry from her own. He prevaricated and grumbled, unsure whether he was free or not, more than a little tetchy with Faith for having accepted without prior discussion with him. Faith found his behaviour incomprehensible. The Jonty she knew was gregarious, extrovert, always up for a good time. It was normally she who looked for reasons not to do things, preferring to stay in. She challenged him with what was wrong.

He pulled a belligerent face. 'I don't know these people, Faith. You'll be talking about medicine all night – blood and guts, that sort of thing. Okay for you but it makes my stomach turn.'

119

'We won't, Jonty. I promise you. Ellie's husband isn't a doctor. We probably won't even mention work. They've twin girls, who are about eight, they have ponies. You'll have lots in common with them, I'm sure.'

'What? With the twin girls? That's charming.'

Jonty grunted. Faith interpreted this as a sign, rightly or wrongly, that he was mellowing.

Saturday evening arrived. Faith had not needed to fall back on any hidden strength of character whatsoever to keep her eating under control; the nervous excitement she felt at the prospect of going to Ellie's was more than enough to cause anorexia. Relieved to find that her hands were steadier, her balance improved and her guts decidedly calmer, she was rushing around most of the afternoon trying to decide what to wear, washing her hair repeatedly and trying to style it and ringing Jonty to suggest outfits for him. After her umpteenth call, which Jonty terminated abruptly by telling her to 'get a grip' and cutting her off, Faith was sent into a panic lest he should decide not to turn up.

Glenda watched the drama of the afternoon unfold with an undisguised smirk on her face and through the fog of many cigarettes. By five o'clock and unable to take any more, she poured them both a large gin and tonic and ordered her daughter to sit down and drink.

'I can't,' wailed Faith, 'I've so much to do yet.'

'Rubbish,' Glenda commented, astutely. 'All you've to do is put on some clothes, a bit of slap and take some deep breaths. It's only dinner, for God's sake.'

'Yes, but it's so vital we make a good impression! If Ellie really likes me and we become closer then perhaps she'll recommend me to the others for a partnership.'

'She'll like you more if you don't behave like a twitchy lunatic!'

Faith looked at her mother, knowing that she was right. She sat down in an armchair opposite her and gulped some of her drink. Unaccustomed to spirits she shivered involuntarily.

Glenda looked pleased. 'That's better. Now just you put your feet up and let's find something banal to watch on the box – take your mind off things for a while.'

120

Glenda snatched up the remote control and flicked rapidly through an array of channels before settling on an ancient but well-loved British sitcom. Faith tried to give it her full attention but could not. She wished her mind would lie still and relax like Otis and Sam at her mother's feet. She watched her mother roar with laughter at the hackneyed jokes, apparently with not a care in the world and wished fervently that she could be like that too. When the final credits started to roll and the catchy theme music came on, Glenda stubbed out her cigarette and turned to Faith.

'You've not finished your drink,' she noticed. 'Never mind, go and get ready now. If you're not down in twenty minutes, I'm coming to get you!'

Faith obeyed and ran upstairs, a little woozy from the drink which had definitely been more gin than tonic and tackled the interminable problem of what to wear. Ellie had said just dress casually. It was just to be an informal supper. But then Ellie's idea of casual might not be the same as hers. She would never forget the dinner party Jonty had once taken her too, stressing that it was informal dress, only to find the men in dinner jackets and the women competing with their diamonds. Faith had hated every moment they were there, feeling that all were laughing at her behind her back as she sat there in a pleated tartan skirt and a voluminous sweater.

Ellie was always beautifully dressed. She had some amazing clothes, or perhaps it was just that she had the enviable ability to make anything look good when she put it on.

On the bed was a mountain of rejected outfits. Glenda's voice bellowed warningly up the stairs and Faith scurried to pick out something. Settling on a short, black, sleeveless dress, having read somewhere that such a garment could never look out of place, she accessorised with sheer black tights, a pearl choker and bracelet and a kingfisher blue pashmina, which was in fact Glenda's. High-heeled court shoes, again black, completed her ensemble. Quickly squirting perfume – Jonty's favourite, of course – onto her pulse points, she tottered back down to her mother's critical eye.

'You look as if you're going to a funeral,' she sniffed.

'Thanks, Ma,' Faith responded, her voice heavy with sarcasm. 'Where's Jonty? He's late.'

'Oh, stop fretting. You're like a nagging old wife and you've not even got him to the altar yet. He's not late and he'll be here, okay? Have another drink.'

'I don't want one. I'm going to phone him.'

Glenda barred the way to the telephone. 'Leave him be. Give him a chance.'

Faith wandered towards the window, picking her way carefully between the dogs, who were keen to sniff her legs. The last thing she needed was for them to drool down her only pair of black tights.

Only minutes later, Jonty arrived and Faith threw her arms around his neck. She could not help but notice that his breath smelled of alcohol. Gently he extracted himself and accepted a drink from Glenda who started pouring it the moment he appeared through the door.

'We haven't time for that.' Faith tried to snatch it away from him, but he was too quick for her.

'Yes, there is,' he raised his glass to Glenda who mirrored his action. 'Cheers!'

'Jonty, we've got to get going,' Faith nattered away.

'The taxi's not here yet, darling. Chill out!'

'I thought you were driving.'

'Well, I decided that it would be nice if we could both have a drink or two. I'm certainly going to need a few to get me through the evening.'

'Jonty, you mustn't get drunk!' she exclaimed but he had stopped listening, totally wrapped up in an anecdote of Glenda's.

Exasperated, Faith rushed back to the window, this time to listen out for the first crunching sound of car wheels on the gravel drive. Glancing over her shoulder she could have wept. Laughing and joking with Glenda, Jonty seemed to have made no effort at all with his appearance. True, he had shaved and, she hoped, showered but he was wearing his old cords and a polo shirt under the jumper he usually wore for riding. She was about to comment but then thought the better of it, aware that there was an undesirable tension in the air already between them. The prospect of a heavenly evening seemed remote if Jonty continued in this vein. Perhaps she should ring and cancel, feigning some type of rapid onset illness but there was no time to put this lie into action as the sound of the taxi's horn interrupted them.

122

'That'll be for us, then,' Jonty yawned, giving Glenda a quick kiss on the cheek as he rose to his feet. 'See you later. I don't expect we'll be back late.'

'Be sure and stop by for a nightcap – I'm longing to hear all about it.' Glenda waved her arm in their direction and returned to the television.

The taxi seemed to take for ever as it meandered down the lanes towards Lambdale. It was not a particularly pleasant evening. The sky was overcast and there was a chilly breeze swirling around the trees and bushes in a way that very much suggested that summer was long gone and autumn well underway. Jonty was not very communicative, staring out of the window but none the less holding Faith's hand in what she hoped was a conciliatory way. She kept squeezing it encouragingly. As they entered Lambdale, Faith wriggled to the edge of her seat, eager to point out to Jonty where the surgery was and other points of interest.

'Look, there's that wonderful delicatessen where I buy you cakes. That's the surgery down there – you can just see it. Isn't it a pretty market square?'

Jonty nodded. Faith was encouraged.

'That's the craft shop where I bought you that painting and – oh look! There's one of my patients!'

She nudged Jonty hard in the ribs.

'Where? Oh, you mean that fat woman eating the takeaway?'

Faith gasped. Pollyanna was sitting on one of the seats in the centre of the square with a nondescript young man wearing a fedora. Both were holding foil containers and tucking into the contents, stopping only to ferret into a paper bag from which they produced chips. They were laughing, merrily.

They disappeared from sight as the taxi turned down to reach the road that led to Ellie's.

'No wonder she doesn't lose weight. She swore to me that she was on a diet!'

'Just goes to show, you shouldn't believe all people tell you.'

'She seemed so genuine, though. I like her a lot. I thought she was being honest with me, that I had her confidence.'

'Oh, get real, Faith. Patients are only human. They'll just tell you what they think you want to hear.'

Faith sighed. 'That's so sad. I must tell Ellie.'

'Faith, you promised me. No shop talk.' There was a warning in Jonty's voice that defied her to disobey. She rushed to assure him that she would postpone the discussion about Pollyanna until Monday.

'Oh, look, we're here! What a charming house.'

Ellie opened the door to meet them, Lydia and Virginia pushing past her to get a glimpse of the guests first.

'Welcome! Faith, how lovely you look! And you must be Jonty. I've really been looking forward to meeting you, I've heard so much about you.' ˉ

Faith had a quick peep at Jonty and noticed with relief that he was smiling and holding his hand out to shake Ellie's, doubtless entranced by her beauty.

'This is my husband Ian. Come on into the lounge. Just leave the door. The girls will be in, in a minute. Lydia's the one with her hair in plaits, by the way. I've lost count of how many there are. Virginia's spent the last hour doing it for her, so it might be wise to pass some sort of compliment, as it was done just for you.'

They followed Ellie into a homely room, with large French windows that opened out onto the back garden. Heavy curtains of dark green fell majestically to the carpet but the focal point of the room was surely the Victorian fireplace, edged on either side by plants, set in burnished old copper and brass jelly pans, their leaves rich and shining with health. Ellie seated her guests on the generously sized, soft sofa and sat opposite on the arm of an easy chair, the seat of which was occupied by a sleepy dog, which had acknowledged their arrival by a thump of its tail and a barely lifted eyelid. Ian asked them what they would like to drink, Jonty asking for a whisky, a choice Faith thought was asking for trouble. She chose a glass of wine, which she proceeded to take minute sips from, aiming to make it last as long as possible. Her eyes darted quickly around the others and she instantly felt foolishly overdressed. Ellie was wearing skinny denims and a whiter than white T-shirt with tiny capped sleeves, somehow making such ordinary wear look extraordinary while Ian looked casually smart in chinos and a dark blue shirt. They made a hugely attractive couple and Faith wondered if she and Jonty presented themselves in the same way to onlookers.

Virginia and Lydia hurtled in to join them like a mini tornado, one carrying bowls of canapés, all home made by Ellie, the other carrying the kitten which was duly deposited on Jonty's lap but quickly passed, almost thrown, to Faith as it sank its claws into his thigh.

She felt her tights snag and pulled down the hem of her dress to hide the imperfection.

Ian started up a conversation with Jonty, asking him about his work and was rewarded with a lengthy speech about bloodlines and thoroughbreds, most of which he found incomprehensible. Jonty ended with, 'I hear you have horses. Are they pure bred?'

'They're just ponies for the girls. There's a bit of Welsh in them, I think.'

'You'll be needing to upgrade as your daughters grow. You just come to me. I could find something suitable for them to compete with and hunt.'

Ian smiled charmingly. 'How kind of you. Actually, I just want my girls to have fun. We all love Smudge and Jester – they're dependable, good natured and part of the family. I don't think we'd ever want to sell them.'

Jonty shrugged, unfamiliar with this attitude to equines.

'Here,' Ian unscrewed the bottle, anxious to keep the peace, 'let me top you up.'

Ellie called them through to eat. Anxious to make things as informal as possible, she had laid the large kitchen table, rather than the one in the dining room. She was aware that Faith felt awkward in her outfit and very much wanted to make her feel at home and relax a little. So far, she had perched on the edge of the cushion, both hands clutching her glass and looking almost too terrified to speak. Her face looked gaunt and sad, while her collarbones stuck out in a frighteningly skeletal fashion. Perpetually, she turned her head to Jonty, as though seeking his approval.

On purpose Ellie was serving soup as a starter. A delicious aroma wafted from the steaming bowls as she put them on the brightly coloured mats before the diners.

'Help yourselves to croutons. Lydia! Guests first!'

Faith was embarrassed to see Jonty taking a more than generous helping, leaving few for the others. He seemed oblivious of his faux pas and tucked in noisily, slurping each mouthful, which made her want to cringe.

Ellie noticed the unmistakable tremor of Faith's hand as she raised the spoon to her mouth, concentrating hard on what she was doing. Impossible to diagnose with certainty, it could equally have been drug induced or just due to simple anxiety.

The whisky had certainly quashed any nerves that Jonty might have had. He was becoming gregarious and garrulous, verging on the crude. Encouraged by the delicious starter, which surely was a sign of more good things to come, he leaned back in his chair and put his arm around Faith, pulling her towards him and causing her to spill her own soup, fortunately only on her side plate. He was keen to talk, mostly about himself, a little about his father but rarely about Faith or the wedding, fielding Ellie's enquiries deftly and re-directing them back to a topic of his own choosing. Whether this was deliberate on his part to make sure that there was no opportunity for matters medical to take centre stage, or whether it was simply his alcohol-fuelled tongue, Faith would never know, but she wished that he would stop either interrupting or talking over the twins, who obviously had some tales of their own that they wanted to delight everyone with.

Ellie did her best, trying to involve everyone equally, the epitome of the good hostess. She repeatedly asked Faith questions, hoping to draw her out of her shell more, disliking the way she seemed to be totally in Jonty's shadow.

Ellie served fajitas as a main course. Soft tortillas on a plate and an array of dishes to wrap up in them – spicy chicken or beef, still sizzling from the pan, shredded lettuce and tomato, sour cream, guacamole, grated cheese – a free for all with everyone helping themselves, guaranteed to break down even the most impenetrable barriers between tricky guests. On this occasion, however, it was unsuccessful.

The extent to which Jonty tried to monopolise the evening was directly proportional to the amount of alcohol he imbibed. Forgetting what manners he had, he reached out for the food first, ignoring Ellie's invitation to Faith to help herself, piled his plate up high and helped himself to more wine, all the while barely drawing breath as his monologue continued.

More embarrassed by the second, Faith attempted to rein him in, rather in the way he might have tackled an undisciplined stallion when out riding. She tried to change the subject away from that of his own achievements, many of which were being described in a highly embroidered fashion, and chat to Ellie and Ian about

126

their house and how long they had lived there and to the twins about their animals and school.

By the end of the main course, as Ellie cleared the plates away, refusing Faith's offer of assistance, Jonty had tipped his chair back, put Faith's pashmina around his own shoulders and was unzipping and zipping up Faith's dress, a humiliating party trick that he saved for special occasions, those being associated with ultimate inebriation. Faith tried to laugh it off, playfully pushing him away, whereupon he lunged at her, almost falling off his chair and planted a sloppy kiss, intended for her lips, on her shoulder.

'I'll make some coffee now,' decided Ellie, loudly and emphatically. 'We can have it with dessert.'

'That'd be a excellent idea,' nodded Ian, getting to his feet and helping clear away, which included moving the half-full bottle of wine out of Jonty's vision.

'I'm not sure how much longer I can be polite,' Ian whispered to his wife as they stacked the dishwasher together. Ellie rolled her eyes in agreement before turning back to the table.

'Let's have dessert in the lounge. Lydia, do you and Virginia want to go and watch television? I'll bring you some ice cream in a moment.'

They needed no persuading, having given up a long time ago on trying to join in the conversation. Normally their parents had nice people round to the house, ones who spoke to them as equals, not ignored them as if they were something rather nasty and best avoided.

Faith led the way back into the lounge, Jonty draped around her neck like an ugly sloth. As she sat down, he spotted the bottle of brandy in the corner of the room and helped himself to a large balloonful, smacking his lips together appreciatively as the first taste trickled down his throat.

'Jonty,' hissed Faith. 'You can't do that!'

He plonked himself next to her, very close, spilling a little on her dress as he did so. 'You're gorgeous, you know that?' he slurred. 'This is a great evening.'

He belched loudly, making not the slightest effort to conceal it and making Ellie recoil as she entered and handed out tiny slices of rich chocolate tart, served with home-made orange ice cream.

'This is to die for,' breathed Faith, genuinely.

'More please!' demanded Jonty, who had polished his off in two or three mouthfuls. He held his plate out to Ellie who had barely sat down.

'It's very rich,' she replied, but put her own plate to one side while she returned to the kitchen to provide second helpings.

The post-prandial part of the evening did not improve. Jonty steadily spiralled into an even more drunken state and Faith willed the hands of the clock on the mantelpiece to move quicker towards a time at which she thought it might not be inappropriate to leave. Ian, as ever, part of a team with Ellie, did his best. He tried talking about politics, sport, computers, economics, the weather, but all his attempts failed to ignite any interest from Jonty, who had moved on from bragging about himself – probably having run out of things to say – to making a laughing stock of Faith. He was critical of her appearance that evening and of her riding, of her taste in music and books and her love of food. He did however concede that she had lost a lot of weight.

'Not much to get hold of now when we're in bed,' he spoke in a loud stage whisper to Ian, which made Ellie want to slap him.

If there was one moment in the entire evening when all four were in complete unison, then it was when Faith announced that they really should be going and rang for a taxi on her mobile phone, not wanting to give either Ellie or Ian the merest chance of offering to give them a lift. Polite good byes and thank yous were said at the door, Faith feeling that she ought to apologise as well and hoping that Ellie could read that sentiment that she tried hard to express in her eyes. Jonty slapped Ian on the back, in the manner bestowed on a close drinking partner and tried to kiss Ellie on the lips, but missed as she had the foresight to move her own head briskly out of the way as she saw his closing in on her.

As the taxi disappeared down the drive, Faith waved tentatively from the back window and saw Ian folding his arms around Ellie and kissing her lovingly before they went indoors. She felt indescribably envious and sighed as she looked down at Jonty, who was snoozing in her lap and uttering noises similar to a contented bulldog with sinus problems.

Chapter Fifteen

Faith had felt angry, enraged, by the time they reached home. Words had not passed between her and Jonty as he had slept the whole journey and Faith had decided that it was probably preferable to leave him in this state rather than wake him for a discussion, which, given his state of inebriation, would certainly have escalated in no time into a blazing row and this would have served no purpose other than to entertain the cab driver.

Glenda, entertaining Hamish, who had apparently just popped round for a chat, noticed in an instant that all was not well. Faith stalked into the room first, Jonty stumbled in chaotically after her. In a rare moment of compassion, she suggested that Jonty, who had sat down groggily at the kitchen table and was resting his head on one hand, repeatedly saying that he thought he might be sick, should definitely not have any more alcohol that evening, even if it was still comparatively early, and would be best served by a large glass of water, some ibuprofen and an early night. Hamish, taking his cue, got up and shoe-horned his son back into the waiting taxi and took him home, leaving a disgruntled Faith alone with her mother.

'Not a good evening, huh?'

Faith burst into tears.

'I'll take that as a no.'

'It was an unmitigated disaster – from start to finish.' Faith sniffed.

'Do you want to talk about it?' Glenda lit a cigarette.

Faith eyed her with suspicion, unfamiliar with her mother being sensitive.

'Not really.'

'Okay then.' Glenda shrugged.

Faith glared at her. 'In a nutshell, nothing went right. Everyone else was in jeans so I looked ridiculous, Jonty got drunk, as I think you might just have spotted. He was rude, I was embarrassed and now I don't think I dare go into work on Monday and face Ellie.'

'Ah,' mused Glenda, wishing she hadn't asked. 'I expect it'll turn out all right in the end.'

Faith's mouth dropped open. 'Is that all you can say? Just for a moment I thought you actually wanted to listen. I should have known better. Oh, I give up.'

She stomped out of the room and upstairs. Glenda felt the whole house shudder as the door was slammed. For a brief moment she thought of going after her but then sighed, poured herself another glass of gin and returned, as her dogs had done, to the sofa and the television.

Faith was curled up in the foetal position on her bed, cuddled up in her dressing gown, the little black dress abandoned in a heap on the carpet. Telephoning Jonty had resulted in voicemail only, which was hardly surprising as he would by now be unrousable until the morning. She felt totally let down and wanted him to know this. His behaviour had been atrocious. Ellie and Ian had gone to such trouble to make them feel welcome and Jonty had humiliated her and he needed to be told. Come the morning and she would summon him to the house and have it out with him.

But as the night wore on and her anger gradually ebbed away, the conviction that a discussion of events was indubitable started to blur. As ever, the nagging doubts started to permeate her conscience. There must be a reason why he had behaved like that? Was it unfair of her to ask him to go there with her in the first place? Had he really been that anxious about meeting her friend? Was this indicative that perhaps his bold and often booming presence was merely a façade that he was hiding behind? The wedding was only six weeks away; were nerves getting the better of him?

By the morning, after a frustrating night of cat-napping and fighting with argumentative thoughts, Faith had come to the conclusion that the last thing that they needed now was a row. Instead, she would quite simply let Jonty know how upset she had been and then leave it at that, or, as a therapist might say, move on. Declining Glenda's offer of a ride out to clear away any cobwebs, she spent the morning catching up on some reading and working on an audit that she had offered to do for John, looking at anticoagulant monitoring in the practice. Aware that physically she felt so much better, she had not restarted the Obesigon, unable to face the return of the miserable side effects and thus far had managed well, starting her day with a healthy breakfast of cereal and banana which had tasted particularly delicious as it was so long since she had had any.

She was preparing jacket potatoes for a snack lunch, anticipating Glenda's return at any time, when a penitent Jonty arrived, clutching a giant bouquet of flowers which he tried to hide behind his back as he dropped onto both knees and begged for forgiveness. He stuck out his bottom lip, which he then wobbled pathetically.

'I know I don't deserve to be forgiven, but I am truly, truly sorry. These are for you and I've taken another bunch, similar but even bigger, round to Ellie and Ian's, plus some sweets for those kids and to offer my apologies.'

He looked so preposterous that Faith's determination to be stern evaporated like breath on a frosty day. She was impressed that he had made amends with Ellie as well. Laughing, she pulled him to his feet and hugged him, happy to close her eyes and inhale the aromas of toothpaste on his breath and expensive aftershave on his chin.

Facing Ellie on the Monday morning was still likely to be difficult. Though Jonty had gone to all that trouble and owned up to his misdemeanours, Faith still worried about what Ellie might be thinking. She had written a card of thanks and was mentally rehearsing a short speech that she wanted to say. Nerves were getting the better of her as she arrived at the surgery and saw Ellie's car already parked there. She planned to go and see her after morning surgery, to catch her in her room before she went up for coffee, knowing that if there were other people present, she would not be able to say what she wanted. But as it happened, like many Mondays, it was hectic, surgeries were overbooked with extras, everyone was running late to a greater or lesser degree and there were more house calls than usual. It was lunchtime before Faith even caught sight of Ellie for the first time when, arriving back from her visits, she found her in the staff room on the telephone, obviously negotiating the admission of a patient to hospital. Ellie's smile of welcome put her at ease.

'I just wanted to say thank you for Saturday evening.' Faith handed the card over as she spoke. 'You'd gone to a huge amount of trouble for us. I'm afraid that Jonty was very nervous about meeting you and made the fatal mistake of having a drink or two before we set off. It's not like him at all. I've never known him do it before. I'm so sorry.'

'Let's forget about it,' Ellie replied in her normal friendly tone. 'Thanks for the card. I expect you know that Jonty came round to see us, to apologise for himself.'

'Yes, he told me afterwards,' Faith was quick to let Ellie know that Jonty's visit had been of his own volition.

'He brought some spectacular flowers. Goodness knows where he got those on a Sunday! Want a cup of something? I'm parched. What a morning.'

Ellie crossed the room to boil the kettle, not wishing to prolong the discussion of Saturday evening any longer and Faith needed no encouragement to swap the topic of conversation to the infinitely safer territory of work. John swept in with Elliot close behind, both weary and rather red in the face after a confrontational meeting about practice-based commissioning and both needing some refreshment. Rob put his head around the door, scanned the room and raised his eyebrows at Ellie.

'Can I have a word, please?' he called.

'Of course,' was the automatic response. 'Are you coming in?'

'It's just some advice I'm needing about a patient. Could you come down please?'

If Faith had been apprehensive of seeing Ellie, Rob could barely contain his excitement. Thwarted for the entire morning, there was no way that anything was going to scupper this chance, which might be the only opportunity the day presented.

He closed the door firmly behind Ellie as she went into his surgery. Without waiting for either of them to sit down he started.

'Well, how did it go?'

Ellie threw her head back and laughed. 'So much for the difficult patient.'

'I had to think of a way to get you on your own,' he confessed. 'Tell me all about it.'

Ellie hitched herself up so she was sitting on the examination couch and crossed her long, slim legs. She reiterated her account of the event that Rob was so keen to hear about. He listened avidly, saying nothing but making appropriate noises to encourage her to go on. Not that she needed any persuasion. She and Ian had debated long into the night after their guests had left, to the point where Ian had wrapped the pillow around his ears and told her to get some sleep.

'What's your verdict, then?' Rob was keen to learn.

'On what? Is she on medication? Hard to tell. She was quite clearly acutely embarrassed by Jonty's conduct, so she could have been shaking for any number of reasons.'

Rob looked crestfallen. 'I'm so sure I was right. What about this Jonty? What did you make of him?'

Ellie considered her reply. 'He's good looking, in an angular sort of way. He's got a voracious appetite for food and wine.' She felt that she had run out of good things to say.

Rob, waiting for her next comment ran out of patience. 'You sound like you're reading a description from a catalogue. What did you really think?'

Not one to highlight the negatives, Ellie was slow to speak.

'Come on...' Rob pushed her.

'I think,' she began, choosing her words with infinite care, 'that he is arrogant, churlish and self-opinionated.'

'I see. Not too good then.'

They giggled. Ellie was getting into her stride.

'I wish you'd been there. I don't know how we managed to be polite for the whole evening. He treated the twins as though they were some sort of lowlife and dismissed all Ian's valiant attempts to chat. My heart went out to Faith as I could see that she was just squirming with embarrassment. Never again!'

'But how did he seem with Faith? Are they a match made in heaven?'

'He seemed affectionate enough, perhaps rather too much so, physically, but he was also really quite critical about her. There was a rather nasty undertone to his comments as well that I didn't feel comfortable with. Oh, I don't know. He was so drunk, it was impossible to come to any sensible conclusions, so we're not really any further forward are we?'

'I guess not. We'll just have to keep our eyes open for further developments.'

Ellie got up and patted him on the shoulder. 'Keep me posted. We need to keep an eye open for any more prescriptions for Obesigon. Apart from that, I don't think there's much else we can do. We can't interfere in the romantic side of things – that's nothing to do with us.'

Reluctantly, Rob acquiesced that this was true, but eagerly accepted the mantle of monitoring Pollyanna Smith's notes.

Chapter Sixteen

As the wedding neared, the passage of time seemed to accelerate, leaving Faith feeling almost dizzy with the daily juggling of work and seeing to the preparations. Her days were packed, from the moment she opened her eyes until her head returned to the pillow to sleep, elusive though this was thanks to the continual barrage of thoughts that whirled around in her head. But gradually, chaos was metamorphosing into order and things seemed to be falling into place.

Seamless management by the supremely efficient staff at the Swindlehurst Castle Hotel guaranteed that there were no hiccups with the reception planning, the florist was utterly content with what creations were expected of him and a few presents from those too far away or too busy to attend were starting to arrive.

She was now relieved that she had decided against the open-top horse-drawn carriage, which Glenda favoured, as autumn was fast making way for winter and there had been several heavy frosts which had resulted in spectacular panoramas that necessitated scarves, hats, gloves and early morning scraping of windscreens.

Faith thrived on being busy. Her exhaustion was a contented one predominantly; there were only brief moments when panic set in. As was her wont, the only way she could accommodate everything that needed to be done was to be organised efficiently, much in the way of a military exercise with Faith as commanding officer. As before, along with the feeling of being in control came the ability to eat sensibly, control her portions and most of all avoid bingeing. What was left of the Obesigon lay untouched in her handbag, perhaps being kept as a talisman in case of crisis, for she did not feel she could consign the tablets to the bin just yet. For the time being, the happy result of combining a normal diet with a lot of rushing around was that her weight remained static and whilst her heart yearned for the loss of a few more pounds, she was content to leave things be.

Uppermost on Faith's agenda that day was picking up her dress, safe in the knowledge that she had chosen the one she wanted, that it had required only the minimum of alteration and that was simply to the length. She had known, as soon as she caught sight of it hanging in the shop, that it was meant for her and nobody else. Timidly, she had stepped out from the changing room and then her breath had been taken away when she watched herself float in front of the mirror the first time she tried it on. Tiny straps, a tight-fitting bodice in ivory with a low waist, emphasised by tiny crystals, and then clouds and clouds of similarly coloured frills cascading to the floor, creating a rippling effect that was enhanced when she walked. Even the assistant in the shop had seemed genuinely moved.

There had followed much discussion about what to have on her head, culminating in the choice of a short veil, held in place by a simple tiara. The entire effect was incredible. No one, including Jonty or Glenda, could fail to be impressed. He would whisper wonderful things to her when she met him at the altar and whilst it was a long shot, her mother might even be moved to tears. For once in her life she looked svelte, amazing and beautiful. So much so, it was hard to believe it truly was her.

If there was a downside then it was the sad fact that she had had to go shopping for it on her own, Glenda having pleaded to be excused on the grounds that the vet was coming. In reality this was probably for the best for, although she would have been delighted by the extortionate price tag that she knew Dennis was going to have to pay, if she had even grasped the merest hint of who had suggested the designer then her reaction was better not even contemplated. Faith had wondered about asking Ellie, having so much admiration for her own style but after the catastrophic evening lost her nerve completely and could not pluck up the courage to do so.

That morning she had received a call to say that the dress was ready. Timetabled for a lunchtime finish, she reckoned that there would be plenty of time to get to Harrogate before the shop shut. In doing so, she forgot the unwritten law that states that if you plan to do anything specific after surgery that necessitates you finishing on time then you can bank on being delayed. True to form, her morning was difficult beyond her wildest expectations. A last-minute cancellation by Mrs Tonbridge lifted her spirits but the space thus created was quickly filled by a patient she had never heard of.

Kenneth Marley avoided any eye contact as he came into Faith's surgery and sat down. Nor did he respond as she would have expected to her usual friendly greeting and proffered hand to shake. He looked bedraggled. Though his suit appeared to be of good quality, it was stained and creased. His white shirt had more of a grey tinge and his tie hung loosely around his neck. Head bowed, he monotonously passed some car keys from one hand to the other, his knees continuously bobbing up and down in a frenetic manner. Faith stared at his greasy, tangled hair, badly combed over the top of his head in an attempt to conceal an incipient bald patch. Her nostrils caught the acrid stench of stale alcohol and tobacco. Studying him from head to toe while she waited for him to speak, she noticed a bottle of some spirit or other protruding from his pocket. It was as though he knew that she had spotted it for his hand left the car keys and tried to force the bottle top out of sight.

She tried her opening gambit of, 'How can I help you?'

No answer was forthcoming. Faith remained silent, listening to the hum of the computer and the jingle of the keys. Finally, without looking up, he spoke.

'I need some help.'

'Go on.' Faith waited.

'I don't know where to start.'

'Wherever you like.'

'I doubt there's anything that you can do. My life's a mess.'

'Tell me about it.'

Kenneth Marley glanced at her. His rheumy eyes were untrusting. 'I'm a failure. I've lost everything. My wife, my house and my job. I've no money and she won't let me see my kids. You don't really want to hear all about that, do you?'

'Yes, if it would help you.'

'Look at the state of me. I never used to look like this. I used to take pride in my appearance – clean shirt every day, different tie – usually one of the cartoon ones that the kids loved to give me, polished shoes, dab of aftershave. People used to remark on how smart I looked.'

'So what happened?'

136

He shook his head and then made Faith jump by banging his fist down on her desk with frightening ferocity. 'Bloody woman!'

'Who? Your wife?'

'No, no, no. Jessica – that's my wife – has nothing to do with all this. It's all my fault. I can't believe I was so bloody stupid. It just started as a bit of fun. No strings – you know the sort of thing? Cath – the other woman, my boss's wife, I can hardly bring myself to talk about her. She was incredible. Sexy, wicked, liked to take risks. At first I was mesmerised by the way she lived life in the fast lane. Champagne, cocaine, lust. We were at this works do. Not your conventional do at some boring hotel or restaurant. Oh no, this was at a fantastic hotel, doubtless very expensive but there was free booze all evening. She followed me all evening. Jessica was at home with the kids – we couldn't get a babysitter. I had way too much to drink. I'd never tried cocaine before but the effect was amazing. I didn't mean to but I was flattered by her advances and afterwards I told myself that it was just the one night and would never happen again; that Jessica never need find out. But of course, it never works out the way you want it to, does it?'

He looked at Faith directly, challenging her to disagree but did not wait for her to speak before continuing. Now that he had started, he was showing no signs of slowing up and as the clock clicked steadily on Faith learned how his infidelity had been revealed, the reactions of not just Jessica but also his boss, his subsequent dismissal and separation from his wife and two children. Holed up in a tiny bedsit, unable to find a job, he was spending most of his time in the pub and all of his money on alcohol. There was little that Faith could do but listen. To come and ask for help was clearly an enormous step for him to have taken, but perhaps a sign that he did have just a smidgeon of pride left somewhere deep inside that he wanted to salvage.

Gently, after thirty minutes, she started to wind up the consultation, explaining to him ways that she could get him help with his drinking problem. He seemed sceptical and expressed doubts that there was anyone who could help him, that he was the instigator of his own destruction and did not deserve help. But he agreed to Faith referring him to the community support team that dealt specifically with drug and alcohol problems and promised her that he would keep his appointment.

Faith opened the window after he had left, for whilst his physical presence had gone, his body odour had stayed to haunt her. He had been her first patient and she was now running almost an hour late. She scanned through her surgery list, hopeful that there might have been some more cancellations but there were none, plus there were several names that made her heart plummet when she saw them and right at the end was Pollyanna Smith.

Thinking rapidly, she rang home. Mercifully, Glenda picked up the phone straightaway. She answered in the thin voice that Faith equated with her having a cigarette in her mouth.

'Ma, it's me. I wonder, could you do something for me?'

'Maybe...' Glenda sounded wary.

'I'm running really late. Could you go into Harrogate and pick up my dress for me? They close at two today and there's no way that I'll get there by then.'

'Why don't you get it another day, then?'

Faith was exasperated. 'Because I've promised I'll pick it up today. I don't know if I'll get another chance to go.'

'Rubbish.' Faith heard Glenda exhale. 'Oh, all right then. I'll get Hamish to take me out for lunch.'

'Thank you so much, Ma. I really appreciate it. See you later.'

Dress crisis averted, Faith relaxed a little and was able to concentrate on the rest of her surgery. She diagnosed a ruptured cruciate ligament in a worried rugby player and thrombosed piles in an uncomfortable-looking middle-aged woman who declined her offer to sit down. More mundane problems such as sick-note renewals, requests for tranquillisers before a holiday flight and a letter for local social services supporting an application for a new washing machine occupied her time until Pollyanna's turn.

It was a different person who bounced into the room in comparison with the sad figure who left last time. Dressed in a smock of enormous proportions, Pollyanna had an unmistakably excited look on her face. She was puffing by the time she sat down.

'Hello, Dr Faber!' There was a huge smile on her face.

'Hello, Pollyanna. You're looking very happy today. Has the diet been going well?'

'Pretty well. I've stuck to it just about all the time. Shall I get on the scales?'

Alas, there was no change but her cheerfulness looked undaunted.

'Are you sure that you're keeping to the diet?' Faith interrogated.

'More or less.'

'Pollyanna, I was driving through Lambdale the other Saturday and saw you eating a takeaway.'

'Oh, that! That was just the once, well maybe a couple of times. But I was so hungry, my stomach rumbles all the time these days and I was just desperate for curry and chips. You must know what it's like when you really crave for something.'

'Well, maybe.' Faith was reluctant to admit to her own failings. 'But that's beside the point. Curry and chips is really fattening. Look, you've not lost any weight, so I suspect that perhaps you've been cheating a bit more than you realise.'

If Faith was hoping to back Pollyanna into a corner and hear some sort of confession, she was to be disappointed.

'I don't care. I've got the money for the operation, Dr Faber!'

Faith was completely taken aback. 'Oh, my word! How have you managed that?' As soon as she had opened her mouth she wondered if this was an appropriate question to ask.

Pollyanna was keen to share this information. 'All my family have chipped in because they know how much it means to me. My uncle and aunt had a car boot sale and my dad won a bit on a sweepstake at work. My mum and I had a few savings and we sold some jewellery that used to be my nan's but nobody ever wears because it's dead ugly. So, now I can go ahead, can't I? Will you write me a referral letter?'

'Of course. How marvellous for you. But you will think about it very carefully, won't you? Listen to everything the consultant tells you. Not just about the operation but also about what happens afterwards. Write a list of questions that you might have before you go and don't be afraid to ask them.'

'I won't. I'm so excited. My tummy's rumbling again, now! It can't wait to be thin! I feel almost sick with excitement.'

It was not possible to fail to be moved by the look of sheer happiness on Pollyanna's round face. Her cheeks were glowing as she sat there, chubby fingers clasped across the top of her vast belly.

Faith was both pleased and fearful for her. She was pinning all her hopes on the fact that the surgery would transform her life, a belief shared by her relatives who had been so self-sacrificing in their efforts to help her by raising such a considerable sum of money. Did she realise though, Faith wondered, that the surgery was just the beginning of a long and arduous relationship with the medical profession, with continual monitoring of her nutritional status and then in the future, further operations to remove the sagging rolls of flesh that would hang redundantly from her body following her dramatic weight loss? Faith decided to leave this for the consultant to explain. She didn't want to spoil this moment for her by casting doubt upon her decision.

'I'm really pleased for you, Pollyanna,' Faith said, quite genuinely. 'I'll do the letter for you in the next few days.'

'As soon as you can please, Dr Faber. I just can't wait any longer!' She burped contentedly. 'Another thing I've got is awful heartburn from this diet. It's all that salad. Cucumber never did agree with me. Could you give me something for it please?'

'Of course,' Faith tapped in a prescription for an antacid and waited for it to print out. 'Is that a new dress? It's a pretty colour.'

Pollyanna nodded. 'Yes, I got it from a catalogue. I can't find clothes that fit me in ordinary shops. But soon I will be able to. I'll be like those photos you see in magazines – me with both my legs down one leg of my jeans, holding the waistband out to show how much weight I've lost.'

'I hope you'll come and show me.'

'Oh, I will, Dr Faber. I couldn't have done this without you. You've been the only doctor who's seemed to understand how I feel.'

Faith smiled and walked with her to the door. 'Keep in touch,' she called as Pollyanna made her way towards the reception desk.

The young man she had been with that Saturday evening was waiting for her, instantly recognisable by his fedora. He stood up, hitched up his jeans and then took her hand and Faith watched until the two of them were out of sight.

Surgery over, she contemplated the pile of paperwork that was waiting for her. Thank goodness Glenda had agreed to go and pick up the dress, for there was no way that she would have been able to finish up here and get over to Harrogate in time. Hurriedly,

Faith sifted through what needed to be done, dealing with the bare minimum and leaving anything that she considered to be non-urgent, which included Pollyanna's referral letter, until the next day. She was eager to get home and see her dress, perhaps model it for her mother but, at the very least, try it on in the privacy of her own bedroom.

She parked her car erratically on the driveway and ran inside.

'Ma, did you get it?' she called, above the noise of the dogs' welcome, a mixture of barks and whines and the thumping of tails.

Glenda and Hamish were in the lounge, surprisingly sharing a pot of tea.

'Hello, Faith. Tea's just brewed. Get yourself a cup if you'd like one.'

'Ma,' Faith's tone was impatient. 'My dress, is it upstairs?'

Glenda dropped cubes of sugar into her tea from a height and then stirred noisily. 'No, but don't panic. It's all sorted and will be arriving any minute. Hamish couldn't go out for lunch, so we decided we'd just meet up for tea. I've had a great schooling session with Caspian. He's really coming into his own now.'

Faith sat down with relief. 'Thank you doing that, Ma. You know how anxious I've been about it. Is the shop delivering it? We don't exactly live on their doorstep, so it's very kind of them.'

'No, nothing like that. Someone else has picked it up for you.'

'Who?' asked Faith as, right on cue, Jonty marched into the room, coat hanger dangling from his crooked finger, the dress over his shoulder and down his back.

Faith screamed. 'Oh no! Jonty – don't look. It's bad luck for you to see my dress.'

Glenda tutted. 'For goodness sake, Faith, it's in a cover. He can't see what it looks like. Anyway it's only bad luck if he sees you actually in it. Isn't that right, Hamish?'

Hamish nodded obligingly. Faith snatched the dress from Jonty.

'I might just have had a little peek,' Jonty taunted her.

'If you have, I'll never forgive you,' she threatened him.

'Of course I haven't, my darling. I was going to Harrogate on business and when your ma told me she had to go too, I offered to save her a trip. Anyway, I got such a hard time from that termagant of a woman in the shop, uttering oaths of terrible consequences if I dared to have a look, that I didn't quite have the nerve. Your dress secret is safe until our big day. All I know is that it doesn't weigh overly much and it rustles a lot. So it could be pink with blue spots for all I know, but I'd rather hoped for something more traditional.'

Faith hugged him effusively. As usual he had won her round with his playful banter.

'You can try and wheedle hints out of me but I'm saying nothing. I'm taking it up to my room immediately, where I know it'll be safe. Thank you for picking it up, Jonty, and thank you for not looking.'

He blew her a kiss as she ran off, carrying the dress as carefully as she could until it was safely stowed away in the dark and secret recesses of her wardrobe.

Chapter Seventeen

'I can't believe I've been at the practice for nearly six months,' Faith was saying to Ellie when Ed and Rob returned with a tray of drinks from the bar.

They were all in the local pub, The Queen's Head, relaxing after another week at work, which had been especially hectic owing to a plethora of seasonal viruses, an outbreak of food poisoning that had resulted in a local hotel being closed down and the annual influenza vaccination campaign. They were planning to stay and eat together, a justified treat for all their efforts. Seated at a round table by the roaring log fire, it was a welcome relief to have come in from the bitterly cold early evening air. Snow was forecast for the higher dales and there were already icy patches on the cobbles of the market square. The pub was welcoming, decorated in reds and browns, which together with the light reflecting off the brass bar top created an atmosphere that exuded warmth and comfort. Tempting smells of bar food wafted through the air and it was hard to ignore the plates piled high with good, home-cooked food that were being served to other customers.

These monthly outings had originally been devised as a team-building exercise, cementing the working relationship between the partners, offering an opportunity to let off steam as well as brainstorm new ideas. But long ago, largely on account of the facts that the partners were fortunate enough to be genuinely good friends with each other, thought along similar lines and were equally enthusiastic, it had transformed into a leisurely get-together with good food and wine, offering time to catch up and have fun. On this particular occasion, however, there was a further purpose to the evening, that of Faith's hen night, or at least the closest she was going to get to one. It had been Ed's suggestion and Faith had been deeply touched, feeling optimistic that maybe this was a sign that she fitted in well and that they thought highly of her. She felt nervous, as if this were some sort of social test for her, which she needed to score highly in.

Ed handed around the drinks. Red wines for Ellie and Faith, pints of the locally brewed beer for himself, John and Rob, who had commandeered two bowls of peanuts from the bar for them to share.

'Cheers, everyone,' toasted John, raising his glass, 'and here's to you, Faith. Good luck and every happiness.'

Faith blushed and felt awkward as the rest of the little party muttered their approval of his statement and drank her good health. Conversation was stilted to begin with, the temptation being to discuss patients they had seen and been amused or bemused by. The very public nature of their chosen place in which to dine forbade this, for fear of breach of confidentiality. Ellie, suspecting Faith's tension, decided to introduce a topic she knew she would be more than happy to talk about.

'Only a week to go, then,' Ellie started, handing the nuts around the table before taking a handful for herself. 'Goodness, I'm hungry.'

'I know,' Faith answered, excitedly. 'I can hardly believe it's come around so fast. When we first got engaged, November seemed an eternity away and now it's here.'

'Where are you going for your honeymoon?'

'I don't know. I've got two weeks off, as you know. Jonty's planned it all and he won't give me any clues until the day before the wedding, so that I can pack the right sort of clothes.'

'Have you much left to do?' Ellie went on, noticing that John and Ed, doubtless not overly keen on the machinations of preparing for a wedding, were engrossed in a conversation about football while Rob appeared to be listening to snatches of both and paying a great deal of attention to his beer.

'Just about everything's done, I hope. My father arrives next week, with his wife, whom my mother loathes and detests, so that's going to be a challenge. They're not staying with us of course; Ma wouldn't have her in the garden, let alone the house. Fortunately, I've got Thursday and Friday off, thanks largely to Rob, who offered to work his half day and do an extra surgery.'

'Anything to help,' murmured Rob, draining his glass with undue haste and getting up to get a refill. 'Anyone else ready for another?'

The football chat paused long enough for the participants to give their orders and then resumed.

144

Ellie rolled her eyes at Faith, who laughed. 'I'm lucky. Jonty isn't particularly interested in football. What about Ian?'

'He loves all sorts of sports.'

Faith took a rather big gulp of her wine. Whilst it was unpalatably warm, it was performing an excellent effect on her jingling nerves and she felt a calmness descending on her in a rather delicious fashion.

'And when you come back from your honeymoon, have you somewhere to live?'

Ellie took more nuts and studied them carefully, choosing which order to eat them in with great care.

'Not of our own,' Faith replied. 'We've looked at a few properties but not seen anything that appeals equally to both of us. I hadn't realised that Jonty was quite so fussy but he's dead set on having outbuildings and stables for his horses. So, we'll be staying with his father for the duration. It's far from ideal –' Ellie watched Faith sigh, '– but Jonty says it's the best thing to do. Luckily, I get on really well with Hamish – that's Jonty's father – and the house is pretty big but still, it would have been nice to have our own place to start married life in.'

Ellie made some sympathetic noises. 'You'll be ready for some time off. You've hardly had any since you started. You must be exhausted. All those preparations plus work's been really busy these last few weeks.'

'But I've enjoyed it so much,' Faith contradicted her. 'I love organising things. I just hope everything will go just according to plan and I'm so pleased that all the partners can come to the evening party.'

'I can't wait,' Ellie assured her. 'I've never been in the Swindlehurst Castle Hotel, so I'm intrigued.' She refrained from telling Faith that Ian had initially refused to go, still reeling from his one encounter with the groom-to-be. Only after Ellie had spent almost an hour convincing him that Jonty diluted by a roomful of wedding guests must surely be tolerable and that it would most probably be possible to avoid any contact with him at all other than the briefest of greetings and farewells did he acquiesce as he usually did to any of Ellie's desires.

Rob appeared back with drinks, including ones for Ellie and Faith, regardless of the fact that they hadn't asked for any, plus menus.

'Specials are on the blackboard,' he told them and they craned their necks to see past the customers standing at the bar to see the selection. There was silence, save for the noise of Ellie still crunching on nuts as they made their decisions, John, predictably slapping the menu shut and announcing without further ado that he would be having sirloin steak, medium rare and all the trimmings. For Faith, the decision was far harder. There was a salad choice which would be low in calories but the temperature of the day decreed that something hot and filling was required. She considered a simple steak and boiled vegetables but, resolve slipping away like water down a plughole, she heard herself ordering chicken breast, stuffed with pancetta and spinach and covered with a rich creamy Stilton sauce. Justifying the side orders of chips and garlic bread was simple. She had had no lunch for the last two days, her weigh-in that morning had showed no gain (but sadly no loss either) and the next few days promised to be a continuous round of high-energy expenditure.

The evening was so enjoyable. Comfortable among her new friends and relishing the experience of being made to feel like an equal, Faith ate a huge meal, drank far more than she usually would have done, pleased by the fact that she had organised a lift home, and ordered the biggest, stickiest toffee pudding with clotted cream that she had ever seen for dessert. She delighted in laughing with the others at the jokes that John and Ed told, some more risqué than others but none even coming near to the insensitivity and crassness that Jonty's would have had.

Coffees were ordered and while they were waiting for these, Faith accepted willingly the offer to finish off Ellie's pudding of crumble and custard, which she could only manage about a third of. Draining the last from his cup, John slipped on his jacket and prepared to leave. Fortunate enough to live a short walk away, he was only faced with a brief dalliance with the elements before he would be home and cosy.

'That's me done. It's been a great evening, as always. I'll see you all on Monday. Have a great weekend.'

'Give our love to Clare,' Ellie called as he turned to go.

'I will,' he promised.

'What was that?' Faith asked quickly, ears pricked up at the mention of Clare's name.

'John's going to see her tomorrow,' Ellie explained.

146

'Oh, that's nice,' Faith commented. 'How is she?'

'Thankfully, she's vastly improved. I expect they may be talking about her coming back to work, hopefully before Christmas.'

Faith felt as though a lead weight had just landed in her heart.

'That's great news.' She put on a brave smile. 'But she needs to be careful that she doesn't rush back too soon, surely.'

'She'll not do that,' Ellie reassured her. 'Anyway, it's about time that I made a move. I promised the girls they could stay up until I got back as it was a Friday, so I expect they'll be up to all sort of mischief by now. Have a nice weekend. Bye, everyone!'

Faith watched Ellie's back as she wound her way in and out of all the other people in the pub, aiming eventually for the door, her mind beginning to race. She had been so sure that the partners were going to ask her to stay on and perhaps even buy into the practice. Relationships between them were affable to say the least, she had worked her hardest, offered to do extra duties to help out, assisted with training Rob and ingratiated herself with the staff and all the other members of the primary health care team. There had been encouraging feedback from the patients to corroborate her beliefs. She had received a couple of thank you cards, a box of chocolates and even the offer of three kittens, though Faith correctly diagnosed that this was more an attempt to house the young, unwanted animals than a token of eternal gratitude. By word of mouth, the receptionists had passed on a number of compliments and they had also commented on how her surgeries were always popular and fully booked well in advance. Only the other week, Joan had said to her that she was very nearly as popular as Dr Jennings.

Secretly she hoped that all these sentiments were filtering back to those who mattered, namely John as senior partner and Elliott, as practice manager. It had been a wonderful six months, with a sense of belonging that she had never before experienced in a job. Even with those while in hospital, she had felt more of a work horse than a valued member of a team. It was this sense of belonging that had made her, rightly or wrongly, feel that she fitted in so well that it was merely a matter of time before she was offered a permanent post.

But now Ellie had razed her hopes to the ground by the very mention of Clare's name and the intimation that she was now well enough for an imminent return. The fluffy white cloud of contentment that Faith had floated through the evening on had turned into one of dyspeptic unease. Lack of self esteem replaced her earlier confidence; feelings of inferiority and failure raged war within her.

Incredibly, Ed and Rob were setting up new drinks, oblivious to her inner turmoil, intent on continuing the evening and glad of her presence. Desperate to regain the mood she had so enjoyed earlier in the evening, Faith downed what was left of her wine, close to half a glassful, in one go, pushed away the empty glass and gratefully accepted the fresh one that was placed in front of her.

'I can't stay too much longer,' volunteered Ed. 'But it's great beer that they do here.'

Rob nodded his agreement, wiping the white foam from his upper lip. Ed regaled them both with stories of his climbing, Rob eager to hear and keen to go out with him for the day, Faith, barely listening as she now suddenly felt awkward, headachy and unattractive.

Automatically, she nodded and smiled in a manner she hoped was appropriate. Beneath her quiet exterior, she was trying to convince herself that a job was just that, nothing more and paled into insignificance when compared to the prospect of a future with Jonty. She was forcing her mind to concentrate on the positives, no easy task with the depressing effect of the alcohol working against her. There was so much to look forward to. The thrill of house hunting, then feathering the nest that was to be their home, the uniqueness of it being just the two of them, which was of course until the arrival of the children which would simply be the icing on the cake.

Jonty had always been reluctant to discuss how many children he would like and Faith, believing that she could read between the lines, interpreted this to mean that he would want a large family but dared not broach the subject, lest she be put off. There was such a rosy image she had built up; that of a large, rambling house, standing in its own grounds with immaculate gardens, though she chose to ignore the question of who might be responsible for keeping them thus. Their days would be filled by a cornucopia of dogs, cats, rabbits and no doubt ponies, together with four or five ruddy-faced, healthy children with tousled hair and grubby jeans, all having the time of their lives as they grew up. Their kitchen walls would be covered by the children's paintings, the rosettes they won at the local gymkhanas and happy photos of them all smiling and laughing.

Family picnics would be spread out on checked table cloths, riotous birthday parties would include amazingly shaped cakes, such as badgers or spaceships and Christmases would be ever memorable thanks to the abundant decorations, festive foods and, of course, presents. It went without saying that the summers would be long and drenched in sunshine and the winters bitingly cold but adorned by that dense, thick snow that is vital for snowmen construction and tobogganing. They would all be out there, wrapped up warm in padded coats, long scarves, shrieking merrily as they careered down the hillside before rushing back inside where she would make hot chocolate with marshmallows and they would all sit together, one happy family, what Faith had always yearned for but never had.

This was what mattered. Staying on at Teviotdale did not. She could easily find another job. In all probability, Jonty might insist that she gave up work to concentrate on being a wife and mother. This idea, deep down, was anathema to Faith, who knew full well that her work was a vocation rather than a means to an end but she also was aware that if it was what Jonty wanted, then that's what she would do.

'Are you all right, Faith?' Rob brought her back down to earth with a thump. 'Ed's about to go and you've gone very quiet.'

Faith looked up and saw Ed standing, zipping up his coat, saying his farewells.

'Yes, I'm fine. I think I'm more tired than I realised.'

'How are you getting home?'

'I've to ring Jonty when I'm about ready and he'll come and pick me up. I might do that now, if you don't mind.'

'Of course, though I'm going to wait until he arrives and make sure that you're all right.'

Faith struggled to hear the dialling tone on her phone. 'It's so noisy in here. I'll have to pop outside to ring. Back in a mo.'

Rob ordered two coffees, noticing that her jacket was still hanging over the arm of the chair and predicting that she would be frozen to the marrow when she came back in. She was not long gone, returning with a frown on her face.

'What's up?' he asked.

Faith sat down inelegantly and slammed her phone on the table.

'He's not coming. He's out at the pub and been drinking. He says he'll see me later maybe at my mother's and told me just to get a taxi.'

Rob could see that she was shaking, fighting back tears and tactfully looked away for a few seconds before speaking. He wondered whether he should offer her a brandy, to steady and calm her, but decided that she had already consumed quite enough alcohol.

'I'm sorry about that. It would have been nice to meet him. Not to worry. Have some more coffee and you can have my mint chocolate. You're lucky that he gets on so well with his prospective mother-in-law.'

Faith sniffed miserably. 'They get on fine. Sometimes I think he gets on better with her than he does with me. He's always round at ours, either in the house or out riding.'

'What about your father? Does he get on as well with him?'

'I don't know. It's years since they met. Jonty would have been in his teens, if that. We're having dinner with Pa and his wife next Thursday. I'm sure that will go well.'

Faith sounded less confident than her words. Rob caught her eye. 'Actually,' she confessed, 'I'm dreading it. I can't wait to see Pa as it's so long since I have done but everything is so rushed. Dinner one night, wedding two days later. I'd like to have time with him on my own, to catch up and just enjoy being with him but it's not going to happen. You know that evening we went to Ellie and Ian's? Well it was an utter disaster. I couldn't bear for something like that to happen with my father.'

Rob watched a solitary tear wend its way down Faith's cheek. Hastily she wiped it away with the back of her hand.

'You're right, you're just tired,' he consoled her. 'Everything looks gloomy when you're too tired to think straight. Let's call that cab. I'll come with you and see that you get home safely.'

'There's no need,' protested Faith.

'Yes there is. You're emotional and need a friend.'

Without more ado, he rummaged in his inside pocket for his own phone and shouted into it to make the necessary arrangements. There was no way that he was going to let her drive off into the night unaccompanied. She looked pale, exhausted and vulnerable.

'Five minutes,' he told her. 'We're lucky that there was a cab free.'

'I need to go to the Ladies before we go. I'll meet you outside.'

150

She shut the toilet door behind her and sat down, still fully clothed, head spinning from the drink, unable to come to terms with Jonty's cavalier attitude to his broken promise. Without even realising what she was doing, she turned around, lifted the seat and leant over, sticking two fingers down her throat, with practised ease, and watching with revulsion as the contents of her stomach splattered into the toilet bowl.

Rob, outside in the freezing air, was stamping his feet to keep warm, his arms wrapped around his body in a futile attempt to protect it from the icy wind. He saw the taxi nearing. As he did so, a couple came running out of the pub, huddled together to outwit the elements as they set out for home. He overheard them talking as they scuttled past him.

'There was some woman being sick in the Ladies.'

'How vile! People should have more sense than to drink so much.'

Faith had been a while. Perhaps there was a medical problem that she was attending to. He was on the point of going back in to look for her when she emerged. Under the street light, her complexion had a greenish tinge and there were dark rings around her eyes.

'Are you okay? I just heard a woman say that there was someone vomiting in the toilet. Was that you?'

Faith stared resolutely at the pavement. The taxi was waiting, engine running impatiently. She reached out for the door handle.

'No, I didn't see or hear anything. Perhaps she was mistaken. Come on, let's get in. I'm frozen.'

They travelled back to Faith's house more or less in silence, Rob convinced that Faith had been sick for it was impossible to look that bad for any other reason and Faith, full of self-loathing, felt that she was not worthy of being spoken to. Just on the outskirts of Lambdale, she fell into an uneasy doze and allowed her head to rest on Rob's shoulder, where it bounced disturbingly until he put his arm around her to support it. There was something very homely about the smell of his jacket, a mixture of open fires and cold night air. There seemed no reason at all why she should not snuggle up against it and go to sleep.

Chapter Eighteen

It was not a good weekend. No matter how hard she tried not to be, Faith was beset with anxieties. To start off with, she felt that she had disgraced herself with Rob. He had helped her into the house, despite her protestations otherwise. Groggy from a short but deep sleep, she had capitulated and allowed Rob to lead her indoors; she had heard him introduce himself to Glenda, who had offered him a cup of tea, which, to Faith's horror, he had accepted. She had left the two of them to it, crawling up to bed and falling, half dressed, under the duvet, only then wondering, as her last waking thought, what on earth had happened to Jonty as there had been no sign of him with her mother.

Rob had rung the next morning, at a respectable hour, asking solicitously how she was feeling. He had told her there was no need for apologies, that was what friends are for and that he would like to think, that if the tables were turned, she could be depended upon to help him. They talked amiably for longer than Faith realised and by the time she replaced the receiver on the hook, she felt more at peace, a feeling that was short lived however as other worries reared their ugly heads above the parapet and shouted abuse at her.

It was Jonty's stag night and, contrary to Faith, he intended to make the most of it. His raucous and unpredictable friends were taking him out to a destination as yet unrevealed and Faith just knew that, if their past record was anything to go by, then the night, for it would surely be just this and not simply an evening, would involve getting paralytically drunk, consuming oily curries, the ingredients of which were unknown and best left that way, and the presence of scantily clad, gyrating women brought in especially for the occasion. She had been so terrified of what might happen that she had actually rung Simon, the mastermind behind the outing, and begged him not to let Jonty fall foul of any practical jokes, such as being put on a train to Inverness or handcuffed naked to a statue somewhere. Simon had roared with laughter at her plea and guffawed that she shouldn't be such a party pooper and of course Jonty would be safe with his friends. Faith had found it hard to believe him, since there was little conviction in his tone as he spoke.

Dawn had phoned in sick, leaving Glenda irate. The stable work had to be shared out between Faith and her mother. As she mucked out Caspian's box, Faith could hear Glenda uttering expletives as she worked in the next stable. Putting down the fork, she went round and suggested to her mother that she have a break and go for a ride instead, promising that by the time she got back, the work would be done. Glenda did not need to be asked twice.

Once left alone, bizarrely, the physical nature of the labour helped Faith feel better, it cleared her head, released the endorphins from her brain and lifted her mood, albeit temporarily. Muck taken out, new beds down, she distributed the morning feeds and then leant on one of the half doors, listening to the soothing sound of the horses' rhythmic, unhurried munching.

Glenda returned in better humour. She cast a critical eye over the work done and then announced her approval and thanked Faith for her help. She even went so far as to say that Dawn could not have done it better, which was doubtless true as a childhood of mucking out for her mother meant that Faith was quite used to her exacting standards and had developed similar ones herself. They went indoors to put on the kettle and warm up some soup for lunch. Faith tried phoning Jonty. She was concerned that he had not contacted her and wanted to speak to him before he left for his evening of hedonism. The lack of reply made her fret all the more. She tried sending a text message but heard nothing back. The afternoon was spent restlessly, as she was unable to concentrate on tasks that needed to be done, all the while unable to stop thinking about Jonty and what he might, or might not, be doing. Half-heartedly she mooched around the fields with the dogs and then toyed with the seating plan for the reception, which true to form was proving to be a nightmare. Thinking that she had it sorted to everyone's satisfaction, she called Glenda in to see it, who promptly tore it to shreds by telling her that there was no way various permutations of people could be allowed to sit together and that three tables away from her was still far too close for Dennis to be.

'Put him behind a pillar, preferably,' she suggested cynically.

154

Faith glared at her. 'Help me please, Ma. This time next week, we should all be sitting down to eat. Surely Aunty Andrea and Uncle Jim would manage to sit at the same table as Winifred and Giles, just for a couple of hours. And you could put Emily Toogood and her husband on the table with the Morrises. They'd keep any conversation going. Once the meal is over, we can all move around to our hearts' content.'

A knock on the door heralded the arrival of Hamish, who was obviously intent on staying for the rest of the day. Faith was disappointed to see him, hoping that he might be going on the stag night and perhaps in some way be able to bring some maturity to the proceedings.

'Are you meeting up with Jonty and his friends later?' she asked optimistically as he leant over the table and viewed the putative table plan.

'Not me. I'm way past all of those sort of shenanigans. Glenda asked me round for supper, she said you were cooking, a more tempting invitation by far. By the way, you can't sit Rosemary with Algie – their decree absolute is due any day now.'

'Do you know where they've gone?' Faith was exasperated.

'Not a clue. They were round at home, about six of them, drinking my vintage champagne as I left and getting pretty rowdy. Don't worry, Faith, it's just boys' games, they'll be fine.'

Leaving her mother and Hamish to argue good-naturedly about the horse-racing that was on the television and rather more heatedly about the seating arrangements, Faith crept into the kitchen and tried to ring Jonty yet again. Still no reply. She rang the house number and was overcome with relief when it was answered, though her heart plummeted when she heard Simon's voice booming down the line at her.

'Give it a rest, Faith. He's fine. No, I won't even let him come to the phone. We're going out now and who knows when we'll get back. Leave us to it. Our phones are going to be switched off. Go and do some girly sort of things like polish your toenails or wax your legs.'

He hung up on her, leaving the sound of the background laughter imprinted in her memory. It sounded very much as though they were all laughing at her.

Faith was distraught. Shouting to her mother and Hamish that she was just popping out to get something for supper, she grabbed her keys, revved up the engine and scrunched down the drive at an alarming rate, scattering gravel as she did so. She had to see Jonty before they all left. With no attention to what might be lurking around each blind bend, she put her foot down hard and covered the short distance in record time but even then was too late. The house was in darkness save for the feeble glow from a small table lamp in the lounge window. No amount of doorbell ringing and frantic knocking produced any human reaction at all, just some aggressive dog barking from deep within the building.

Irrationally, Faith considered driving to the Green Dragon and other local hostelries that she knew Jonty frequented intermittently but the prospect of having to enter those buildings on her own and scour amongst the customers was enough to put her off. For all she knew they had headed for town, perhaps even as far as Harrogate, in search of the potentially more sophisticated club scene and the possibility of more nefarious entertainment. Faith clenched her fists around the steering wheel and wailed. It was no consolation that in just seven days time she would be Jonty's wife and that their futures would be forever entwined. It was imperative that she saw him now, she needed to hear him say that he loved her and vow to her that there would never be anyone else in his life but her.

She looked wistfully at her engagement ring but there was nothing more she could do. Sadly accepting this fact, she backed the car into the road and drove recklessly into the village where she parked untidily and went into the little shop that sold everything from dishcloths to pâté de fois gras. Glenda had requested a soufflé for supper, so she bought eggs, cheese and one of those part-baked French sticks that only needed minutes in a hot oven in order to turn into fresh crusty bread. On her way to the counter, she passed the chocolate and with little thought filled up her basket with an indecent number of bars, knowing that this was the only panacea that could ameliorate the way she felt. If the elderly man behind the till thought it odd that someone should buy such an obscene quantity of one food then he knew better than to say anything. As it was, any customer was welcome; the future of his empire was constantly in jeopardy, so money that might boost his profits was well received, what was purchased was irrelevant.

Not wanting to be detained and have to chat, Faith haphazardly filled a carrier bag, paid and made her way home, stopping briefly only to open one bar of chocolate which she then ate as she drove.

The soufflé rose spectacularly and then sank as soon as it emerged from the oven. Helpings fell on the plates with a soggy thud. Hamish, ever tactful, begged Faith not to worry and reassured her that it did not detract from the taste one iota. Glenda mashed hers into a pulp before feeding it to the dogs and commented caustically that she would have asked for an omelette if she'd wanted one. Sighing, Faith scooped up the plates and threw them in the dishwasher. When her mother asked what was for dessert, she snapped and said there wasn't one. She had not stopped thinking about what Jonty might be up to and there was a decidedly unsavoury recurring image in her mind of some sinuous, toned and probably well-endowed young woman sitting on his knee and whispering words of a sexual nature into his receptive ear, his friends shouting encouragement all the while.

She spent the evening trying to find solace by eating chocolate, bar after bar until it was all gone. If anyone had asked her whether it was plain or milk, toffee stuffed or fruit and nut, she would not have had a clue. All that mattered was that while she was eating she felt better. She chose to dismiss the fact that when she had finished the feeling she was left with was infinitely worse.

Sunday passed at a snail's pace. Hamish rang to tell Faith that Jonty returned mid-morning, looking horrendous and had gone to sleep off the excesses of the night before. Faith was grateful that he had gone to the trouble to let her know but upset that Jonty could not have done this personally. It would only have taken him a couple of minutes. Quite why he had not got back before was something she was keen to find out but as the day drew on she came to the inevitable conclusion that at least he was intact, that the awful event was now a thing of the past and would surely have been the worst thing she had to endure before the wedding. She spent the afternoon prevaricating. Should she call him or wait for him to ring her?

'You're driving me stark staring bonkers, Faith,' Glenda told her. 'Leave the poor guy alone to sleep. He'll have one hell of a hangover and the last thing he needs is you bleating down the phone at him. Act your age and wait for him to ring you. Come on, let's go through this hideously long check list and see what's been done and what still needs to be done.'

Faith ate continually all day, grazing distractedly like some elderly donkey in a rich pasture. Glenda raised an eyebrow on several occasions as she watched her daughter consume buttered toast, with and without jam, biscuits, sweets, half a rhubarb pie with tinned custard and a batch of rock buns. She refrained from comment for once. Though she would have been loathe to admit it, there was something about Faith and her behaviour that really bothered her. For all her blousy bravado, deep down she genuinely desired to see Faith happy and to have a good, solid marriage that lasted for life. There was no way in which she would inflict the same pain and agony that she had had to endure on her own flesh and blood.

Monday dawned imperceptibly. It was a dark grey morning that was virtually indistinguishable from the previous night. Driving was made more hazardous by a low-lying fog and invisible icy patches on the road. It was not a pleasant journey to the surgery, made worse by the facts that Faith had slept badly as Jonty had still not telephoned and also because she was wondering what had happened when John had been to see Clare.

Up in the staff room the partners were all subdued. Faith misinterpreted this to mean that they had all made a decision about her and she was going to be asked to leave. The reality of the situation was that the gloominess of the day had seeped into their bones too and it was with heavy hearts that they set about their work on what was bound to be a tediously busy day.

The patients seemed drab also. Winter coats were the order of the day, with boots and mufflers. Layers of clothes had to be removed before adequate physical examinations could take place. Runny noses and coughs predominated, closely followed by sore throats, earache and headache. It came almost as a relief when a diabetic check or prescription review presented a different challenge.

Pollyanna came in to see Faith. She looked as happy as she had done before, making Faith feel guilty that she had not yet written the referral letter. Today she was dressed in a shapeless, quilted coat and had a purple and orange toorie pulled down over her head.

'Hello,' began Faith.

'Hi, Dr Faber. Don't worry, I'll not keep you long today. Just two things. The indigestion mixture you gave me is really good, so I wondered if I could have some more and I think I've got cystitis. I've lost count of the number of times I've had to go for a wee recently.'

Faith breathed a sigh of relief inwardly, looking forward to an easy consultation.

'Is it painful?' asked Faith.

'No, I just feel I need to go all the time.'

'Have you seen any blood in your urine?'

'No, nothing like that.'

'Any pain in your tummy?'

Pollyanna lifted up her belly and rubbed her pubic area. 'A little, not much. More of an ache really.'

'It sounds as if it is an infection, though usually patients have pain as well. Never mind, leave a sample with the nurse; I'll give you some antibiotics to start on and just be sure to drink plenty.'

'Thanks, Dr Faber. Sorry to bother you.'

Faith smiled. 'It's no trouble. Take care.'

At the door Pollyanna paused and looked back. 'Have you done my letter?'

'It'll be in the post today, I promise.'

'Thank you. Bye!'

Three patients later and Faith had finished and felt a sense of achievement for having successfully completed the first part of the day. Checking her phone she was delighted to find a suitably sloppy message from Jonty, which made her squirm with pleasure, plus he gave his word that he would see her later. She was just texting back, a rather daringly suggestive message, when her phone rang and John Britton asked her if she would be so kind as to step into his surgery for a quick word.

Adrenaline ran riot around her blood stream resulting in a racing heart, sweaty palms and rapid breathing. This was the moment that she had not been waiting for. She gently tapped on his door and entered quietly. He was sitting in his cherished, if moth-eaten, chair behind his old-fashioned desk, dark wood with a scroll top. The appearance was incongruous in the otherwise modern room but he refused to be parted from either, having worked with them both for decades. Little of the walls were visible, for they were covered with photographs of his wife Faye and their family, children and grandchildren. The family dog smiled out from several photos and on closer inspection of another, there was a rather blurred but unmistakable cat running across a vast lawn. He smiled in an avuncular fashion and motioned for her to come and sit down.

Faith could feel herself trembling as she pretended to get comfortable.

'Thanks for looking in, Faith. I know it's a busy morning but I don't think house calls are too onerous, from what I've heard so far.'

'Oh, that's good,' answered Faith and then instantly worried that her comment might make her look less than enthusiastic. John nodded.

'I went to see Clare yesterday.'

'How is she?' Faith asked, not wanting to hear the answer.

'I'm pleased to say that she is very much better.'

'Oh that is good.' Faith did mean it.

'Yes, she's beginning to talk about coming back to work again. Perhaps starting next month.'

'Oh?' Faith tried to sound nonchalant.

'I spoke to the partners last night when I got home. We're very keen to let her come back but of course anxious lest she should overdo it.'

'Of course.'

'So we wondered how you felt about staying on. We're all unanimous in our praise for your hard work. You've really been a great help to us. You fit in well and your work ethos is very similar to ours.'

'Thank you very much.'

'I suggested to the others that we offer you a contract for a further year, with a view to extending it at that time. Everyone was very pleased with the idea. That way, Clare could feel her way back in, under no pressure to do too much. Even if she's back full time after a couple of months, which personally I doubt, but if she were then having an extra pair of hands will be no bad thing. How do you feel about that? Obviously you may have your own plans and I would hate to intrude on those. So if you want to take some time to think about the offer…'

160

'No, not at all. I love it here. I'd love to stay on. Thank you so much.' She felt her words sounded woefully inadequate.

'Excellent, that's settled. Elliot will draw up the contract. A good start to your wedding week, eh? Shall we go and have a coffee. I know I need one. I've brought in some biscuits that Faye made, oaty flips. They're delicious. She thought they might brighten up an otherwise dreary day.'

'Thank you so, so much. That's simply wonderful. I'll meet you up there, I just need to fetch my bag.'

By the time she reached the coffee room, John had obviously briefed the others. Congratulations were offered to Faith who repeated over and over again how grateful she was and how happy she was to have been asked. She listened while they discussed Clare, John particularly emphatic that she should not be allowed to be stressed in any way.

'That means you'll have to keep seeing Mrs Tonbridge, Faith!' laughed Ellie.

Just at that precise moment, Faith would have gladly volunteered to have that patient as her matron of honour, so happy was she.

'That's precisely what I mean,' agreed John, with a more serious note to his voice. 'Clare has a huge following and a lot of them are really hard work. We've to ensure that she doesn't just try to pick up where she left off. I'll have a word with Elliot about sorting out a few hours for her. But we'll all need to be very vigilant, yet without seeming overprotective. I want Clare to feel that we are all supporting her to the hilt.'

Nods of agreement came from everyone.

'Everybody happy? Good, then let's divide up these house calls. Oh, Lord, what's this? I thought someone said there weren't very many of them?'

To show extra willing, Faith took the biggest share of the calls and then enjoyed driving around the town and out into the countryside, no longer aware of the dark, damp day which made sidelights obligatory, now that her future was secure. Well, at least the next year of it was and to have had that offer made to her must surely be a good omen. She made a secret vow that she would work even harder and be a huge help to Clare and then felt giddy with excitement at the thought of the vows she would be making in but a few days' time.

At lunchtime, Faith contacted Glenda, to make sure that she was hard at work with the list of tasks that she had been left to do and then went and pressed her nose up against the window of a local estate agent's office, praying that there might be some suitable property for them to view on return from their honeymoon. She would love to live on the outskirts of Lambdale. Not only was it such an attractive location but how splendid it would be not to have that longish drive to work each day. Sadly, there were none, which was perhaps as well seeing that Jonty had already intimated that he wanted to live no more than a stone's throw away from his father, in view of the family business. Shielding her eyes with her cupped hands so that she could see better, Faith vaguely made out the unmistakable shape of Pollyanna, towards the back of the office. She was wearing a great tent of a dress and appeared to be making a pot of tea but waved cheerily when she spotted Faith, who of course returned the compliment.

The afternoon sped by, as is often the way when there is not a moment to take stock and draw breath. The surgeries were all over booked, thanks to the clamouring patients who were insistent that their problem came under the category of urgent and thus necessitated an appointment the same day. Quite how neck pain for ten years could be deemed worthy of such a description, Faith had no idea but she knew better than to waste time giving it her consideration; she simply smiled her way through the session and then looked to tackle some, it not all, of her paperwork before she set off for home.

She felt ambivalent about Pollyanna's referral letter and contemplated asking her to come in for a further chat. But then she visualised the joy and anticipation on Pollyanna's face and felt that there was no way she could let her down. She had promised that the letter would go in the evening's post, so after careful composition, in which she stressed that she was unsure just how much the patient understood about the nature of the surgery and the gravity of the consequences, Faith printed off the letter, signed it and put it on the pile of work for the secretaries to deal with. She would be interested to hear what the consultant's comments were.

Reaching home, later than expected but with an empty in-tray, it was as though the weekend had never happened. There was Jonty, admittedly still looking rather wan around the edges and drinking a huge mug of tea rather than a gin and tonic, sitting with Glenda. Faith rushed to him and hugged him, receiving a tepid reception in return.

'Sorry, darling, I'm still quite rough. Go easy on me. Have you any aspirin in your bag? My head's thumping like nobody's business.' His voice was croaky.

Glenda threw her head back and laughed sardonically. 'You've only yourself to blame. Serves you right.'

Sam and Rex started barking for no reason and Jonty put his hands over his ears. 'Somebody shut them up, please.'

Faith poured a cup of tea for herself, gearing up for an inquisition.

'So,' she began, 'did you have a good stag night?'

'Absolutely bloody marvellous. Simon's an ace party planner. Not sure what we did, though. It's all a bit of a blur.'

'Where did you go to?'

'Not sure. I had to be blindfolded on the journey.'

'But you must have recognised where you were when you got there?'

'Nope, they didn't let me see until we were inside. We had some cocktails in a few bars and went to a club. That's about it.'

More information did not appear to be forthcoming and Faith decided to quit while she felt more or less ahead. It was certainly true, in some circumstances, that ignorance was bliss.

'Oh well, it's a good job you've got some time to recover before the wedding. Just imagine what it would have been like if you'd gone out the night before!'

Jonty groaned softly.

'Aspirin, please. And more tea. Then I think I'd better go to bed. How I've managed to work today will forever be one of the mysteries of mankind.'

Wallowing in his self-inflicted aches and pains, he reacted minimally when Faith told him and her mother about the job offer she had had at work.

Glenda was more generous with her congratulations. 'You've done well, Faith. Show a bit more interest, Jonty.' She punched him on the shoulder. 'She's doing all this hard work for you.'

He slurped his tea noisily before laying his head on the table and closing his eyes. 'Thank you, darling. That's just great.'

'I'll put him to bed, shall I, Ma?' Faith made to help him off the chair. 'Will you help me get him up the stairs?'

'Leave him where he is. Ring Hamish, or rather, I will. He'll come and get him. Get the supper on, in the meantime but don't make any for Jonty. All he needs is sleep.'

Chapter Nineteen

Faith woke up after an excellent night's sleep and stretched out beneath the duvet like a contented kitten. She could see a glimmer of sunlight coming through a small gap in the curtains and hoped that this was an omen of continuing good weather, cold but bright. There was still enough colour in some of the trees to make a pleasing backdrop for the wedding photographs if the sun was shining and she dearly wanted them to be taken outside if possible. She had studied several different forecasts to check the prospects. Those on the television had concurred with the radio but conflicted with the local newspaper and an on-line source that she had found. Regardless of which she chose to put her trust in, it was completely out of her hands; all that she could do was hope and pray that the sun would shine and there would be no wind, either of which was a tall order for the month of November.

The forty-eight hours that stretched ahead promised to be hectic but enjoyable, allowing little time for meteorological divinations. Her father and his wife were due to arrive in the late afternoon and would go directly to the small but ridiculously expensive hotel that they had booked into, with Faith and Jonty due to meet them there for dinner that evening in the award-winning restaurant. They had turned down the welcoming arms of the Swindlehurst Castle, feeling that it would be wise to be distanced as much as possible, for Glenda's sake. Whilst this was in theory an excellent plan, Glenda of course had chosen to misinterpret it as a sign that they were frightened to face her, refusing to accept the possibility that they were capable of being diplomatic.

'Ha!' she'd snorted, when Faith had broken the news of the arrangements over a relatively relaxed supper one evening. 'Still as spineless as ever! If he were a real father he'd want to be in the thick of things. I can't wait to see his face when he sees the bill for all this.'

Faith had tried, unsuccessfully, to soothe things over but Glenda, true to form, wanted to feel that she had the upper hand in the proceedings.

Jonty, to Faith's relief, was showing none of the reluctance that he had exhibited before the meal with Ellie and Ian. For someone about to spend time with his future father-in-law and presumably keen to make an appropriately good impression, he appeared remarkably unruffled. He had even accepted Faith's suggestion of what he should wear without a murmur, given her a huge hug and told her that he couldn't wait for Saturday and why didn't they just elope right now. Faith hoped that this was yet another demonstration of his passionate commitment and nothing to do with not wanting to meet Dennis.

Remarkably, Glenda appeared at the bedroom door, not bothering to knock, carrying a cup of tea which she put on Faith's bedside table. Without waiting for any comment she marched out. She smelled of horse dung and the cold morning air. Some shreds of straw had fallen from her jacket onto the carpet. Plumping up her pillows, Faith sat up in bed, luxuriating in the fact that she had been given tacit permission to stay there for a few precious moments longer.

Smiling, she thought back to the previous day at the surgery where a special drinks party, rather in the style of Elliot's birthday, had been put on especially for her. The staff room had been transformed with dozens of silver balloons, corkscrewed ribbons dangled from the ceiling and a huge banner looped from one side to the other which shouted 'Congratulations' in garishly coloured letters. Small tables were covered with matching cloths and an array of the finest canapés, savouries and little cakes from Delicious. Faith, who had had no idea that anything of the sort was being planned, had been completely speechless when she had gone in there to pick up her coat and bag before setting off for home. A glass of champagne had been thrust into one hand while she tried not to blush furiously as the doctors and staff of the Teviotdale Medical Centre gave her the best welcome she had ever had. If she had any lingering doubt that she was not respected and liked at her current place of employment then surely this should have been enough to erase it. John had given one of his speeches – even now, twelve hours later, Faith had to smile at some of the hilarious stories he had told – wished her and Jonty well and then everyone had raised their glasses and toasted the happy couple in one voice.

Somehow, Faith, who was not in any way adept at public speaking, had managed to cobble together a few stumbling sentences of thanks, not just for the party but for the vouchers that they had given her, which she had promised would be spent wisely and that she would let them all know what they had chosen to buy.

She had been so happy as she drove home that the disappointment she felt when she found that Jonty was not waiting for her was only transient. Still hiccoughing a little from the champagne, she had been able to sit down and compile one of her lists of jobs that needed to be attended to and compose her plan of campaign for the next couple of days before spending the rest of the evening sitting convivially with her mother and the dogs, while watching a reasonably good thriller on television.

Glenda was back out with the horses when Faith came down; Dawn had rung in to say that she was still unwell but hoped to be back the following day. Faith was rather glad that she had not been there to witness her mother's reaction, both verbal and physical. But now the kitchen was quiet, save for the deep, steady hum of the fridge. Faith made a hot drink and sat at the table, cradling the mug in her hands and gazed at the familiar surroundings. A trail of biscuit crumbs that led to the back door suggested that the dogs had been eating on the run, torn between their breakfast and their yearning to be outside. By the stove were the dogs' wicker beds, for occasional daytime use only, filled with cushions and pieces of the picnic rugs that they had used years ago when out for the day at shows. A bridle hung over one chair, the throat lash broken, waiting for the next trip to the saddlers. It was spotlessly clean and smelled of recently applied saddle soap. On the dresser were the cookery books that Glenda had received over the years as unappreciated birthday and Christmas gifts but never opened, almost hidden from sight by the trophies on display and a selection of the more prestigious rosettes, a testament to the successful summer just passed. At one end of the table were piles of magazines, either medical or equestrian which neither of them could ever quite pluck up the courage to throw away, just in case they might be of some use in the future. In the centre was the dish that had once been used for Faith's food, when she was a baby. With rabbits chasing each other around the rim, it had miraculously never been damaged, apart from a small chip which meant that one rabbit had no tail. Through domestic disputes, house moves and years serving as a water bowl for the dogs, it had survived against the odds and now stood in pride of place, only demoted to continual use as an ash tray.

Faith sighed, wondering what it would be like, not seeing these emblems of home life, which she knew so well and took for granted, on a daily basis and realised that in fact she was going to miss them terribly. What was more, she was going to miss her mother. Much as she loathed her smoking and winced at her acerbic comments, it would seem strange living with Hamish, easy-going and happily disorganised, trying not to upset his daily routines while at the same time trying to make it feel like home. He was never anything less than charming and welcoming but was hopelessly set in his ways, with a dreadful habit of leaving rubbish for someone else to clear up and a trail of dirty clothes and used crockery in his wake.

She had tried on innumerable occasions to explain to Jonty what she was thinking, hoping that he might understand and agree to look for somewhere to rent temporarily. In desperation, she had even tried the tack that it would be unfair on Hamish to have them both living with him, disrupting his comforts, but it had been hopeless, like trying to talk to someone who didn't speak English. He had been totally unable to empathise with her at all, unable to see past the point of how much money they would be saving by not paying rent. The last time she had dared to raise the subject he had turned round and snapped at her. What was her problem he had asked. She ought to be grateful. Their house might not be as big as hers but it was warm, comfortable, full of his belongings, which would save him having to pack, and nearer to Lambdale by five minutes. His father would be delighted to have his meals cooked and their laundry could easily all go in together, which would work out quite splendidly for all concerned. It was just as easy to shop and cater for three as it was for two.

The didactic way in which he had delivered his verdict had stunned Faith into silence, afraid to fight back, and thus the matter was considered to be closed. His arguments had done nothing to assuage Faith's mounting fear that when the three of them were living together, it would be she who felt like the proverbial gooseberry, rather than Hamish.

Faith shook her head and sipped at her drink, now unpleasantly cold, having been forgotten while she was day-dreaming. Of course it would be fine. It was imperative that she focus on the positives, that she and Jonty would be together every night and that it would surely be no time at all until they found their dream home or, at the very least, somewhere that had the potential to transform into one. She made a mental note to contact estate agents to send them details of suitable houses to view when they got back from their honeymoon.

Time was slipping through her fingers and there was much to be done. She poured what was left in her mug into the sink and then ran down to the stables to find her mother, who had promised to go out with her to the hotel, the florists and various other last-minute checks.

Glenda, regretting her offer to help, became increasingly tetchy as the day wore on and by mid-afternoon was marching about with the sternest of faces and barely speaking at all. At the cake maker's, which was their final port of call, she refused to get out of the car and sat listening to a discordant and crashing piece of music on the CD player. It was as though she had an invisible antenna that was able to pick up the proximity of her ex-husband. On their return to the house, she reached immediately for the bottle of gin and recklessly splashed a more than medicinal measure into a glass, topping it up with the merest hint of tonic while simultaneously lighting and inhaling long and hard on a cigarette. With no regard for femininity she knocked back her drink in large, noisy gulps as though her survival depended on it. Faith watched her with sadness, wishing that she could exorcise the pain that her mother continued to feel, even after so many years. She contemplated saying something and was constructing a sentence that she hoped could not be construed as confrontational when Glenda stubbed out her spent cigarette, lit another and disappeared into the drawing room to turn on the television, the volume overpowering to all but the completely deaf. Faith correctly assumed that she wanted to be left alone for a while. Tactfully, she refrained from following her and sat alone, as she had done in the morning, but now aware of a weariness that was out of proportion to the day's exertions and the effort of keeping her mother in a good mood.

To her horror she was aware of the unmistakable feeling of the beginnings of a cold – a solid, bunged-up sensation was starting to irritate behind her nose and a scratchy, sore throat made its presence felt when she swallowed. Not daring to take any chances, she took some paracetamol and made a warm lemon drink, adding runny honey, opting for the more conventional approach than the one Glenda would have chosen which would

169

have relied heavily on a bottle of whisky. Her shoulders shuddered as a shiver ran across them and a one-man band was starting to thump in her head. This was the last thing she needed.

Glancing at the clock, she calculated that her father should be arriving at his hotel any minute. Eager to ring and check, she held back, wanting him to have time to unpack and settle in, so instead she logged onto her computer to see if she had any emails. There were several but as usual most of them could be deleted immediately. She smiled as she read a gushing note of good wishes from the shop where she had bought her dress, imploring her to send them a photo and then clicked on one from her father that would probably just be some last-minute instructions about this evening. He was like that, so organised, so reliable, so efficient.

For a message of such brevity, the impact it created was earth-shattering. In fewer than three lines, he managed to catapult his daughter from her pinnacle of excitement into the darkest chasm of disappointment by telling her that he was sorry, but a problem had come up at work and much though he regretted it and sent a million apologies and a similar number of promises to make amends, he would not be able to attend the wedding and give her away.

Faith re-read the message again and again, hoping to find some mistake, believing that perhaps her incipient fever was causing her to hallucinate. It made no difference. However she grouped the words together the end point was the same. Her father was not coming to her wedding. Scrabbling for her phone, she dialled his number, ignoring the fact that it was the middle of the night on the other side of the world, and let it ring and ring, hoping that it did disturb him for it was no less than he deserved after what he had done. Whether he heard or not, she would never know for there was no response.

Jonty, typically, was not answering his mobile phone either, nor was anyone in at his house. Faith uttered some extraordinary profanities and snapped her own phone shut and threw it back in her bag. Where was he when she needed him?

The sound of canned laughter together with Glenda's chuckling reminded Faith that someone else needed to be informed of this new development. Much as she might dread breaking this news to her mother, it had to be done. Hopefully the sounds of mirth were encouraging, a sign that her humour was improved, though she was going to have a field day when she heard what Faith had to tell her.

170

'Ma.' Faith entered the drawing room cautiously, keeping an eye open for signs that her mother was in a receptive mood.

'What is it now?' Though curt, this was not said in an unfriendly way.

'I've something to tell you,' Faith began. 'Could you turn the sound down a little?'

'Hang on, I've lost the remote control,' shouted Glenda, burrowing under a Labrador and triumphantly retrieving it. 'Okay, I'm all ears. Whatever's up? You look terrible.'

'It's Pa – he's sent an email. He can't come to the wedding.'

Glenda exploded into her gin and tonic. 'Bastard! He's let me down but I never thought he would sink so low as to do the same to you. Just let me get my hands on him.'

Faith automatically sided with her father, irrespective of the disappointment she felt so keenly. 'I'm sure he'd have been here if he could. His visit was all planned down to the last detail, so something of paramount importance must have come up.'

'Know your problem? You're too naïve. You can't see anything but good in people. How could anything be more important than his own daughter's wedding?'

Faith was unable to come up with a counter argument owing to the fact that, deep down, she agreed with her mother.

'What shall I do, Ma? Who'll give me away?'

Glenda sucked in her cheeks, inhaling on her umpteenth cigarette. She shook her head. 'Hamish?' she suggested after some cogitation.

'No way!' expostulated Faith. 'I can't be given away by my father-in-law to be.'

'I don't see why not.'

'Because...' Faith was adamant.

'Well, how about your Uncle James?'

Faith wrinkled up her nose.

'But I haven't seen him for years. It would be rather like being given away by a stranger.'

Glenda rolled her eyes at what she considered to be her daughter's obstinacy.

'Time's short, Faith. You can't afford to be picky.'

'Ma,' stormed Faith, which caused a bout of croupy coughing. 'This is supposed to be my wedding and it's all falling apart. Plus I feel as if I'm coming down with the flu.'

Glenda studied her daughter. 'As I said, you look terrible. Go to bed. I'll bring you up something shortly. Get a good night's sleep. We can sort this in the morning.' She turned back to her programme.

'But I can't get hold of Jonty and he ought to know.... He's supposed to be picking me up to go out to dinner.'

'Go to bed. I'll ring Hamish.'

'I've tried – there's no reply.'

'Faith, I will sort all this out for you. Now go to bed.'

Tears were rolling down Faith's hot cheeks. She coughed harshly. 'Oh, Ma, I can't be ill. Not now.'

Glenda heaved her body off the settee, unsettling the dogs who had been arranged on top of her in various positions of repose. They uttered grumbling noises as she did so and then instantly returned to their dreams. Taking Faith by the elbow, aware of the abnormally hot, sweaty skin beneath her fingers, Glenda steered her daughter, not ungently, upstairs to her bedroom, waiting while she undressed and slid gratefully under the duvet onto the soft and inviting mattress, then sat on the edge of the bed, wiping Faith's burning forehead with a cold flannel.

'Poor you. What a let down. It'll work out for the best, you'll see. It always does. Don't give it another thought tonight. Just try to get some sleep and you'll feel better in the morning. You're made of strong stuff. You take after me, which is fortunate, considering the alternative.'

Faith needed no encouraging. If she hadn't felt so terrible and the situation were not so tragic, Faith might have broken into a grin at her mother's unfailing ability to cast yet another stone at her object of hate.

She was dozing before Glenda had managed to creep as far as the door. It was a fitful, restless sleep, fraught with vivid, mad dreams of tearing around, racing against time, never quite reaching her goals. In a brief moment when she woke, desperate to have a drink of water and turn the pillow over so that it was refreshingly cool against her prickling skin, she heard voices below, those of her mother and Hamish but no amount of straining her ears reassured her that Jonty had come round too.

Chapter Twenty

Her temperature was nearly down to normal when she crawled out of bed shortly before nine o'clock the next morning, bursting to empty her bladder. She felt sticky and was aware that she exuded a most unpleasant body odour. Marshmallow seemed to have replaced the bones in her legs and she wobbled to the bathroom, holding on to the furniture as she did so. Not only did she feel thirsty but hungry as well, which was barely surprising as it was nearly twenty-four hours since she had eaten, having been quite content to skip lunch when she was out with her mother. It was an effective way to lose weight, Faith surmised as she stood on the scales and saw a satisfying decrease since she had last done so, but not one to be recommended. Minimising her intake for this last day should be easy and ensure that she looked what she considered to be perfect for her wedding day. Her brief foray to the bathroom used up what little energy she had and it was a relief to sink back down into bed.

For the second day in a row, Glenda appeared, this time bearing a tray with breakfast. Memories of childhood illness came flooding back as she surveyed a piece of toast, cut into triangles and denuded of all crusts, thickly spread with real butter and marmalade, and a little pot of tea.

'I could get used to this,' Faith thanked her.

'How're you feeling?' Glenda went over to open the curtains and let in the unwelcome sight of a dreary day, sombre and damp.

'Better, thanks,' admitted Faith. 'Just like a half-wrung-out dishcloth.'

'You still look pretty peaky. Good job you've nothing much to do today. Make the most of it and rest, plus do all the sorts of things you would tell your patients to do.'

'Okay, Ma.' Faith was glad to be given instructions.

'We've solved the problem your father has created with his thoughtlessness,' Glenda started.

Faith looked up from her toast, suddenly interested. 'How?'

'Hamish has offered. He wants to do it for you. He wouldn't take no for an answer.'

Faith's face fell. 'Oh, Ma. You know I didn't want that.'

'It's the logical solution. He knows you well, he'll look good in that rig-out you'd got for your father plus they're about the same size, so it should fit nicely.'

'I'd hoped you might give me away, Ma,' Faith ventured timidly.

Glenda threw her head back and roared with laughter. 'No way. Come on, Faith – think about it. Hamish is the obvious solution.'

'There's something that's just a bit incestuous about it though, Ma.'

'Rubbish. He'll do a far better job than that man who purports to be your father would have done.' Glenda turned to leave. 'I'm off down to the stables. Dawn's back, thank goodness, but she looks a wreck.'

'What?' laughed Faith, 'no make up?'

Glenda smirked. 'Oh, that's as perfect as ever. I just want to check she's up to the job. You stay there for the morning. I'm expecting a call about an indoor event next month – come and get me if they ring.'

Faith put the tray on the floor and snuggled back under her bed clothes.

'Oh and Jonty rang.'

'Did he?'

Glenda secretly thought that the eagerness in Faith's voice was pathetic.

'Yes, he's coming round later. I've told him that you're ill and staying in bed for the morning, so I expect he'll appear this afternoon. He sounded most concerned.'

Faith smiled and gazed devotedly at the finger that wore her engagement ring. Not long now – only hours in fact, until it had a wedding band to keep it company. She closed her eyes and hoped for more sleep. Accepting of the fact that Hamish was going to give her away and knowing instinctively that the viral infection that had ravaged her body overnight had almost been beaten into submission by her immune system, she was able to relax.

174

She managed to catnap only, but as her temperature was stable the rest was far more refreshing and devoid of lunatic adventures. In fact, she felt so much more human that, even though it was only midmorning, she dared to go against the regulations of her dictatorial nurse, showered, washed her hair and dressed in jeans and a polo-necked cashmere jumper, soft as chinchilla fur, which clung to her skin like a security blanket. Still a bit shivery, she draped a woolly cardigan over her shoulders and then made her way tentatively downstairs, a little ashamed that she felt safer when holding on to the banister.

A generous handful of post lay scattered on the mat, spilling over onto the floor. Faith bent over to scoop it up and had to steady herself as a wave of light-headedness engulfed her when she stood upright again. Apart from the usual bills and circulars there was a wealth of cards, which she carefully stacked on one side, looking forward to opening them together with Jonty, tomorrow. She paused to pick some dead leaves off a plant, feeling exhausted just from the effort of getting up. Shuffling into the kitchen in her old slippers, she chose the chair nearest the range, where it was warm and soothing, and settled down to flick through the newspaper and a magazine on home interior design she had bought the previous day, hoping to be able to enthuse Jonty with some attractive ideas.

It was strange how when you were under par, the crossword seemed impossible, the sudoku unfathomable and ideal home ideas unattainable. She threw down her pen with more than a little frustration and reverted to a paperback that she was halfway through. This proved more successful and she was able to while away a reasonable period of time before being disturbed by the front doorbell ringing insistently. Her immediate reaction was that it would be Jonty, though common sense reminded her that he always came to the back door and simply walked in. Still cherishing a small but burning hope that it was him, she ran her hands through her still-damp hair, hoping that she looked presentable, and made her way to find out.

No Jonty but instead, a globular, cheery lady from the bakers, delivering the cake. Looking as though she had indulged in rather more of her own cooking than was wise, she breathlessly heaved three large boxes from the back of her van and carried them with immeasurable care into the house. Faith accepted her wishes of good will and thanked her profusely before watching her choose to back the van erratically down the drive veering this way and that before exiting the gate with a branch of evergreen attached to one wing mirror.

There had been no dispute about the cake. Both were adamant that they did not want the traditional fruit cake, neither being particularly fond of the mixture, or marzipan nor icing so hard that it threatened to fracture your teeth. Without a moment's deliberation, a sponge cake was first choice. They had viewed a variety of designs before Faith amalgamated a few ideas and came up with one of her own. Three circular cakes of different diameters would be balanced one on top of the other, each one covered with a myriad of chocolate petals – white, plain and milk, all hand made at great expense. Concealed beneath this breath-taking exterior lay soft, moist layers of vanilla sponge sandwiched together by creamy orange filling which boasted the subtlest hint of Cointreau.

Faith peeped into each box to check that it was as beautiful as she had anticipated. Tomorrow she would be permitted to have a large slice, for her diet would be suspended for the day and she would need plenty of energy to dance the night away in Jonty's arms. The end result was indisputably spectacular. When it was finally arranged, there would be nobody who had ever seen, or tasted, anything like it before. This was going to be a day to remember, not just for her and Jonty but for all their guests.

She sighed, recalling that her father would not be there. He would just have to make do with the photographs, her emails and phone calls. She had forgiven him, as she always did and always would. The fact that she never saw him and conducted almost the entirety of their relationship through cyberspace was irrelevant. If she ever needed him, she knew that he would be there for her (at this point she deliberately subtracted her wedding from this calculation), fighting her corner for her, making sure that she was safe. How he managed to achieve this without his physical presence would remain a mystery for ever but somehow he did and his ability to supply a seemingly bottomless pot of money for her only served to help.

Reimmersed in her novel, it was only moments before she was interrupted again, this time by the telephone, shattering the comfortable silence with its harsh tones. It was the call that Glenda had warned her about. Resting the receiver on the dresser top, Faith went into the hall and shouted up the stairs, in case her mother had nipped indoors when she wasn't looking but reckoning that it was unlikely as there was no sign of the dogs, who followed their mistress as if magnetised and would happily have forfeited their perpetual search for rats and rabbits if it meant that they would not lose sight of her.

'She must be down with the horses. I'll get her for you straight away. Do you want to hold or shall I ask her to ring you back?'

Faith recited the number back as she was given it, hastily scribbled it down and then went to find a coat and some more appropriate footwear. Outside the air was wet with a malignant drizzle that quickly sank into her clothes and drenched her recently dried hair. She shivered, still feeling frail. Pulling her jacket hood over her head, she broke into a half trot, all that she was capable of having been too lazy to fasten the laces on her trainers. Out of the corner of her eye she observed to her delight that Jonty's car was parked in the drive. He must have just arrived and spotted Glenda in the stables, so gone to announce his arrival and enquire tenderly after his fiancée's state of health before bouncing in to see her. This would also explain why Glenda had not come back up to the house before now. They would, as ever, be talking horse.

As she neared the stable block, she saw no sign of either Jonty or her mother and wondered if they had gone out riding. She peered into each of the six loose boxes but all were full and the only occupants were equine, snug in their rugs, tugging on their haynets contentedly. They turned their heads inquisitively to see who was watching them. Caspian, alone, came over to be stroked and kicked the door, hoping this might be a sign they were going out. Unlike his rider, he was nonplussed by miserable wet weather and raring to go.

Further down the yard, Faith noticed that the door to the tack room was ajar, as was the one to the small barn where the feed, hay and straw was kept. Thinking that she could hear voices, Faith checked the former, which was, as ever, meticulously neat and tidy. Bridles hung in symmetry, saddles shone on their racks. Shelves were divided up into compartments which held neatly stacked brushes and bandages, bottles of shampoo, show sheen and various veterinary products. A small wood-burning stove in the

177

corner of the room was lit and inviting. Two near-empty mugs sat on a bench nearby, together with a half-full packet of digestive biscuits and a bag of apples. Next to this was Dawn's coat and bag from which a neat aluminium foil-wrapped parcel of sandwiches had fallen onto the recently swept floor. Faith bent over and picked it up, placing it out of the way of any hungry passing Labrador. To her amazement, she noticed that the ashtray on the windowsill was empty.

Finding that the radio was on, Faith listened briefly to a snatch of political debate and then switched it off, curious that it was not tuned into the usual station which played continuous popular music for twenty-four hours a day. She was also flummoxed that she had still not found any evidence of her mother or Jonty. More puzzling still was the absence of wagging tails and dangling dogs' tongues.

The only place left to check was the barn where she was likely to draw another blank unless they had darted in there to escape the rain, but still a strange choice when there was the warmth of the tackroom, with its tea-making facilities and licence to smoke. Faith splashed her way through a large puddle and took hold of the handle to the barn door. On doing so, she heard noises inside. Something made her stop and listen. Clearly human in origin, it was far from the normal conversational tones of two adults. Breathy and in gasps, they were punctuated by moans and utterances of encouragement. Familiar though these noises were, it took Faith a little time to identify what she was listening to. Realisation sinking in, she panicked, wondering what to do. Whilst it might be inappropriate for Dawn to entertain her boyfriend on the premises, Faith felt it was not her responsibility to interrupt a moment of intimacy that was obviously becoming increasingly heated and her preferred option would have been to tiptoe away and then weigh up the pros and cons of whether to tell her mother about it later on.

She half turned to go, sure that they had no idea of her presence, but a particularly passionate and identifiable grunt made her stop in her tracks. As if drawn by an invisible force, she slunk inside, holding her breath, willing that she would not start to cough. The darkness made it hard to make out where anyone was. A recent delivery meant that there were huge bales of hay and straw stretching from floor to ceiling, blocking out what little light was allowed in by the tiny opaque skylights. Try as she might, there was no way of finding out what was going on without putting on the main light. The only torch she possessed was back at the house, possibly in the kitchen but more likely lost somewhere.

The further she made her way into the barn, the noisier her footsteps became, crackling straw telling of each stride she took. Surely they would hear her now.

The logical course of action was to retreat and go back to the house but still she could not go. An orgasmic cry shuddered through the dusty air, followed by the hideously clear words of 'Oh, Jonty'.

It was all she needed to hear. Faith sped back to the door, flicked on all the lights and was rewarded by the sight of her fiancé and Dawn, both naked from the waist down, their shirts unbuttoned and in disarray. Their heads spun round to see who had come in, expecting to see Glenda, which would have been bad enough but found that it was a far worse scenario that met their eyes.

Faith thought of all the cutting comments that it would have been clever to utter about half an hour later when it was too late. Instead, now she was speechless, standing with her mouth hanging open, looking idiotic. The disturbed lovers, initially frozen by shock, suddenly started to shove their limbs frenetically back into their clothes in a belated attempt to conceal their nudity and pretend that nothing had happened. Faith watched them with escalating horror, unable to take her eyes off Dawn's gorgeously slim body and Jonty's familiar musculature.

'Say something, Jonty,' hissed Dawn, dragging a fleece over her head and pulling on her boots.

'Such as?' he retorted. They stared at each other in desperation.

'Faith,' they started in unison.

'It's not what it looks like— ' added Jonty, breathlessly.

That was all Faith needed to break the spell of immobility. She found that her feet now agreed to move at the behest of her brain and, emitting a heart-rending sob, she turned on her heels and ran as best she could, oblivious of the puddles and the now-persistent rain, back to the house, slamming the door behind her and locking it.

Glenda was in the kitchen, on the telephone, and looked up, irritated at the noise that Faith was making and on the verge of telling her to be quiet before she noticed with her innate maternal instinct that she usually kept well hidden that something serious was amiss. Faith ran through the room, pushing the welcoming dogs out of her way, tearing off her trainers at the foot of the stairs and throwing her coat in a heap on the floor. She was halfway up before Glenda, phone call hurriedly terminated, came after her and stood, one hand on the bottom of the banisters.

'What is it, Faith?' she called after her.

'Ask Jonty! But do not let him anywhere near me ever again. Or you could ask Dawn!'

Glenda felt the house shake from the violence with which her daughter hurled the bedroom door shut and let out an enormous sigh. She was on the point of going up to find out more when she heard a loud knocking at the back door and went to answer it, feeling her heart sink as she spotted Jonty's distraught face pressed up against the window on which he was also banging simultaneously. It would be simpler to walk away and not let him in and she toyed with the idea briefly before acknowledging the fact that this would not achieve anything at all.

Unlocking the door, she let him in and cast a disapproving look over his dishevelled look, shirt only half tucked in, trouser flies unzipped and no coat. A telltale smear of vermilion lipstick stood out on his left cheek. Glenda was visited by a chilling feeling of déjà vu. It didn't take a genius to identify the source of the lipstick and work out what had been going on.

'Glenda!' Jonty did his best to sound normal, but he would have fooled no one.

'Jonty!' Glenda mimicked, more than a touch of sarcasm in her voice.

'How nice to see you. I thought you'd gone out.'

Glenda nodded in confirmation.

'I had but I'm back now and it would appear to be a good job that I am.'

'Can I come in and see Faith? It's pouring with rain out here. How is she feeling?'

Glenda shook her head. 'Would that really be a good idea? I'm not sure what's been going on but I'm beginning to put the pieces together.'

'I can explain,' promised Jonty with feeling.

'You forget that you are speaking to an expert in the matter of infidelity, so don't try to belittle me with puerile comments.'

'Glenda, we're good friends. Why don't we talk first and then I'll talk to Faith?'

'Are we good friends?' was the echo. 'I'm starting to wonder. For months, you've sat in my kitchen, helped yourself to my hospitality, all the while getting your feet further under my table. Did you really come round to my house so often because you enjoyed my company? Did you really value my opinion on your horses? Or did you just want an opportunity to screw my groom behind your fiancée's back?'

Jonty paled. 'It's all a terrible misunderstanding...'

'Spare me all the hackneyed phrases. I've heard them all before.'

'I can explain... honestly...'

Glenda let him into the kitchen as the rain was splashing onto her face too, but made a point of blocking his way to the door to the hall. They sat down facing each other, Jonty fiddling with a tablemat, Glenda with a look of defiance in her eyes.

'I doubt very much that you can. I also presume that when you were off on your supposed stag weekend, Dawn was with you, rather than too ill to come to work for me. How it's all starting to fall into place.'

He looked awkward. 'Well, funnily enough, we did bump into her in a club.'

Glenda lit a cigarette, taking time over her actions, considering her reply. She exhaled smoke directly into his face, causing him to cough uncontrollably and cackled, the only way to describe the noise that she made when she cleared her throat and laughed concurrently.

'You're dafter than you look and that's saying something. Don't insult me by presuming that I've just dropped off a Christmas tree. How long has this sordid business been going on?'

'I'll put the kettle on, shall I? Faith could probably do with a drink. I know I could. How about you?'

'Bugger the kettle,' Glenda replied curtly. 'Answer my question.'

Jonty hung his head. 'Not long, just a few months.' His voice had gone very quiet.

'Does your father know about this?' Her eyes narrowed.

'No, no, he knows nothing,' Jonty's reply was so vehement that Glenda knew, if nothing else, then this much was true.

'I can't wait to tell him,' Glenda soundly hideously smug.

'Please don't,' begged Jonty.

'Don't be absurd. Isn't he going to suspect something when there's no wedding tomorrow?'

'What do you mean?'

Glenda ran her fingers through her thick, blond hair, making a mental note to keep her hairdresser's appointment for that afternoon as her roots badly needed retouching.

'Hmmm, let me think. What could I mean? Shall I speak in words of one syllable? Perhaps I'm trying to tell you that the wedding's off.'

'No!' Jonty stuttered. 'Let me talk to Faith. She'll understand it was just last-minute nerves. I love her, Glenda, you know I do.'

'What a curious way you have of showing it.'

'All I need is some time with Faith. Just the two of us. It'll all be all right, I promise you.'

Glenda assumed the air of one who was giving due consideration to a question. She scratched her head, thoughtfully, and cast her eye over Jonty critically. He was a forlorn sight. To her mind there was nothing quite so pathetic as a man grovelling, particularly when he didn't really mean it. Still, there was something about the situation that she found incredibly enjoyable. All these years of pent-up anger were proving to have been of use after all. She switched on a quite bewitching smile.

'Jonty,' she started softly, watching his eyes light up with hope. 'Watch my lips. I am privileged to have had the dubious honour of knowing you. Single-handedly you have managed to qualify as a new subspecies of scum. The wedding will not be taking place. Faith has informed me that she does not wish to speak to you and I think that that's for the best, don't you? I can't say I blame her. You've hurt her enough, so now just leave her alone. Bear in mind that in her distressed state, if my daughter so much as hinted that she might forgive you, I would lock her up and throw away the key so that you couldn't get your slimy hands on her.'

'Glenda,' wheedled Jonty, not yet ready to capitulate.

'I think it would be best if you went now. I'm going to ring your father and then between us we will cancel tomorrow. As if I didn't have better things to do with my time. At least he appears to be dependable, which is more than can be said for his son. I hope you can live with yourself and the damage and havoc you have caused. People like you shouldn't be allowed out in the daylight and, thinking about it, preferably not at night either.'

Jonty opened his mouth but backed off as Glenda called the dogs to her side.

'I'll ring later,' he muttered, not meaning it.

'Don't bother.'

She watched him as he neared the door. 'Oh, and Jonty?'

'Yes?' His face was full of last-minute pathos.

'Take Dawn with you. I never want to see either of you again.'

184

Chapter Twenty-One

Unbeknown to Glenda, while she was engaged in defending her daughter's honour, Faith was crouched on the landing, hands clutching the spindles of the staircase, striving to hear every word that passed between her mother and her now ex-fiancé. She had been unable to ignore Jonty's persistent hammering at the door and had crept out of her bedroom to try to find out what was happening. Her heart was thumping, loud enough for them to hear she was sure and her face flushed hotter and hotter as she listened.

Unable to decide how she felt, her mind was a whirl of different emotions. One second she longed to dash down and hug him, sure that there must be some mistake, the next she hated the very sound of his voice, now so insincere, almost mocking. She felt foolish, humiliated and sad that she had ever been taken in by his charms. So close to the wedding of her dreams, to the man whom she had trusted and believed in when he had professed his love for her, she listened aghast as he revealed to her mother the duration of his liaison with Dawn. A one-night stand, a last moment of bachelor madness, she might just have been able to come to terms with, or would she? Did she really want to commit herself to a life with someone who failed to value their relationship in the same way that she did? The engagement ring on her finger winked provocatively at her. Such a shame, as it was beautiful beyond belief but so much of its beauty came from the sentiment with which it had been given. Now it looked cheap and tacky. Suddenly she doubted whether it was real. Tearing it off, she threw it as hard as she could down into the hall, listening to the metallic ping as it bounced across the tiled floor, never wanting to see it again.

When the back door closed, Faith heard the familiar sound of the top being unscrewed off the gin bottle followed by the fizz of the tonic being opened. Shaking, she got up, retreated to her bedroom and shut herself in. From the window she watched Jonty walk away, tucking in the back of his wet shirt, which clung to his body, and hitching up his trousers. Waiting for him by his car was

Dawn. He gave her a perfunctory hug and indicated with his head that she should get in. Faith flinched as Jonty looked up towards her window, one last final gesture before he revved up the engine and accelerated off with his normal panache and screeched out of the gate with a squealing of his tyres.

Turning back to her room it was impossible to ignore the sight in front of her. There on a hanger, completely obscuring one of the wardrobe doors, was her wonderful dress, the dress she loved so much, that made her look so fantastic and that she had so been looking forward to wearing just for one memorable day. She stroked the fine material as if it were a rare animal and struggled to fight back tears. Sitting back onto the bed, she reached out for one of the few remaining relics of her childhood, a teddy bear, fur worn away in places from so much love and recipient of a lifetime of secrets shared with it, safely stored behind its beady eyes. Faith hugged it tight, inhaling the familiar smell, taking comfort from the softness of what fur remained and wept, suddenly unable to contain her emotions a moment longer. Her shoulders heaved while every bone in her specially prepared tiny body shuddered with grief.

Glenda heard the sobs from the kitchen and swore. Woe betide Jonty if she ever saw him again. She could not think of a punishment that was heinous enough to equate to the damage he had done. Memories of how she had felt when she had discovered that Dennis and his secretary had put a unique interpretation on dictating some letters descended like a radioactive cloud, making her tremble unpleasantly from head to toe. Grinding her cigarette stub to a pulp with a vengeance – she had lost count of how many she had just smoked, one after the other – she made a quick phone call, picked up the car keys and a large box file which was entitled 'Faith's wedding' and shouted up to her daughter.

'I'm just off to see Hamish. Don't worry, I'll sort everything. I'll not be long.'

Faith held her breath as she listened to her mother's parting comments followed by the obvious noises of her departure, dogs in tow and barking as normal, unaware that they were simply going for a ride in the car and not for a walk. The house was suddenly chilly and eerily quiet. There was a tap dripping in her bathroom metronomically. Outside an insipid sun had ventured out from behind a cloud. How dare it?

Her eyes fell again on her dress. Sniffing and using the sleeve of her cardigan as a handkerchief, she undressed, wanting to see for one last time how she would have looked. Parading in front of the mirror, there was no denying that, from the neck downwards, she would have made a bride of singular exquisiteness. The effect was ruined by the blotchy cheeks, harrowing red eyes and puffy nose, a sight which only caused a fresh burst of tears. Faith wandered around her room, luxuriating in the sensual feel of the dress as it swayed around her, foolishly imagining that it was the next day and that she had just awoken from some warped night terror, before stopping for a final time in front of the mirror, giving herself a long, hard, calculating stare and then removing the dress and carefully placing it back on the hanger.

With Glenda out of the way, it was safe to leave the confines of her bedroom knowing that she would not have to be faced for several hours which might give her time to pluck up the courage to withstand the barbed comments that she would doubtless have stored up to hurl at her. There was no denying the fact, however, that Glenda had certainly turned up trumps when she was needed. She had acted as an effective gatekeeper and provided an impenetrable barrier which Jonty was not allowed to pass through, had treated him in a manner which he thoroughly deserved, failing to fall for his little boy looks and whines, facts for which Faith knew that she would be eternally grateful.

Faith wished that the dogs had been left behind. A cuddle with an adoring Labrador or even a fidgety terrier who wanted to play on her knee would have been most welcome. Much as she wanted to be on her own, to wallow in her misery, she also desperately needed a presence there with her, to look after her. She could not keep warm, despite layers of clothes. Aimlessly, she mooched about, idly picking up things and putting them down again, checking the answering machine on the landline and voicemail on her mobile. The crossword was no more solvable now than it had been earlier. She put a number in the sudoku, realised that it was wrong and threw the paper on the floor. Having the benefit of satellite television proved to be dubious as she flicked in a bored fashion through dozens of channels completely unable to find something that vaguely caught her interest.

Her engagement photograph beamed at her. She pulled the sleeves of her jumper over her hands and pulled her knees up to her chest, rocking on the settee. Closing her eyes, she could still see it and now it was as clear as day that the look in Jonty's eyes was one to be treated with suspicion. He seemed to be laughing at her. Glenda had been right – she, Faith, looked far too submissive. How easy it was to be wise with hindsight. All those alarm bells, now ringing so clearly, that she had chosen to dismiss, thinking that she knew better.

Having exhausted all possibilities of distraction in the drawing room, Faith's next port of call was the kitchen, supposing that she would make that universal panacea to all ills, a cup of hot tea. There was no milk save a few drops which just caused a small, momentary cloud in the strong dark drink. It was poured down the plughole without further ado. Nor in the fridge was there any juice or even a can of pop, just two bottles of tonic water, chilling ready for the next glass of gin. It had served her mother well enough over all these years, so maybe it had properties that she was as yet unfamiliar with. Pouring herself a larger measure than she had intended, Faith diluted it considerably with tonic and started to sip. On an empty stomach, its restorative properties were soon felt and for several minutes the world looked a more optimistic place to live in and the continuing sunshine outside a good omen.

As is often the case with gin, hot on the tail of the euphoria was the gloom of wretchedness. As fast as her spirits had soared, Faith found that she was hurtling back down to earth and into a dark gaping hole that was waiting to swallow her up. She started to cry again, inelegantly and angrily, banging her fists on the table over and over. Her gesticulations became more frantic the more she wept and one extraordinarily energetic lashing out hit the nearest cake box and the lid flew off. Pulling the box towards her, she knew in a flash was what going to happen next. Powerless to change predestination, she viewed the cake and then picked off one of the chocolate petals and put it in her mouth. Another followed, then two at a time, then three, then a handful. Which was most delicious? The plain, the milk or the white? It no longer mattered, just as long as it ended up in her mouth. Her fingers were besmirched with melted chocolate but regardless she sucked them carelessly and dug into the soft sponge, bringing out a fistful which she shoved gracelessly in the direction of her mouth, not waiting until it was empty, not caring that half of it ended up either on the table or all over her face. The initial frenzy passed, she sat crying but robotically eating her way

188

through the entire cake, feeling that if she ate more, she might exorcise the revulsion that she felt, revulsion that by now was not just for Jonty but for herself as well.

Full to bursting, her stomach's pleading with her to stop almost audible, she rushed to the sink and vomited, only just having the foresight to remove the washing-up bowl first. Her breath was coming in short, panting gasps as she stood back trying not to look at the stomach-turning mess that she had made. Half-heartedly she tried to swill the debris away, taking handfuls of water to rinse out her mouth.

Empty again, she wiped her mouth as if preparing for action, returned to the next cake box and started picking off the petals, hysterically crying out, 'He loves me, he loves me not! He loves me, no he bloody doesn't!'

So absorbed in her own gluttony, Faith never heard the back door open and Glenda come in. Having delegated a list of cancellation duties to a horrified but supportive Hamish, she had returned sooner than expected, on the pretext of having left something behind but in reality worried out of her mind about her daughter. Expecting her to be up in her room, still sobbing, nothing could have prepared her for the sight that met her eyes. It was as though there had been a food fight in her absence. The kitchen seemed to be smeared in chocolate from the floor and dresser to the chairs and range. Crumbs littered the floor and dollops of creamy filling sat like recent bird droppings on the table. In the midst of this bedlam sat her daughter, looking like a cross between a wild woman and a six- year-old child who has been caught in the act, hair sticking out this way and that, eyelids swollen, face bloated and both her hands assaulting one of her wedding cakes.

Glenda's eyes darted round the room, weighing up the situation, only too capable of comprehending what was going on. Faith, who had temporarily stopped eating when she had become aware of her mother's presence, had thrown caution to the winds and was now carrying on.

'Want some?' she asked casually. 'It's very good. It's a shame to see it go to waste. Could do with a bit more Cointreau though. I was going to take the third cake and throw it on Jonty's head but it's too good for that, so I'm going to eat it.'

Glenda watched as another fistful of cake was rammed into Faith's mouth. She felt as though she might vomit too, but for entirely different reasons. Slowly, she moved the cake boxes away from Faith, out of her reach, and finding that she was met by no resistance replaced the lids and carried them into the utility room, out of sight. Returning she was just in time to see Faith race from the room, hand clasped over her mouth, into the cloakroom where the incontrovertible sounds of retching were then to be heard, followed by the toilet flushing.

'Faith?'

She was not quick enough. Faith was back in her bedroom and the door firmly closed.

Glenda pondered on her next actions and reflexively lit a cigarette and poured a drink. The glass halfway to her lips, she put it down, stubbed out the cigarette and took a deep breath in to prepare herself.

'Go away,' yelled Faith when her mother knocked on her door. It was impossible for her to cope with the ignominy of the marriage debacle, let alone the revelation of her eating disorder.

The door opened.

'Ma, I said go away.'

'I never did do as I was told,' announced Glenda, marching in. 'Come here.'

Faith looked up and before she knew what was happening found that her mother's arms had closed around her and that she was being hugged for all she was worth. She stiffened, unaccustomed to this show of caring, but then buried her head into her mother's shoulder. Though the body that was pressed against her was bony and smelled of a mixture of expensive perfume, smoke and drying dog, it was immeasurably comforting and the new tears that started to flow down Faith's face were no longer those of anger but mere unhappiness.

Glenda held her close and let her cry, trying to fight back her own tears that were threatening to fall also.

'Hang on to me, Faith. It'll be all right. I promise.'

'Oh, Ma. I just don't know what to do about anything any more.'

'Poor Faith. I'll help you, don't worry. What a day you've had.'

'How could he do that to me, Ma?' Faith wailed.

'It's his loss, not yours, just you remember that,' Glenda shifted her position slightly for her left arm was going numb.

'Don't leave me, Ma.' Faith was anxious.

'I'm not going anywhere. You have a good cry and get it all out of your system.' Glenda squirmed a little, aware that her words sounded inadequate but unable to come up with anything more profound. 'Once you've finished crying, I'm going to run you a hot bath, then you're to put on your pyjamas and dressing gown and come down to the drawing room where it'll be nice and cosy and we'll spend the evening together and talk. We don't do that often enough, do we? I'm afraid that's rather more my fault that it is yours.' Faith halted mid hiccup, taken aback by her mother's admission.

She took her time in the bath, wallowing in the scented water, Glenda having provided some very eclectic essence for her. It was peaceful to be cocooned in the warm water. She wondered if this is what it had been like in the womb and would not have protested if it had been suggested she return there. The prospect of the evening ahead was strangely appealing, not exactly the night before the wedding that she had planned but none the less not without its own attractions.

By the time Faith retired to bed, exhausted, at just after ten, having already fallen asleep once in a chair, Glenda was still reeling from what she had heard.

Faith, emboldened by her mother's recent exhibition of affection and vulnerable in her nightwear, had poured out her heart. She had shared not just the worries she had nurtured for Jonty since she had first met him and how she had never felt good enough for him but also the hopes she had had that he would change and so would she – into what he wanted her to be. Try as she might, the fear of losing him had never quite gone away but she had dreamed that if they married then they would live happily ever after. Into her flow, out came the secret of her bingeing, the love-hate relationship that she had with food, the compulsive desire to be thin, because this meant you would be popular and well liked and the horrors of what it was like to make yourself vomit.

At this juncture, Glenda had had to look away, able to feel bile rising in her own throat for Faith wasted no words on her description. Amazingly, Glenda had been so wrapped up in her daughter's monologue that she had not smoked one cigarette and there was still a glass half full on the coffee table, left forgotten as the reality of what went on in her daughter's life came out into the open at last.

But once Faith had gone to bed, the cigarettes were back, fast and furious, helping her deal with the facts that she had heard, problems that she felt more than partly responsible for and revelations that were only too familiar as she realised that her daughter's early adult life was an exact parallel of how her own had been.

Chapter Twenty-Two

Faith slept soundly that night, exhausted by having bared her soul to her mother, of all people, telling her things that nobody had ever heard before, things which she had hoped would never see the light of day for she had filed them away in little boxes and nailed down the lids. Somehow though, one of those boxes had been opened, precipitating the domino effect and before she knew it, one embarrassing confession after another came cascading out. She was like a clockwork toy, wound up to the full and then unable to stop until worn out. Whilst her mother had not passed any comment – in truth she had hardly said a word of any sort – or indeed sought to provide any solutions, Faith had been left with a feeling of unexpected but welcome ease and inner peace as if some ticking time bomb had been defused at the eleventh hour. To her surprise, she had felt more than ready when her mother suggested she went to bed and they had exchanged rather stiff hugs and chaste kisses on the cheek before she left the room.

Glenda, left alone, was alert, mind racing, and unable to contemplate retiring for the night, let alone trying to sleep. She sat up in the drawing room, idly tickling the dogs' ears, to all intents and purposes glued to the television screen but her thoughts were far away as she replayed the evening over and over. It was a huge relief that Faith had not seemed to expect her to pass judgement, that she was happy for her mother just to sit and listen, for there was no way she would have known what to say. There had been one fleeting moment when she had been about to tell Faith that she understood exactly what she was talking about, that she, her mother, had had first-hand experience of using food as an emotional crutch, a means to console or to celebrate, whichever the occasion demanded and the subsequent bingeing and purging. It was a part of her life that she had chosen to bury and ignore many years ago, an addiction she had replaced with cigarettes, gin and escalating hatred for her ex-husband. She could still shudder, even now, at the memory of Dennis coming home unexpectedly one day when Faith, aged perhaps no more than five, had gone to tea with a friend from pony club. Glenda had been in the kitchen, well into a humongous binge, scoffing biscuits, cakes, chocolate and even baking some scones, which took no time to prepare and were irresistible when still warm and smothered with an unhealthy layer of butter and jam.

Unbeknown to her, Dennis had chosen to stand just behind the door and observe in a clandestine manner as her self-inflicted force-feeding continued, as she worked her way into a frenzy, vomited with an ease born of much practice and then start all over again with more food. He had said nothing until they were lying in bed that night, the lights out, his voice sounding, to Glenda, accusatory and unnatural in the blackness. He had kept his distance, not wanting to touch even the smallest part of her and had bombarded her with questions, trying to find out why she did it, how long it had been going on for and would she like some help. Devastated that she had been observed, she had lain there, wishing that he would hold her, every muscle clenched, lost for words as she realised that she had no idea why she did do it. What she did know was that she hated every moment, from the first prodrome of temptation as it infiltrated into her thought processes with an insidious stealth to the point at which she collapsed in a heap, shattered, bloated, aching but grateful because she knew the binge was finally at an end.

He had watched her like a hawk from that moment on, barely leaving her side when at home and checking the waste bins and the toilets for telltale signs on his return from work. She had never talked to him about it. Her refusal to confront the problem had infuriated him and her ostrich-like avoidance of the subject may well have driven the first nails into the coffin of their relationship. Instead, she had chosen to spend even more of her life with her horses, the only time, if she were ever honest, when she felt completely happy. To be fair, the bingeing did decrease dramatically but the substitutes started to winkle their way in and take a hold, her addictive personality needing something to rely on.

All those years ago and she had never spoken about it and there was nothing that was going to make her start now, even if it would be beneficial for Faith. To give Dennis his due, though she was not prepared to admit it, the subject of her eating disorder had never been mentioned in the divorce, much to her secret relief. Channelling all her energies into loathing Dennis, rather than herself, Glenda had found a new way of coping with life and it had served her well, she felt. But tonight, it had all come back to her. Everything that Faith had come out with, she could relate to only too well. Talk about history repeating itself. She wished fervently that Faith could have inherited some of her more endearing traits and been spared this particular horror.

It was past three when she finally traipsed up to bed, dogs, indignant at being woken up, lumbering behind her. Even then, as she lay under the cool covers, listening to the sound of the wind in the trees and buffeting around the house, sleep would not come near.

What would have been Faith's wedding day dawned late, a sure sign that winter was just around the corner. The wind was even stronger and stormy-looking clouds were racing across the sky at a rapid rate. Short sharp showers rattled against the windowpanes intermittently, occasionally even some hailstones.

They made a curious pair as they met for breakfast. Faith, puffy from deep sleep, preceded by too much crying and Glenda, gaunt and hollow eyed from insomnia. Sitting in silence, Glenda poured coffee and made toast which neither of them wanted. Faith kept sighing as she looked at the pile of presents and cards piled in one corner of the room, knowing that they would have to be opened and returned with an explanation of why they could not be accepted. She rested her elbows on the table, all the better to support her weary head on her hands. Feeling a soft, moist sensation under one arm, she identified, after inspection, that she had placed it in a blob of Cointreau-flavoured cake filling that had not been wiped up. Miserably she fetched a cloth, cleaned up and sat down again, feeling Glenda's eyes watching her every move.

'How are you feeling?' Glenda managed to ask, having struggled to think of something uncontroversial to say.

'Okay,' whimpered Faith. 'I slept better than I expected.'

She paused before looking down and continuing. 'I don't suppose Jonty's been in touch has he?'

She was spared her mother's vituperative reply as the telephone started to ring and calls came in thick and fast from friends and relatives, who had been contacted by Hamish, expressing their condolences. Glenda nobly chose to field these, if for no other reason than it spared her from awkward attempts at conversation with her daughter, who sat shaking her head with vehemence when asked if she wished to speak herself. At that present moment in time, Faith very much doubted that she would be able to face anyone ever again. Sam and Otis lay curled up in their beds, sighing occasionally, intuitively aware that quiet was the order of the day. Only Rex, bouncy as ever, pawed at Faith with a toy, wanting her to play. He cowered when, unfairly, she raised her voice at him and he too retreated, tail between his legs, to curl up with his canine friends.

Faith watched the hands of the clock creep round, calculating what she should have been doing by rights. Just now, she should have been at the hairdresser's, having her unruly tresses cajoled into a style of elegance that would last for the day and be immortalised in the photographs that she had envisaged sharing with her grandchildren.

Never far from her thoughts was the image of Jonty and she wondered if she dared to ring him. Glancing at her mother, who was deep in animated conversation with someone horsy, Faith reckoned that she could sneak out of the room and try to contact him, but then again, maybe she should wait. He would surely come round today to make peace.

A tiny flicker of hope ignited as she began to imagine that the situation was salvageable. Anyone could make a mistake. It must just have been a last-minute fling, a final celebration of bachelordom, an act of animal instinct rather than one where affection was involved. The wedding could be rearranged. Perhaps she'd been wrong to want such a showy affair, reeking of affluence and aplomb. Maybe, it had been the opposite of what Jonty had really wanted but he had just gone along with her to make her happy. Hadn't he suggested that they elope? This time they would sit down and discuss it reasonably and openly; there was nothing wrong with a registry office wedding, a few close friends and family at a cosy party afterwards. In many ways it would be far less stressful for all concerned and after all, so long as they actually became man and wife, what did it matter how they achieved this status?

Faith's reveries of resolving her marital crisis were disrupted by the back door opening and a wet and bedraggled Hamish being blown in. He shook his head and raindrops leapt wildly into the air. Glenda gesticulated that he should hang up his soaked coat, which he did before coming over to Faith and giving her a hug.

'I'm so sorry, darling,' he whispered, bringing fresh tears to her eyes. She had believed that she was incapable of crying any more.

'Thanks, Hamish. How is he?'

Hamish poured a cup of coffee and dunked a biscuit into it. His face had hardened from his usual amiable, approachable features.

'He left last night,' he replied tersely.

'Left?' echoed Faith, aghast. 'To go where?'

'I don't know…'

Faith scrutinised his face, looking for clues. 'Yes you do. I can see it in your eyes. Please tell me. I need to contact him, to see him, to tell him that we can work all of this out. I've realised why he didn't want to get married today. I've been so selfish but I won't be in the future.'

Hamish looked up at Glenda who had finally terminated her phone call. He raised his eyebrows questioningly. Faith turned towards her mother and saw her nod, briefly. Her head whipped back towards Hamish, who cleared his throat purposefully.

'What?' Faith urged him.

'He left with Dawn. They've gone away together for a few weeks until, as he puts it, the dust has settled. Faith, I'm appalled by his behaviour. I cannot believe any son of mine would behave in such a despicable manner. I've told him so, in no uncertain words. We had a huge falling out, I think that's one of the reasons he's gone.'

That barely glowing ember in Faith's heart was extinguished. Her shoulders sagged, her hair fell over her face and her body contorted in spasms of sobs.

'I'm so sorry,' Hamish repeated. 'I wish there was more I could do.'

'You had to know the truth, Faith,' Glenda remarked. 'There's no point in pretending that he's coming back to you. He's an out and out bastard. Someone should cut his balls off, preferably with no anaesthetic. Sorry, Hamish.'

The father of the much maligned shrugged his shoulders. 'Don't apologise. Fair comment, I'm afraid.'

He patted Faith on the shoulder. 'Better that you should find out now than after you were married.'

It was hard to tell how this comment affected Faith as all that could be heard from beneath her unbrushed hair was repeated sniffs.

Glenda rolled her eyes. 'I'm having a drink. It's after twelve already. Can I get you one, Hamish?'

'We'd be getting ready to set off for the church now,' blurted Faith through the tissues she was using to blow her nose.

'Better make that one each,' suggested Hamish. 'Might do us all the power of good.'

Rallying to the cause, Hamish rooted through the cupboards and prepared a rudimentary lunch of biscuits and cheese, plus some yoghurts that were only just past their sell-by date. Invigorated by his presence, Glenda found it easier to keep up some sort of pretence at chatting about inane subjects, hoping that it would be better for Faith if she did so. She stayed studiously away from the subject of Jonty, preferring to opt for the safety of the latest goings-on in her favourite soap opera, an article she had read recently on Irish bloodlines and some scatterbrained plan that she was hatching about trying her hand at carriage driving next spring when the weather was more clement.

Faith barely heard a word but was thankful for their presence and the sounds of normality as they talked. Her forehead furrowed as they laughed, feeling that this was disrespectful and that the whole world should be joining her in her mourning. She somehow managed to eat a cracker with some blue cheese. It was dry and stuck to the sides of her mouth and teeth. Though poured for her, she rebuffed the glass of wine, preferring to stick to tea, which Glenda was lacing with sugar, thinking that being jilted was certainly a form of shock and thus this was the appropriate cure. Funnily enough, despite its outrageous sweetness, the drink was soothing and did cheer her ever so slightly.

After they had eaten, on Glenda's instructions that it was better to get this job over and done with, they all opened the presents and cards, Faith feeling that she was living in someone else's dream, trying to be dispassionate, but repeatedly dissolving into tears as she recognised the items that she had put on her wedding list and read messages of love and wishes for a happy future. Glenda and Hamish, able to be dispassionate about this process, efficiently wrote a list of who had sent what and then tactfully removed everything to the little study by the front door, so that there was nothing left for Faith to see.

It was starting to grow dark when Glenda dragged her daughter out for a horrible walk with the dogs in the early part of the afternoon. The rain was almost horizontal when the wind blew and at times, when the gusts were at their most malevolent, it was nigh on impossible to stay upright. Faith had tried her hardest to wriggle out of this enforced exercise, she had whined, moaned and cried, arguing that she couldn't possibly be expected to go out in weather like this and that it was better that she stayed alone to fester with her gloom. But Glenda was back in authoritative mode and made the most of it. She sent Hamish to the shops for provisions and turned a deaf ear to Faith's pathos. They were drenched before they had crossed the first paddock. Shivering, Faith trudged along next to her mother, glad that the roaring wind made conversation difficult, for she had nothing to say. Imagining what she might have looked like after walking up the short path to the church wearing her highly impractical wedding dress, tiara and veil in this weather was small consolation. So much for her view of them standing in the grounds of the hotel, surrounded by autumnal hues, sipping champagne and laughing.

The dogs were filthy by the time they returned, Glenda having led them down muddy paths in the woods, where puddles had to be negotiated with care and their boots slipped repeatedly in the wet. Much as she would have liked to retreat into the house and divest herself of her sodden garments, Faith felt obliged to help her mother with the dog bathing, a job performed in the stable yard, rather too close to the scene of the recent crime of passion to be comfortable. If they had been wet before, they were soaked all the more by the time they had finished lathering, scrubbing and hosing off the animals, who treated the whole procedure like a great game devised solely for their entertainment.

Hamish was back and had unpacked the shopping, which he had left on the worktop in an uninspiring heap muttering the excuse that he wasn't sure where anything went. Glenda told, rather than asked, Faith to sort it out but after she'd had a bath and warmed up.

'Don't be long, though. You're not to disappear and be maudlin on your own. That won't do you any good at all. What you need is company. Hamish, I'm off for a quick shower. Answer the phone if it rings, would you?'

From the hot steamy waters, Faith heard several calls being taken and then her mother going back downstairs, presumably rejuvenated. Envying Glenda's indefatigability she sighed and looked down at her scrawny body, the one she had gone to such lengths to sculpt, especially for today. The vigorous waxing that she gritted her teeth through in preparation for bikini wear on her honeymoon gave her a strangely pre-pubescent look which she found disturbing and she placed her hands over the area so it was no longer visible. The agonies she had put herself through – depilation, eyebrow shaping and extreme dieting – had all been for nothing. Hadn't someone once said, 'no pain, no gain'? Nothing could be further from the truth. Faith felt as if she had lost everything.

She found dry clothes, not paying any attention to what they were but just pulling out the first things she came across. Glenda's voice bellowed menacingly from the kitchen, demanding her presence as soon as possible.

'Ah, there you are, at last,' was her greeting. 'Here, have a cup of tea and a biscuit and sit down. We've something to tell you.'

Faith looked at the two of them. Surely they weren't about to announce their engagement. Not even her mother could stoop so low.

'Your father's been on the phone,' Glenda began.

'Actually, it was your mother who rang him,' corrected Hamish.

'What?' Faith asked with disbelief.

Glenda tried to look nonchalant and lit up a cigarette. 'Well, all right, if you want to be pedantic about it, yes, I rang him. Not that it matters in the slightest. I woke him up.' There was more than a hint of triumph in her voice.

'What did he say?' Faith was eager to hear.

'Well, all that you'd expect. How sorry he was et cetera, et cetera.'

'Is he going to ring me?'

'Better than that. He wants to see you. He rang back just now and you're booked on a flight to Japan tomorrow. It's just what you need.'

'I can't go to Japan—'

'Why not? You've two weeks off work.'

'Yes, but…'

Glenda tilted her head on one side. 'Yes, but what?'

Faith was lost for words, still reeling from the shock of hearing that her mother had voluntarily made contact with her father.

'See – you can't come up with any reason why you can't go. We'll take you to the airport. You'd better go and start packing. Go on.'

Their promise held good and the next morning Hamish and Glenda watched as Faith, having hugged them both tightly, in a manner that suggested she may never see them again, disappeared down a corridor towards the departure lounge for international flights. Had Hamish looked closely, he might have spotted the tiniest tear in the corner of Glenda's eye but he was too busy worrying about where to pay for his parking. Instinctively, however, he put his arm around her shoulders as they walked back into the open air, as different a day again with the sun shining and the trees unmoved by even the merest whiff of a breeze.

Back at the house, the two of them spent the day as though nothing had happened; they rode, had a pub lunch, mostly liquid, and then relaxed watching television for the afternoon. It was only when Glenda, with some reluctance, struggled to her feet, having lost when they tossed a coin to see who was going to make supper, in the form of beans on toast with grated cheese, that she saw that the rubbish bag under the sink was full, already starting to tear under the strain of all that had been pushed into it. Cursing, she gingerly extracted it and made her way outside to the dustbin. Lifting the lid, there was no mistaking the crumpled mass that had been squashed in there. Faith's beloved wedding dress had been consigned to a smelly fate at the nearest landfill site.

Chapter Twenty-Three

Monday morning and by the time the first patient had come and gone, Faith felt that she had never been away.

Her return had been far easier than she had anticipated. Everyone was quietly supportive without constantly reminding her of what had happened by asking intrusive questions that she had no desire to answer. What she had dreaded being a humiliating experience proved on the contrary to reassure her that she was surrounded by people who cared for her. Each one of the partners and Rob had, quite independently, taken her to one side and offered to let her talk if she wanted to and whilst there was no way that she would ever contemplate baring her soul to the senior partner, or indeed any of the men, Ellie's proffered shoulder to cry on was one she might just consider.

Japan had been therapeutic.

Dennis had been all that she had hoped. He and his wife had listened to her and commiserated with her. But they had also refused to let her vegetate in her room and had insisted that she go out and about. They had organised trips for her and taken her not only on amazing sight-seeing tours but also to shops and restaurants where they had spoiled her with delicious if strange-tasting meals and bought her more presents than she could cope with.

Away from home, she had been able distance herself from her problems. There was nothing to remind her of Jonty – this was new, exciting and uncharted territory in a busy, chaotic city, a far cry from the rural existence she was used to. She found that she stopped thinking of him, that many hours would pass when she did not so much as spare him a passing thought, surely a sign that recovery was possible and perhaps already in its infancy.

In many ways, she wished that she hadn't had to come home. Dennis had suggested she stay as long as she wanted or needed to. It was tempting, of that there was no doubt. Her escapist holiday had been wonderful and she had not wanted it to end but

203

duty called and this meant a return to reality which had to be met head on.

Mrs Tonbridge, if she was pleased to see Faith, gave nothing away. The doctor's private life did not even feature on her agenda. Her face was set in its usual fixed expression of pessimism, the corners of her mouth downturned, her lower lids drooping in the manner of a morose bloodhound's. Her varicose eczema was bad, the rash under her pendulent breasts was on fire and as for her bowels, it took her several minutes to describe in minute detail just exactly what was going on in that part of her anatomy.

Faith smiled inwardly. Much as her heart might sink when the likes of Mrs Tonbridge came into the surgery, this was what she loved and what she was good at. Here she could be herself, no need to adopt airs and graces and pretend to be someone she wasn't. Most of the patients had elected to see her, for her personality and the quality of service that she offered. It was both gratifying and stimulating to think that she was going to be working here for a minimum of at least another year. Today, everything was enjoyable, from the fungal toenails to the removal of the forgotten tampon with its aroma once smelt, never forgotten.

She relished the challenge of the thirty year old who complained of being tired all the time and sat, in a demonstration of text-book empathy, as a recently bereaved elderly man imploded before her into a morass of grief. Finally, she felt powerful and in control.

But try as she might, little things kept jogging her memory about Jonty. From the moment she walked into her consulting room and saw the photograph of him, her day was sabotaged by little traps that brought him back to the forefront of her thoughts. There was a toddler with the same name, dragged in as he screamed with temper by his overwrought mother. She thought he might have tonsillitis and a wrestling match ensued while Faith tried to examine his ears, throat and chest, before admitting defeat and prescribing some antibiotics which, if she were lucky, would deal with most of her provisional diagnoses. Promises of lollipops from the chemist were ineffective as his shrieks continued, still audible even after they had left the room.

Hot on his heels was a middle-aged farmer, whose jacket was remarkably similar to the one Faith had given Jonty for his last birthday and her last patient of the morning teetered in on ridiculously high heels to ask for a repeat prescription for her contraceptives. As Faith checked her blood pressure, she spotted a sparkling engagement ring that made her long for hers, which she had hidden in the bottom compartment of her jewellery box so that she didn't keep coming across it every time she brushed her hair.

She was divided as to whether to go upstairs for coffee with the others or simply take some house calls and disappear. Having chosen the latter as her preferred course of action, she was thwarted in her plans by the arrival of Ellie, who wanted to let her know about a patient she had been seeing whilst Faith had been away. This dealt with, it was then inevitable that the two of them set off together for the coffee room, Ellie chattering away ten to the dozen, wanting to know all about Japan and what Faith had seen and done, steering tactfully away from any subject that might be more emotive. There was time enough to find out all about that.

Already drinking coffee were John, Rob and Ed, who glanced up as the two women entered and pointed to large piles of paperwork that were waiting to be dealt with in their respective trays.

'How I hate Mondays,' sighed Ellie, switching on the kettle. 'There are loads of visits as well.'

They all worked doggedly for the next half hour, taking it in turns to answer telephone calls from patients or the receptionists. Regardless of their best efforts, little inroad appeared to have been made by the time Ed was due back in surgery and the others pondered over the house calls.

'Let's split them geographically. It'll make it far easier for all of us. There's only one who has asked for a specific doctor and that's one of mine, so I'll also do those two chest infections, the possible stroke and the one who says she can't walk, but seeing who it is, I'll put money on her being able to get to the door to let me in.'

John scribbled down the five names in his diary and ambled off, not bothered in the slightest about the amount of work either that he faced or was leaving behind. It would all get done, in the fullness of time, as it always did, so to his mind there was no point in letting it bother him. Faith watched him go, envious of his calm character, before offering to do more than her share of the calls so that she could keep busy. Rob and Ellie vetoed this immediately, shared out the calls democratically and arranged that the three of them should meet back afterwards and have a working lunch during which they would continue to attack the paperwork.

It was a nondescript day, unseasonably mild and damp. Wet leaves on the pavements made for slippery walking and Faith had to grab onto a fence at one point when she was gingerly negotiating her way up a particularly steep drive to see an elderly couple who both believed that they were in the grips of influenza. They lived in an inventively designed bungalow, decorated in what would have been the height of fashion some three decades ago but now looked dull and jaded. Both of them were only ambulant with the aid of wheeled trolleys, each one resplendent with a string bag attached to the handlebars, so that they could transfer their more important possessions, such as knitting, newspapers, dog- eared paperbacks and reading spectacles from room to room. The thought of either of them tackling the precipitous drive made Faith fear for their osteoporotic bones and arthritic joints.

Neither was very ill, Faith was glad to establish, simply catarrhal and coughing, but as the precarious balance which existed to allow them to live at home was dependent on one or other of them being in good health, they were struggling to cope with the day to day aspects of living. Faith made several calls and was fortunate enough to be able to enlist the help of the various agencies who would come in several times a day until they were well enough to manage on their own again. It was a simple visit but one which took time and while she was in the throes of hanging on waiting for the appropriate people either to answer or return her calls, she was treated to a cup of weak tea and a guided tour through the family photo album, starting with their wedding memories which prompted questions to Faith about her own marital status and whether there was anyone special in her life.

She was glad to escape. The last thing she needed was to be interrogated, albeit innocently, by a garrulous old couple whose lives took a turn for the better when they had somebody new to chat to. In her hurry, she forgot about the wet leaves and with no warning found that she was sitting at the bottom of the drive, her tights torn to shreds and her buttocks and elbows muddy and bruised.

Considerably shaken she had to sit in her car for some time before she felt able to carry on. Warily she checked around her, hoping that her fall had gone unwitnessed by the residents of Plover Close. Reaching into the glove compartment for some tissues to wipe her hands on, she found one of Jonty's ties that he had stashed away there when she had picked him up from a meeting one day, glad to be rid of its restrictions. Sadly she stroked it gently and held it up to her nose, hoping for the merest whiff of his aftershave.

Driving to the next visit, feeling melancholy, she thought she saw Jonty walking down the pavement. It felt as though her heart had stopped. There was no mistaking that tall outline, that loping walk and the floppy hair. Quite what he was doing in this part of the town was irrelevant as she madly rehearsed what might be the best thing to say. Keep calm, that was the first rule, she ordered herself ineffectually. If nothing else, I've got to stay in control. Momentarily she heard her mother's voice, commanding her to drive past without a second glance or alternatively and perhaps preferably, mount the kerb and run him down.

Easing the car to a halt a little way past him, she ran her dirty fingers through her hair before opening the door and getting out, feeling self-conscious about the muddy state she was in. Opening her mouth to utter a cheery greeting, she shut it abruptly and dived back into the safety of her car. It wasn't Jonty, nor indeed anyone who bore the slightest resemblance to him. Embarrassed by her error, she revved up the engine and pulled out in a rush, failing to check in her rear view mirror and receiving an abrasive hoot from the car coming up behind her which had to screech on its brakes to avoid contact. As soon as she could, safely, Faith pulled into the side to let the car pass, fixing her eyes on her hands that were gripping the steering wheel so that she could avoid the one finger wave she got from the irate driver, who was delighted to have acquired more evidence for his dossier on the implausibility of women drivers.

More by luck than good clinical skills, Faith finished her house calls without putting any human life in jeopardy and arrived back at the surgery, a little battered both physically and psychologically but still in one piece. Rob, who had finished first, had bought sandwiches and crisps for the three of them and was working on the computer when Faith joined him.

'Hi,' he started and then noticed the mud. 'Whatever happened to you?'

Faith explained, noticing that both her knees were protruding from holes in her tights and found that she was able to laugh about it. 'It's not been my best morning,' she apologised.

Rob smiled. 'We all have them, don't worry about it. Here, you can have first choice on the sandwiches, cheese and pickle, chicken salad or egg mayo.'

'I'll cut them into quarters and then we can all share,' suggested Faith, taking the bags over to the little worktop and ferreting in the drawer for a suitable knife, all the while thinking that Jonty would never had said anything as understanding as that. He would have laughed at her, rather than with her.

The afternoon was long. The patients were impatient as most of them had to wait a long time to be seen. Everyone was running late as extras had been squashed in to cope with the Monday demand and ease the pressure on the receptionists who were being bombarded with demands for appointments. As far as Faith was concerned, none of her patients had a definitive problem, making each consultation unsatisfactory and a mystery. They presented with a variety of the vaguest symptoms, which failed to fit any specific complaint. The nebulous nature of their description was very suggestive that in fact there was little, if anything, amiss but there was always that nagging worry that perhaps there was something she was missing. Unable to be decisive, she sent the majority of them off for blood and urine tests, promising to see them again next week for review, in the hopes that time would have yet again have proven to be a far better healer than she would ever be.

Difficult though the day had been, she was reluctant to leave and go home, where there would be even more reminders and so sat around plodding her way through letters, while the cleaners dusted, polished and vacuumed around her.

Predictably, Glenda was sitting with Hamish, the two of them drinking, the former smoking as well. Lavishing care from the moment she stepped into the house, they sat her down, poured her a glass of wine and asked after her day. Hamish made supper, which amounted to putting a ready meal into the oven and when Faith admitted that she was not really hungry, she was frogmarched to the table by her mother who sat and watched while she ate every scrap of lasagne that was on her plate.

'You look dead beat,' Glenda told her, brusquely. 'Let's all sit in the drawing room for a while and then you have an early night. Hamish is a dab hand at cocoa.'

'Thanks, Ma. And can I just say thank you both for everything that you've done for me over the past couple of weeks. I know that it's been a huge amount of work, which by rights I should have done but you let me go off on that fantastic holiday and have time with Pa. It's helped enormously. I still hurt desperately and cannot for the life of me understand what's happened or why but at least I feel better than I did and I couldn't have got to this point without you.'

'It's nice to see you looking a bit more like your old self. Some colour in your cheeks and less haggard. Perhaps your father does have some uses after all.' Glenda sniffed, begrudgingly.

'Faith, darling, it's the least I could do.' Hamish came over and hugged her, his jacket rough against her face. 'We've both been so worried about you. We're always here for you, come what may.'

Faith curled up on one of the sofas and rested her head on one of the cushions. It had been a long, long day, one that felt more like a week than just twelve or so hours, but it had been a major hurdle surmounted and surely the days to come would gradually get easier.

Chapter Twenty-Four

It was Faith's half day. She wasn't looking forward to it in the way she usually did; she felt immeasurably better when she had something to keep her busy and demand her full concentration. Ironically, just when she would have celebrated running late and a handful of visits, she finished on time. Try as she might to grab opportunistic moments when she might discuss health promotion with her patients, they refused to accept the bait, preferring to be off and away, to Christmas shop or get back to their warm homes. There was a minimum of paperwork to be tackled and the morning's post brought in an unimpressive amount of letters.

She sat, idly surfing the internet, looking for something to read that might be vaguely medical but nothing caught her eye. Much as relations between her and her mother had improved, superficially at any rate, Faith was not keen to go home just yet. There was nothing tempting about the weather to make her want to ride, it was far too muddy to walk the dogs with any enjoyment, for her at least, and the thought of sitting in the house for the rest of the day was about as inspiring as watching paint dry.

Halfway through the morning, she had volunteered to do an extra surgery that afternoon, to help ease the pressure of earlier in the week but she was emphatically reassured by Joan and Gary that plenty of appointments were available and so she should just go and enjoy her time off. Faith had been on the verge of asking them if she could help out on reception for the afternoon but correctly guessed that they would turn down that request as well, not wishing her to encroach on their territory.

When Rob suggested lunch at Delicious, she was ambivalent. This would provide a means of passing the next hour or so but she was not sure if she wanted to spend that much time with him alone, fearing a cross-examination. So when Ellie asked if she could accompany them, the idea sounded far more attractive. Safety in numbers.

They ran across the square, pulling their coats tight around their bodies to keep out the biting wind. Steamy windows made it impossible to see how busy it was and first impressions, when they made their entrance along with a gust of icy air which made those seated at the table nearest the door turn their heads with annoyance, was that it was overflowing. Rob, hawk eyed, spotted a space right in the corner and they squeezed their way past customers and shopping bags to stake their claim. Rob and Ellie prevaricated about what to have, spoilt for choice by the options on the blackboard while Faith was more interested in the company than the food but settled on a bowl of broccoli and stilton soup which sounded both warming and comforting.

What seemed like an age passed before their meals arrived; usually the service was slick and speedy. Ellie was starting to check her watch, fearful about being late for the start of afternoon surgery and Faith was scared that she might leave them.

'I've arranged to start early,' she explained. 'Lydia and Virginia have dental appointments after school and I must be there to go with them.' She turned her head, 'Where *is* our lunch?'

On cue, the owner of Delicious appeared to serve them herself, apologising profusely for the delay. Her cheeks were glowing from the exertion of serving so many and trying to keep everyone happy but even then, she still had time for a smile and a quick chat with her regular customers.

'It's been bedlam all morning. We've barely stopped to draw breath. Still, I'm not complaining. It's all good business. I'm so sorry you've had to wait. If you want coffee and cake afterwards, it's on the house. Oh,' she looked directly at Rob, 'there's rhubarb crumble and custard.'

He rubbed his hands together with delight.

Faith stirred her soup, a huge bowlful, far too hot to eat and enough to feed three or more probably four. In no hurry for it to cool, she played with a homemade bread roll, still warm from the oven, tearing it into little pieces, buttering one of them but not actually eating any. She still had little appetite. Since that evening with her mother she had not binged once. All the time she was in Japan she had never even considered it and since her return, she genuinely had not been hungry, food having lost its appeal, to say nothing of its taste.

They chatted about inconsequentialities as they ate, Ellie wanted to know more about Japan and Rob had spent a day rock-climbing with Ed, the details of which he was keen to share with them. Ellie told them what the twins had put on their Christmas lists for although the festivities were still over a month away, there were constant reminders wherever you looked. Shop windows were already decorated, the tree was up in the centre of the market square and yards of multicoloured lights stretched from one lamppost to another.

The season of good will filled Faith with dread. She had had all manner of plans for her and Jonty but a fat lot of use those were now. She wondered what he would be doing instead. It didn't bear thinking about.

Rob was deliberating over whether he had room for crumble after his toasted sandwich and chips when his phone rang. Putting a finger in one ear so that he could hear more clearly, he said little, saying only words like 'yes', 'no', 'okay' and finally 'I'll be back in a couple of minutes', which left the other two in no doubt that he had been talking to someone at the surgery.

'It's a late call,' he announced, putting his phone back in his pocket. 'Abdominal pain. I suppose I'd better deny myself of the crumble.'

Ellie laughed. 'I'll make you one, I promise. Anyway, I've got to go too, so we'd better pay the bill. My treat.'

With nothing better to do, Faith jogged back to the medical centre with them. They arrived en masse at the reception desk, blowing on their hands which had frozen in the brief trip from the café. Gary looked up and admired their red noses.

'Very seasonal,' he chuckled.

'What's the visit?' inquired Rob, waving to Ellie as she set off across the waiting area to her room.

'Let me see... Oh yes. It's just come in. For Pollyanna Smith, thirteen Lapwing Avenue. Abdominal pain since this morning.'

'I'll go,' Faith insisted. 'I know her well. She's waiting to see about bariatric surgery. Maybe she's had it done while I've been away. I'll have a look at her notes first, in case there are any letters about her.'

'Faith, it's your half day. I'm on for late visits, so leave it for me.' Rob was resolute.

'No, Rob, I'd like to go. I've nothing else to do. If I'm honest, there's nothing to do at home and so I'd be glad of an excuse to stay.'

Rob studied her closely. 'We could go together...'

Faith shook her head a little too rapidly. 'No, you go and do some reading or write up your visits from this morning. I don't expect this will be very exciting and I'll be back before you know it.'

'Are you sure? I feel bad about you doing my work for me.'

'You did some extra for me, didn't you, before my— I mean before I went off, so look on this as me repaying your kindness.'

'Okay, but consider it repaid now, all right?'

'Come on, let's go and look at her notes.' Faith pushed him towards the staircase and up to the coffee room. Logging in, she pulled up Pollyanna's notes. The last entry was her referral letter to the consultant. No letters back and definitely nothing about an operation.

'She could only just have been discharged,' suggested Rob. 'You know that the discharge letters take a while to come through.'

'True,' agreed Faith, copying down the address, presuming from its ornithological reference that it was on the same little council estate as Plover Close. 'I'll find out soon enough. See you later.'

In the car, she turned the heater on full, glad when some warm air finally filtered around her. On the radio, one of Jonty's favourite songs began to play, a soulful female vocalist whom Faith had never been able to see the attraction of and she angrily switched over to a CD of her own choice, one that she knew he would have poured scorn on. Some temporary roadworks meant that she was sent on a diversion around town, crawling in a caterpillar of traffic that moved at an infuriatingly cautious rate. Wishing that perhaps it would have been more sensible to let Rob do the call, she spotted the sign to Flamingo Street and turned off, recognising that there was a way she could attain Lapwing Avenue.

Blocks of terraced houses, overdue for renovation by the council, lined each side of the road, inappropriately called avenue, for there was not a tree in sight and where once had been grass verges there was just mud, the end result of indiscriminate parking and unruly cyclists. Most gates were battered and falling apart, just a few had been replaced by home-proud tenants who had also taken meticulous care with their tiny front gardens, laying out plants with perfect symmetry and clipping the privet hedges into neat little rectangles.

Other houses were not so lucky. Paint peeled off the woodwork, rubbish lay where the wind had blown it and discarded children's toys cluttered the overgrown lawns and weed-infested flower beds. A posse of dogs trotted across the road in front of Faith's car as she stopped, one of them taking the time to sniff and then urinate up against the front wheel before baring its teeth at her in an expression that was about as far from a smile as she could envisage.

Working out which was number thirteen took a little time as most houses were bereft of any means of identification. Only by counting back from thirty-seven, did Faith find her destination. With some relief she noted that it was one of the better-loved houses. It was the only one where, as a result of some amateur topiary, the hedge had been sculptured into a shape, possibly a mouse but then it could just as easily have been a cat or even a peacock. A little wrought-iron gate led the way under a wooden trellis, doubtless an archway of colour at the height of summer and on to a narrow pathway of carefully laid-out crazy paving. Pruned rose bushes crouched on either side of the path, alternating with a variety of garden ornaments, a selection of gnomes, moles and rabbits perched idiosyncratically on stone toadstools. The front door had its own trellis around it and straggles of climbing rose still clutched to it, one late, bewildered bloom drooping down sadly.

Faith rang the bell and was treated to a trumpet fanfare that lasted several seconds. She wiped her feet on a very clean mat and waited for someone to answer. Mrs Smith, a facsimile of her daughter, though smaller in height and wider in diameter, ushered Faith in, shaking her hand and thanking her for coming out.

'There's no way she could have come to the surgery, doctor. The receptionists tried to get us to but I told them over and over that she was in too much pain to move.'

'That's quite all right, Mrs Smith. Don't give it another thought. Where is Pollyanna? Upstairs?'

Mrs Smith nodded and led the way, her huge bulk taking one stair at a time and pausing to reclaim her breath halfway up.

'I think it's something she's eaten. She had a takeaway last night.'

Faith, following patiently, murmured that it might be a possibility. So much for the diet. She took in the well-hung, if hideously flowered, wallpaper, matching curtains and swags with tasselled rope tiebacks and a twee telephone table adorned with green onyx ornaments. The tiny landing was just as spotless. The walls were covered with Mrs Smith's thimble collection, the result of heirlooms, holiday souvenirs, birthday and Christmas presents and special edition offers from the penultimate pages of Sunday magazines.

'Over two thousand,' Mrs Smith announced proudly, as she saw Faith gazing at them all and reading her mind. 'Must be worth a small fortune, so Mr Smith says. I clean them all every week. What a job that is. Come on, she's in here. That's the bathroom, if you'd like to wash your hands when you've finished. I've left a little towel in there for you on the side of the bath.'

'That's very thoughtful,' Faith thanked her.

Mrs Smith approached the door that was helpfully emblazoned with a china plaque bearing Pollyanna's name in gothic script and knocked.

'Polly? Are you awake? The doctor's come to see you. In you go. I'll leave you to it. Just call if you want anything, I'll be doing the ironing.'

Faith wriggled past the rotund Mrs Smith and gained access to a small but very yellow bedroom, most of which was taken up by a double bed. Fitted wardrobes and a matching dressing table took up what little space was left.

'Hello, Pollyanna,' Faith tried to sit on the edge of the quilted stool, pushing an array of well-worn underwear out of the way first.

Pollyanna was half lying, half sitting in bed by the side of which someone, probably her mother, had considerately left a bucket as a receptacle for any vomiting. She looked flushed and unwell. Her brow was wet and tendrils of her hair clung to her skin.

'Hello, Dr Faber. I'm glad it's you.'

'What's been happening?'

'It started in the night. I woke up and was sick and then my tummy started to hurt. Down here at first but now all over.'

'What sort of pain is it?' asked Faith.

'Awful. It keeps coming and going. Mum says that's colic.'

'Have you vomited any more?'

'No, but I feel sick when the pain comes on.'

'Any upset with your bowels?'

'No.'

216

'No diarrhoea?'

'No.' Pollyanna was definite.

'Any problems when you have a wee? Does it hurt?' Faith went on, remembering the not too distant urinary tract infection.

'No. Oh, oh no, the pain's coming again.'

Faith waited until it had eased off, watching the girl's contorted face as she held her breath before starting to relax as the pain subsided.

'Poor you,' she patted her hand. 'Let's see, have you eaten today?'

'No, I can't face it.'

'Your mum says you had a takeaway last night...'

'Yes I did, but it tasted fine and we regularly go to that place and have never had any trouble before.'

'Okay. I'd better examine you now. I'll start by taking your temperature then your pulse and blood pressure.'

She rummaged in her bag for the equipment needed to perform these basic tasks and then had to wait as Pollyanna experienced another wave of pain.

'I think it's getting worse, Doctor. It's definitely coming more often than it was.'

Faith wrapped the cuff around Pollyanna's arm and pumped it up. Her blood pressure was fine, her pulse rapid but not absurdly so. Her temperature, for all that she was red in the face and perspiring, was normal.

'I'd better feel your tummy now, please,' Faith started to fold back the yellow duvet and pull up Pollyanna's nightdress. The acres of her abdomen spilled over on each side like a waterfall of fat.

'Any word about your operation? Faith asked, more to make conversation than anything else.

'I've got an appointment for next week to see the consultant— ' Pollyanna's voice tailed off as she clutched her abdomen in the grips of another spasm. Faith waited patiently for her to calm down again, struggling to come up with tentative diagnoses but not really able to.

As with any obese patient, the abdominal examination was very difficult to assess. Her belly appeared soft and not particularly tender and the bowel sounds were active, excluding obstruction or peritonitis, but the sheer size of it made it an imprecise tool to use.

Faith had no idea what to do. It didn't take a doctor to see the amount of pain that Pollyanna was in but the absence of any diarrhoea and no vomiting to speak of made the putative diagnosis of food poisoning look less likely by the minute. Should she administer some strong pain relief and then check back in a couple of hours or should she admit her and risk being on the receiving end of the withering comments of the surgical team on call when it proved to be something trivial?

She played for time, oscillating from one option to the other as she repeated the blood pressure. Pollyanna shouted out as the pain returned.

'That was the worst yet, Dr Faber. What's wrong, do you think?'

'I'm not sure, Pollyanna. I don't think it's food poisoning though. Could you manage to get to the bathroom and do a urine sample for me?' She had moved on to the possibility of renal colic, caused by a stone in the kidney. Legend had it that this is one of the worst pains known to mankind.

'I think so. Let me just wait until this pain has gone though.'

Faith produced a small bottle with a red top and handed it over.

'Phew. That's a bit better. Could you help me up please? I feel quite weak.'

Somehow, without injuring either of them, Faith got Pollyanna to her feet and sat on the edge of the bed to wait while she waddled off to the bathroom. She picked up the pile of dog-eared paperbacks on the bedside table and put them down again. Romances – doctors and nurses, pilots and air hostesses, somehow not a surprise but not her sort of thing. Just in case, she checked her phone for messages but as was usually the case these days, there were none. A gripping discomfort in her own lower abdomen reminded her that her period was about due and also scolded her for not asking Pollyanna any questions of a gynaecological nature, something she determined to amend as soon as she returned and got into bed.

A shriek that rattled the walls of the house rang out and Faith dashed from the room and banged on the bathroom door.

'Aaaaaaaaaagh. Help, help me.'

Faith tried the handle and was relieved to find it unlocked. Pollyanna was standing by the washbasin, legs apart in a pool of fluid that was also dripping down her legs. Frantically trying to make some sense of the situation, Faith's first thought was that she had spilt tap water all over herself and her second that she had spilt her urine sample.

'Don't worry, you can do another one.'

Pollyanna, holding her abdomen in both her hands, fell to her knees. Moving onto all fours she yelled out as the agony beset her again. 'Oh what's happening? Please help me. It's so awful when it comes.'

'I'm going to help,' promised Faith, hoping that her voice carried more conviction than she felt. 'I think we need to get you to hospital for some tests. I can't leave you here with such pain. I'm just going to ring for an ambulance.'

'No, don't leave me. Aaagh, it's coming again.'

More fluid gushed onto the floor and in one horrifying moment Faith realised what was going on. Pulling the door ajar, she called out as loudly as she could. 'Mrs Smith? Call an ambulance immediately.'

A bustling noise was followed by some huffing, puffing and footsteps on the stairs. Mrs Smith's face appeared between the spindles on the landing. 'What's going on?'

'Dial 999 now! Your daughter's having a baby.'

'Whaaaaaaaat?' Pollyanna sobbed. 'I can't be. I don't want one. It's that curry from last night. Ooooooooooooh no, make this pain go away.'

'Pollyanna, listen to me. You're in labour, you're having contractions. The ambulance is on its way. Think about your breathing, long deep breaths. Count to ten as you breathe in and then to ten again as you breathe out. Hold my hand. You're going to be fine.'

'Where's Mum? You'd better get Phil as well.'

'Who's Phil?'

'My boyfriend. OOOOOOOOOOH. They're coming so often now, these pains. Sorry, I think I might just have broken your fingers.'

Faith smiled. She reached for a flannel and moistened it with cold water before handing it to Pollyanna to wipe her burning face. Where was the ambulance? She felt powerless. In a nice, sterile obstetric unit, like the one where she had done her training, there would be instruments to monitor the contractions and listen to the baby's heartbeat. Pollyanna would be on a practical, if uncomfortable, bed, which facilitated examinations both internal and external, and competent midwives would be buzzing around in total control of the situation. Yet here she was on a bathroom floor, the coldness of the tiles seeping through her skirt, her knees stiff from having been fully flexed for so long and eye to eye with an avocado toilet and matching bidet. Beside her was a terrified young girl whose body was making short work of a process that should be the most natural thing in the world.

'You're doing really well,' Faith comforted her. 'Really, really well. Do you think that you could get back into bed?'

'Maybe...I mean no! Oh, oh, please. Make it go away.'

'What about sitting down?' Faith waited for a moment of calm.

'I don't think I can go anywhere. I'm sorry.'

Mrs Smith tried to come in but the tiny room was already packed.

'How's she doing? I've boiled some water and brought you some clean towels.'

'Thanks.' Faith had them handed to her. She had never been exactly sure what the purpose of either of these rudimentary elements of the Victorian delivery room was. Still, with any luck, she would be saved from needing either by the well- timed arrival of an ambulance crew who were only too delighted to take over. And if the current volume of Pollyanna's shouts were anything to go by then this baby would be making its first appearance en route to the hospital.

Pretending that she was busy with the towels and positioning the kettle, Faith turned away from her patient momentarily. A guttural voice spoke between gritted teeth.

'I think I need to have a shit.'

'What?' Faith was terrified.

'There's something going on, I want to bear down. I can't help it, Dr Faber. Oh, it hurts so much. Urrrrrgh.'

I've got to do something, Faith told herself. Her gloves were next door.

'Mrs Smith, please could you fetch me my bag from Pollyanna's bedroom? Thanks. Now if you open it up and look down there on the left – that's it, yes, pass me a pair of those gloves. Is there any sign of that ambulance?'

She strained her ears optimistically. Nothing apart from the sound of the radio in the lounge.

'The pain, it's coming again. Oh, I've got to push. It feels as if I'm tearing open. Mnnnnnnnnnn.'

Somehow, Faith managed to manouevre her way round to Pollyanna's bottom. She lifted up the hem of the bloodstained nightdress. Parting her buttocks gently, she could just see a small piece of the baby's head, about the size of a fifty-pence coin.

'Pollyanna, the baby's nearly here. You've done so well. I can see its head. Try and do as I say next time when the pain comes. I know it hurts more than anything but try and listen to me. Tell me when it's starting.'

There was a lull in the contractions. Pollyanna wiped her face and sucked on the flannel, her mouth parched from all the shouting. Faith waited, heart in her mouth, hoping against hope that she could remember what to do.

Pollyanna started to grunt. 'It's coming.'

'Right, now when I say push, push. When I ask you to stop, stop and pant like a dog.'

The niceties of the second stage of labour were not to be experienced by either of them and there was no time for controlled pushing and panting for, with one almighty push, a small, slimy baby with a mass of black hair slid into Faith's hands.

'Oh, Pollyanna, it's a boy! Well done. Look at him. He's beautiful.'

Chapter Twenty-Five

'You are nothing short of amazing! I'm sure that I'd never have been able to cope like that. I'd have been a bag of nerves.'

Ellie was sitting with Rob, Faith and Ed, surgeries over for the day, in the nearby pub, sharing a bottle of wine. Faith had returned to the surgery, shaking from head to foot, needing the support of her peers rather than Glenda's insistence that she did not want to listen to anything that involved blood and guts and they had persuaded her to go with them for a drink. They were agog to hear the details of her supposed afternoon off and she, in her turn, was longing to tell them.

'It hasn't quite sunk in yet,' she confessed. 'It seems more like a dream.'

'That's hardly surprising,' Ed concurred. 'None of us would have anticipated that if we'd taken that house call we'd come face to face with someone in labour.'

'Didn't she have any clue that she was pregnant?' Rob asked.

'Apparently not,' Faith informed them.

'Lucky thing, I say.' Ellie thought back to her own, arduous and uncomfortable pregnancy, most of which had been spent in hospital, the only time in her life when she had been vast in size, with swollen ankles and blood pressure so high it made her consultant obstetrician go pale.

'Good job it wasn't a breech,' mused Ed.

'Or twins,' volunteered Rob.

'Don't even go there,' agreed Faith. 'I was just fortunate that it was all so easy – well, not for Pollyanna, I know, but at least the actual delivery bit was quick. I almost didn't catch him. Can you imagine if he'd slithered out of my hands? He could have ended up in the toilet!'

Her look of abject horror made the others laugh.

'Has she given him a name yet?' Ellie's motherly side was coming out.

223

'Yes, she'd decided on that by the time the ambulance arrived. He's called Zak. Apparently it's the name of a film star that she thinks is really good looking.'

'Shame it wasn't a girl, she could have called her after you,' Ellie became whimsical.

'I don't think so,' Faith doubted, who had never been very fond of her own name.

'What about her parents? Whatever did they say?'

'Her father was out. Her mother was incredible. You'd think that babies were born in her bathroom on a regular basis. For someone who has just become a grandmother with no warning, she took it remarkably well.'

'Bloody hell.' Ed shook his head. 'I must say, I'm glad it wasn't me.'

'What?' laughed Ellie. 'Having the baby, becoming a grandparent or being the doctor?'

'All three!'

They all giggled into their drinks and Faith felt special, part of an exclusive clan that shared secrets that no one else was allowed to be privy to.

'I do feel bad about it though,' she began.

'Why?' Ellie asked, filling the glasses and poking Rob in the side, indicating that he should go and fetch another bottle.

'I should have diagnosed it months ago. Looking back, there were all sorts of clues. She felt sick, which I thought was the Obesigon, she had urinary symptoms and oedematous feet. Oh, and there were the rumblings that she thought were her bowels. I bet that was foetal movement.'

'You can't blame yourself.'

'I do rather. I couldn't understand why she wasn't losing weight. She seemed so determined.'

'Loads of patients sound full of motivation in surgery. They don't want to disappoint us and so say the things that they think we want to hear,' Ellie reminded her.

'But I thought she was different. That's why I spent so much time with her, encouraging her, trying to keep the impetus going.'

'I'm sure she appreciated it.'

'Then I never asked about her periods.'

'Was there any need to? Did she complain of a problem?'

'No,' declared Faith. 'But I should have asked. I should have taken a more comprehensive history before starting her on the tablets. She was so desperate for help. Never mind about her wanting to please me, I just wanted to please her. I know that's not what our job's about but if you'd seen her...'

Faith's voice tailed off. The others were sitting silently rapt, waiting for her to continue, a captivated audience.

'To be honest, I never even considered that she might have a boyfriend, which sounds just the worst thing to admit. I mean, she's such a size. I assumed, wrongly I know now, that that was one of the reasons why she wanted to be slim – you know, to be more attractive.'

'What's he like, the boyfriend? Was he there?'

'He appeared as they were wheeling Pollyanna and Zak into the ambulance. He's just the opposite. Stick thin, skin-tight black jeans that make him look like an insect, long hair, a hat that seems to be welded to his head. I was quite worried about him – he was as white as a sheet. Probably shock, I suppose, but I thought he might faint. He went to hospital with them. It was getting a bit crowded in the back because Mrs Smith wanted to go too.'

'And the baby, Zak, he's okay?'

'Fine. When last seen he was bawling away ferociously apparently none the worse for his precipitate arrival in the world.'

'Thank goodness for that.'

'Not bad for someone whose first view of life was a green bathmat.'

They all roared.

'I don't think we'd have done anything any differently,' Ed reassured her, suddenly sombre.

'There were so many cues that I missed though.'

'We can all be wise using the retrospectoscope,' Rob added.

Faith shook her head. 'I'm not so sure.'

Gloom had fallen on the previously merry party. Ellie sat upright and coughed to attract attention. 'We all still think you did a fantastic job. So well done.'

The four of them raised their glasses to Faith, who smiled wanly.

'Now,' continued Ellie, 'I think it's only right that we drink a toast to Pollyanna, Zak and his father, whatever his name is.'

'Phil,' muttered Faith.

They drank again.

'What do you think I should do next?'

Ed thought briefly before replying. 'Visit her and the baby. Either in hospital or when she comes home.'

'Do you think I should take her something? You know, flowers or a present for the baby?'

'No,' advised Ed. 'Perhaps later. To start with I would keep your visit on a professional level. I'm sure she'll be thrilled to see you.'

'I hope so… No, don't give me any more to drink, please.' Faith put her hand over her glass. 'I've got to drive home.'

She waited until the others had finished their drinks and they walked together back to the car park before driving off, waving and promising to see each other the next morning.

Rob waited and walked Faith to her car, holding the door open while she settled in the seat.

'You did a great job, Faith. Be happy about it. It's a real privilege to deliver a baby.'

She looked into his eyes and saw something she had rarely seen in Jonty's – sincerity.

It was a look that stayed with her for the rest of the evening and the last thing she recalled before she fell asleep.

The sister in charge of Burnsall Ward was deep in conversation with two student midwives when Faith approached the nursing station the following day. She had elected to drive over to the hospital rather than go for lunch with Ellie, wanting to get this visit over and done with, fearing the outcome. Unappetising smells of gravy and overcooked cabbage hung in the air as Faith entered the ward and a care assistant was scraping piles of leftovers into a large metal bin. In the nursery a row of cribs was occupied by newborn babies, each one wrapped up tightly in identical blankets, giving them the appearance of small grubs rather than human life. One, scarlet in the face, was screaming for all it was worth, fury all over its tiny features, demanding the delivery of some food as soon as possible. Women shuffled about in their slippers, all postnatal but still looking pregnant, their dressing-gown belts tied above their still well-defined bulges. There was a definite atmosphere of proud, if weary, joy.

'Can I help?' The Sister looked up at Faith.

'Hello, I'm Dr Faber, Pollyanna Smith's GP. I wondered if I might be able to see her. How are they doing?'

'Ah, the famous Dr Faber. She's not stopped talking about you since she arrived. Of course you can see her. Mother and baby are fine. She's in bay two, the bed by the window. Well done, you.'

'Thanks. It was pretty scary actually,' Faith confessed.

'Not enough home deliveries these days, if you ask me. Anyway, I've lots to do, so if you'll excuse me but don't hesitate to let me know if you need anything.'

Tentatively Faith made her way to bay two. A woman, who was half lying on her bed, propped up with half a dozen pillows, and becoming frustrated as her baby refused to latch onto her breast and feed, looked up inquisitively, curious to know why someone was visiting out of hours. Another was snoring gently, catching up after a bad night and a third was munching her way through a sandwich and flicking through a magazine.

Pollyanna was sitting on the edge of her bed, her back to Faith, stroking the little boy in the cot beside her. Vases of flowers covered the top of her locker and a blue helium balloon floated aimlessly above the bed head. An open box of chocolates lay on the bedspread, Faith noticed that half of them had been eaten.

'Hello, Pollyanna,' Faith cleared her throat.

'Dr Faber! How wonderful to see you! I hoped you'd come but Mum said you'd be far too busy. Come and see Zak. He is just so handsome, like his dad.' Pollyanna patted the bed beside her invitingly and Faith accepted.

'Here, you'll want to hold him, won't you? Oops, I'm not very good at this yet. I keep forgetting to support his head.'

Clumsily she scooped up Zak and managed to pass him to Faith without incident. Faith moved the hem of the blanket which had fallen over his face and a pair of dark beady eyes blinked back at her. He grimaced.

'Look!' Pollyanna pointed proudly. 'He's smiling at you.'

'Maybe. I suspect it's probably just wind,' Faith told her.

'Nope, he's smiling. Zak, this is the doctor who brought you into the world. She's just the best doctor you could hope for.'

Faith blushed. She stammered, struggling to find the words she wanted. 'Aren't you angry with me? I mean, if I'd realised you were pregnant you could have had the proper antenatal care and given birth in the hospital. It must have been petrifying for you yesterday.'

Pollyanna gazed adoringly at Zak and adjusted the little bonnet he was wearing. She stroked his perfect fingers, marvelling at his long nails.

'How could I be angry? I had no idea what was going on. I was just worried about my weight. Speaking of which, I stood on the scales this morning and I've lost over a stone! I'll be cancelling next week's appointment. I've only just had him but he's already become the most important thing in my life. He needs and wants a mum who loves him and looks after him, he doesn't want someone who's trying to be something they'll never be.'

'What about your boyfriend? How's he?'

'He's had the fright of his life. Says he'll never trust condoms again. But he's tickled pink to be a dad. Scared of holding him, 'cos he's so fragile. But he'll learn, just like I will.'

'I think you're going to be the best mum ever,' Faith said, meaning every word.

Pollyanna gave her an ungainly hug. 'He's just the very best thing that ever happened to me. I can't thank you enough, Dr Faber. Just you wait until you have kids of your own, then you'll understand just how I'm feeling.'

Faith said nothing.

'I'm going to breast feed,' Pollyanna informed her. 'They say you get your figure back quicker if you do. I've had a few tries and it's going quite well but I still need a nurse around to give me a hand. I'm a bit sore as he's got quite a suck on him. Thank heavens he hasn't got any teeth. I expect Mum'll help when I go home. She says she breast fed me and my brothers.'

'When are you going home?'

'I'd go now. I feel fine. But they've suggested I stay at least a couple of days, so hopefully I'll be off at the weekend. Will you come and see us at home? We'd love that, wouldn't we, Zak?'

'I would love it too. I'll pop in next week and see how you're all getting on.'

Faith had lost track of time and was amazed to see that if she didn't leave now and get a move on then she would be late for her first patient. She reluctantly said her goodbyes – he was a most adorable baby – and ran back to where she had left the car, hoping that no parking ticket had been stuck on the windscreen as she had left her vehicle illegally on a double yellow line in the corner of the staff car park, which was overflowing, as was the norm. She was in luck.

How she envied Pollyanna and the instantaneous contentment she felt with her new role in life. That such a small, totally dependent baby could have such a phenomenal impact in so short a space of time was truly mind blowing. Maternal instinct had kicked in automatically, despite the fact that she had been denied months of preparation. Wallowing in self-pity, Faith reflected that she wished it were her, that it was she who was lying in that bed, in a new, sexy negligee, with Jonty sitting by her side cuddling his son and heir, or perhaps his daughter, but she presumed he would expect a son first to perpetuate the family name. He was always a bit old fashioned when it came to matters such as these.

Would she ever see him again? Now that she had had time to recover from the initial disbelief of what he had done to her, as each day passed, the yearning to talk to him was growing stronger, building up inside like her own pregnancy, developing rapidly, taking shape. With no one she dared admit this to, she nurtured the feeling on her own, feeding it with rosy thoughts of her and Jonty meeting up and getting back together. She became expert at ignoring the negatives and she could think up a tangible excuse for all his misdemeanours. By this time, she expected that he would have seen the error of his ways, be ruing the day he first let Dawn seduce him – it was impossible that he could have seduced her – and he would be going mad trying to come up with a reason for getting in touch. How was he to know that she was willing him to do just that?

Perhaps, thought Faith, she should make the first move and put him out of his misery. She could just ring to see how he was, tell him chattily about Pollyanna's baby (though his reaction was likely to be very similar to Glenda's) and then shyly suggest that they meet up for a drink. There were still some of his things at her house. Jumpers, trousers, riding boots. He'd be needing them, surely. It would have been simple for him to arrange for his father to take them back for him, but he hadn't. There must be a reason and Faith thought that she knew what it was. Without a doubt this was his way of letting her know that he wanted to come back to her, that there was no way that his life had any meaning if she were not in it.

Glenda, who was covertly keeping a close eye on her daughter, wrongly assumed that she was just quiet, but coping. Had she been granted access to her daughter's neuronal perambulations, she would have wasted no time at all in bringing her down to earth with a heavy thud as she listed, in detail, all of Jonty's innumerable shortcomings, including a fiery diatribe on how he had been unfaithful without so much as turning a hair. Nor would Glenda have allocated any time for Faith to put forward her own arguments to the contrary, for her opinion of Jonty would never change; he had been banished to the same pit of revulsion that up until recently had been reserved solely for Dennis Faber.

Faith was late for starting surgery, having fallen foul of the one-way traffic system around town for the second day running. She bluffed her way with the first few patients, who had been sitting impatiently waiting for her, telling them that she had been called to the hospital, which seemed to placate them as they imagined scenes of carnage and emergency medicine like the ones they were glued to on television most nights.

Working consistently, the worry about Pollyanna now consigned to the past, she juggled long and short consultations, thinking she was catching up, only to be held up again. As a result she finished late and found that it looked as though she was the last one in the building, save for Gary, who was just wrapping his scarf several times around his neck about to set off and the cleaners who were emptying rubbish bins and tidying the magazines and self-help leaflets which had strayed off the tables onto the floor.

Rob was waiting for her upstairs when she went to fetch her coat.

'Hi! How was your afternoon?'

'Good, thanks, how about yours?'

'Great. Did you go to the hospital?'

'Yes, I did. She was fine about things.'

'There – what did we tell you?'

'I'm so relieved, I can't begin to tell you. It could all have gone so wrong.'

'Faith, of course it could but it didn't.'

Faith mellowed. 'The baby is so cute. He doesn't look like either of his parents. Oh, I didn't mean that to come out quite the

230

way it did! I'm going to pop in next week when they've all been at home for a few days. See how things are getting on.'

'That's more like it. You've done something very special.'

'I know. I can't believe it was only yesterday.'

'Quick drink at the pub before you go?' Rob asked, hopefully.

Faith hesitated before declining.

'Not tonight, thanks. I'm tired out.'

'Probably yesterday catching up with you.'

'Probably.'

They walked downstairs, calling good night to the cleaners on their way. At the door, Faith fumbled with her key.

'Would you come out with me another night? Just the two of us?' Rob gulped.

There was no reply.

'I'm so sorry. I should have thought. Is it too soon?'

'Yes, but thank you anyway.'

Chapter Twenty-Six

Christmas came and went with its customary haste after the long build-up which seemed to have started earlier than ever that year. Glenda and Faith spent the time together, alternating between hacking out and watching television, sighing with relief as advertisements for toys and hair straighteners gave way to ones for tropical holidays and sales with rock-bottom prices. Neither of them over-ate and the boxes of chocolates that Faith had been surprised and delighted to receive from grateful patients – nothing from Mrs Tonbridge – lay unopened in a heap next to the Christmas tree. The dogs ended up with the lion's share of the turkey breast that Faith had gone to the trouble to cook, along with the usual trimmings. Only Hamish, who spent the day with them, did justice to the food, having second helpings of everything, proclaiming that he would never eat another morsel but ready a few hours later to tuck into sandwiches, Christmas cake and yuletide log. Glenda preferred to stick to liquid refreshment and Faith was not bothered one way or the other. She was eating a little better, perhaps not amount-wise but regularly. Occasionally she felt hungry but mostly after a couple of mouthfuls was full and picked at the remains. For once food was lowest on her list of priorities.

Seizing an opportunity when Glenda had slipped out to the toilet, her euphemism for refilling her glass, Faith asked Hamish, as nonchalantly as she could, whether he had heard from Jonty at all. His answer was in the negative, not so much as a call or even a card. He had no idea where his son was and he was still angry enough not to care.

'Don't lose any sleep over him. You deserve better,' he told her, sounding frighteningly like Glenda, Faith thought.

'Oh, I'm not. I just wondered, that's all. He might have wanted to get in touch to say Happy Christmas.'

'What are you doing for New Year?' Hamish changed the subject.

'Not a lot, just staying in.'

'Your mother and I are off to a party at the Widdowsons'. You're welcome to come if you like.'

'Thanks, Hamish. I don't think so, but I'll bear it in mind.'

'Good girl. Try to come with us. It'd do you good to get out and about a bit.'

'What's all this?' Glenda returned, glass refilled to the brim, ice cubes clunking.

'Just telling her about the New Year's Eve party that we're going to.'

'She won't want to come,' Glenda predicted, ignoring Faith's presence in the room.

'I might,' Faith retorted, knowing full well that her mother was right but not wanting to admit it.

'Huh!' Glenda shoved one of the dogs that had rolled over and taken her space on the couch out of the way and reclaimed her seat. 'I'll believe that when I see it.'

'I've been invited to a party too, you know.' Faith sat up, indignantly on the defensive.

Glenda peeped at her through half-closed eyes as she inhaled the first, gloriously satisfying lungful of a new cigarette.

'Ellie, one of the partners, is having a party and has invited us all. So I might go to that.'

'Of course you might,' replied Glenda sarcastically.

They sat through yet another Christmas special tensely but by the end of the action-packed adventure film that was actually rather good, the atmosphere had relaxed. In the true spirit of Christmas, they bid a congenial good night to one another, agreeing in one voice that the film had been excellent entertainment and kept them on tenterhooks right until the end.

Faith drove them to the Boxing Day meet which was being held in the market square at Lambdale. She was doing it as a big, big favour to her mother. Under normal circumstances she hated towing a trailer behind the car and had to plan her journey so that there would always be room for her to turn round in a forwards circle, knowing that she did not possess the knack of reversing. Glenda, fully conversant with this fact, persuaded her to make an exception this once, convincing her that if the hunt ended up close enough back to home, then she and Hamish would be able to hack back and not bother her. Faith, who had done enough hunting in her time to know that there was just as much chance that the hunt would end up on the far side of Lambdale, had unenthusiastically agreed to help out.

Whatever your thoughts on the subject of hunting, there was no denying the splendid spectacle that met their eyes on arrival. To start with, it was text-book hibernal weather, cold and crisp with a bright sun low in the azure sky.

They had woken to a heavy frost which lay all day, coating the trees and plants, roofs and fences and creating a festive look which had coaxed supporters and spectators out in their droves. Horses of all sizes were stamping their hooves on the flags of the square, well aware of what was to come, eager to be off. Small ponies with big grass bellies had been brushed and polished, their equally small riders sitting up straight in clean jodhpurs and tweed jackets that were almost completely hidden by their back protectors. Adults on fine thoroughbreds, heavy cobs and prize-winning hunters milled around, weaving in and out, calling out greetings while adjusting their girths and gloves. Faces pink with excitement, the cold and perhaps too much stirrup cup. The master in his scarlet coat, resplendent on a powerful dapple grey, whippers-in trying to control the mischievious hounds who were threading their way through people's legs, scavenging and ingratiating themselves with the public, one even making a brief foray into the mini-mart that had opened to make the most of the hunt followers and the usual suspects who had run out of bread and milk.

Glenda was riding Caspian who was snorting almost hysterically when unloaded, having kicked the door continuously from the moment they set off. Faith, whose blood ran cold at the thought of riding him when he was in that sort of mood, was impressed as her mother swung easily into the saddle and sat, unperturbed by his antics, chatting away to Hamish who was astride a far calmer, more experienced bay gelding called Toby.

A short, sharp blow on the horn and the hounds appeared as if by magic, sterns waving, tongues lolling, sensing it was time to set off. They made a picturesque cavalcade as they clattered off and down the main street to the woods. Faith watched them all go, dozens of horses and then even more folk following on foot, a walking advertisement for waxed jackets and long Wellington boots. Turning to go back to the car – judiciously parked in the surgery car park, which was otherwise empty, she spotted Jonty, urging his horse into an extended trot as he tried to catch up with the main pack. Automatically, she called out. His head turned; momentarily he was unable to locate where the sound came from and then he caught her eye and waved before disappearing round the corner.

Faith's heart was pounding, her stomach performing gymnastics, her mouth dry. It had definitely been Jonty. There was no mistaking that angular profile and his handsome looks. He looked thinner than Faith recalled; she found this made her feel happy as it must be a sign that he was missing her. Knowing that Hamish had no idea where he was, then Jonty must have planned this, hoping that he would see Faith. Most importantly, he was on his own. There was no sign of Dawn – another good sign.

What should she do now? Faith had enough sense to dismiss the ridiculous notion of following the hunt in her car, abandoning the trailer in the car park until she came back later. Even in the few minutes that had passed, they would be into the woods and heading off for open countryside. Should she ring him later? Just a quick call to acknowledge that she had seen him and ask how he was. Perhaps a text message would look more casual. Or should she wait and see if he contacted her. The third idea appealed to her the most, but did involve the strain of waiting to see if it happened.

She returned home cautiously, feeling the trailer skid more than once on the icy lane, which was rarely in receipt of a visit by the gritter lorries, no matter how bad the weather. By the time Hamish and Glenda rang for a lift home, it would be even more slippery, a hazard offset slightly by the possibility that Caspian might be worn out and thus not thrash around as he had done earlier.

Chilled to the bone, Faith heated up soup and sat huddled close to the radiator while she drank it, trying to thaw out. She managed a brief, brisk walk with the dogs before curling up with a new paperback which lulled her to sleep within the first chapter.

The surgery was open as normal the following day. Back to the usual routine, thought Faith, as she dealt with cases of indigestion, otitis media and requests for the morning-after pill. Not everyone had had a happy Christmas. There was no let up for the whole day. Patients were prepared to let their doctors have one day off but two was stretching their tolerance. Elliott begged everyone to squeeze in an extra surgery at lunchtime to ease the pressure and they met periodically for coffee, tea and melt-in-the-mouth mince pies that John's wife had made to keep them going.

Mrs Tonbridge, not one to let a matter as trivial as celebrating the birthday of the baby Jesus interfere with her regular visits to the doctor, was sporting a new tam o'shanter, jauntily sited on one side of her head with matching scarf and gloves. Faith went out of her way to admire it, hoping that this would be well received. Sadly not, for the rich food, all that dried fruit and several glasses of sherry had played havoc with her bowels and now she was all out of sorts. What did Dr Faber intend to do about it?

By midday, the only reminders that it was Christmas were the decorations in the surgery, already looking tawdry and past their best and the half-empty giant tin of chocolates and sweets on the reception desk. There was however another holiday to look forward to, though Faith and the others agreed that in many ways it might be less stressful to open every day of the year, offer a reduced service on Bank Holidays and take time off in lieu in the summer when demand slackened off, to a degree.

Faith had no intention of attending either party. At the Widdowsons', she would be subjected to interrogations as to what had happened to her and Jonty and the thought of repeated post mortems did not fill her with good cheer. As for Ellie's party, she would feel embarrassed seeing Ian again, after their one and only meeting and there would be dozens of people she did not know, a situation that always made her feel awkward and tongue-tied. So despite Glenda and Hamish's best efforts to persuade her otherwise, she stuck to her ground and announced that she had a date with a cheese omelette, glass of wine and whatever eclectic mix of programmes was on offer to see out the old year and welcome the new one.

Glenda looked astonishing. Rarely seen, what she called, scrubbed up, Faith could be forgiven for forgetting what an attractive woman her mother was. After only thirty minutes' preparation, she appeared at the foot of the stairs, a vision in a dress of flame colours, which allowed a lot of well-toned thigh to be on view, her hair shining and make up perfectly applied. Both Faith and Hamish were speechless when they saw her.

'You look fantastic, Ma,' breathed Faith. 'Doesn't she, Hamish?'

'Belle of the ball, if you ask me. Shall we go?' He offered her his arm, which Glenda took, elegantly.

'Have a wonderful time. Happy New Year! Don't wake me when you come back,' Faith shouted after them.

It was peaceful in the house on her own. She poured a glass of wine, whisked up the eggs absent-mindedly and threw scraps of cheese to the dogs. Much to her amazement, she had not contacted Jonty, finding the will power from some previously forgotten corner to wait and let him get in touch with her. Nothing had transpired. She had even got other people to text and phone her, just to make sure that her mobile was working, which it seemed to be. If Hamish or Glenda had seen Jonty hunting that day, they said nothing and Faith, who longed to ask them, knew better than dare to raise the subject first.

She alternately sighed, ate and drank. What a year, she reflected, and now a new one ahead. If only she had the power to see into the future, what a help that would be. Her attempts at divination were curtailed abruptly by the sound of knocking on the back door. The dogs barked warningly. Could it be?

Pulling back the thick curtain that kept out draughts, she saw that it was not Jonty, but Rob. She ushered him in and closed the door quickly, for the freezing weather showed no sign of letting up.

'Hi,' he said, audaciously kissing her on one cheek before stooping to pat the dogs.

'Er, hi,' she replied, pulling away.

'Are you on your own?'

'Yes, Ma and Hamish have gone to a party.'

He looked quite nice, she decided. He had had his hair trimmed and was wearing some well-cut trousers and a smart shirt and plain jumper.

'Talking of parties, I just wondered if you might change your mind about coming to Ellie's.'

'I don't think so. Sorry, I was forgetting my manners, can I get you a drink?'

'Thanks. I'll have a glass of what you're having. Ellie has said I can stay over at hers if I want so I don't need to worry about driving. It'd be great if you came too. You'd enjoy it. She puts on brilliant parties.'

Faith passed his drink and unscrewed the jar of salted peanuts, offering them to him.

'I'm sure she does. Any other time and perhaps I would come. As it is, I don't feel like being amongst lots of people, particularly ones I don't know, getting drunk and then all hysterical at midnight.'

'Okay. You know best. Shame though. Mmm, this is very pleasant.'

'Come in the drawing room and sit down. Or are you in a rush?'

'No, I've plenty of time. I made sure of that in case I could persuade you to come with me and needed time to change.'

Faith was impressed by his forward planning.

They sat talking, in a stilted fashion, Faith feeling uncomfortable with his presence but bizarrely not wanting him to go. After a long, increasingly awkward silence during which Faith was reduced to staring at her hands in her lap, Rob started to speak again.

'I'd really like to take you out one evening, Faith. Sooner rather than later, if possible. What do you think?'

Faith opened her mouth to say no but again was mesmerised by the look in his eyes. He really wanted to take her and not because he felt sorry for her but because he wanted to spend time with her.

'I'm not sure...'

'Nothing heavy, a pub meal and a drink. I promise no subdued lighting and dark corners. Please?'

It was hard to ignore his plea and certainly easier to agree to go than explain that she wasn't over Jonty yet and suspected that she never would be. 'Go on then. But just a meal and a drink.'

'Sure thing,' Rob agreed, delighted. 'Next week sometime? What about Friday, then neither of us have work the next morning?'

'Sounds good to me.'

'Excellent. I'll book somewhere, just to be on the safe side and then speak to you at work about what time et cetera. All very casual, hand on heart. Look, I'd better be off now. You can still change your mind and I'll wait ...'

'No thanks. You go and have a good time and give my love to Ellie. I'll see you the day after tomorrow, back with our noses to the grindstone.'

He kissed her again, his lips lingering a little longer on her cheek, taking advantage of the fact that this time she did not move away.

'Don't be too lonely. Remember that you can always ring me. Happy New Year!'

Faith smiled.

'Happy New Year to you too.'

Chapter Twenty-Seven

No one was more surprised than Faith when she came out of work a few days later to find Jonty waiting for her. He was loitering in a dark corner, keeping out of the way of everyone else until he spotted Faith. She almost fell over on the ice when she heard his voice.

'Jonty!' Faith's incredulity echoed round the quiet and empty car park.

'Hello, Faith. How are you?'

'Er, fine.'

'Good.'

'How about you?'

'Yes, good, too.'

They laughed nervously.

'Listen to us!' exclaimed Jonty. 'You'd think we were meeting for the first time.'

'Silly, isn't it?' agreed Faith, still lost for intelligent conversation, her tongue dry and sticking to the roof of her mouth.

'Fancy a drink?'

Hesitating, Faith heard two voices in her head. Get in your car and drive away as fast as possible before you say or do anything you might regret later, said one, while the other more temptingly argued that going for a drink was surely not going to do any harm. There was nothing wrong with two old friends catching up, two adults, reminiscing, sharing a sociable glass of something before each going their separate ways by mid-evening. Technically speaking, it was still Christmas, just, and wasn't the purpose of this to spread peace and good will to all men?

In other words, Faith, who had known all along precisely what her decision was going to be, nodded her head and accepted his proffered arm, which felt comfortingly familiar. She was going to suggest they went to a recently opened wine bar down a ginnel at the far side of the square but Jonty, happily slipping back into his role of taking command, led her into the Queen's Head, the pub that she and the partners frequented. On entering, Faith spotted Rob and Ed in one corner, pint glasses in their hands, deep in conversation, perhaps debriefing after another long day's work but more probably having a friendly chat. Noticing her they waved and indicated to empty seats next to them. Turning to Jonty, Faith suggested they joined her friends. Jonty turned his head, made a point of scrutinising the two men and then pointedly led Faith away to the other side of the room to a table that very definitely was for only two. Making sure that Faith sat with her back to Ed and Rob, Jonty switched on the charm. Monopolising her attention, he asked tenderly how she had been, stressing how attractive she looked, so slim and pretty but tired and worried at the same time.

'Are you eating properly, my darling?' he enquired tenderly. 'You've lost so much weight.'

He waxed lyrical about how wretched he had felt since the moment she had found him in the barn, how he had suffered from insomnia or nightmares, lost his appetite and even lost the desire to ride. Dawn, it transpired, had been the most awful mistake of his life.

'I can't begin to tell you, Faith.' He shook his head theatrically. 'Under all that make-up, she had the most dreadful complexion. She had no personality. All she wanted to do was talk about pop music, that new boy band that's on the scene and clothes.'

With a choke in his voice, Jonty went on to explain that Dawn had developed a crush on Simon, who was good enough to put them up and they had slept together. He had learned his errors the hard way, Jonty was at pains to point out. It was going to take time but he was going to make amends with all those he had upset. He had approached his father, asked for forgiveness and if he might be allowed to move back in. Simon's sofa was not the most comfortable of sleeping arrangements and Simon had begun to make noises suggesting that he was outstaying his welcome. Though not yet given a definitive answer, the omens were looking optimistic. Jonty chose to draw a veil over the humiliating talking-to he had had to endure when his father first set eyes on him.

'So, it looks as if I'll be moving back home very soon. But,' Jonty took hold of Faith's hand, 'my happiness can only be complete if you will allow me back into your life. No! Don't say a word now. I'm not expecting you to give me an answer straight away. I don't deserve it. But at least say you'll think about it, which gives me hope. After what I did to you, it's understandable that I've bridges to build. However, I will. You'll see. I've changed. Learned my lesson. Faith? Say something.'

Faith opened her mouth but nothing came out.

'I'm sorry, this has all been a big shock to you. I'm just off to the gents, give you a bit of time to think. I'll get us another drink, shall I? Same again?'

'Orange juice please,' croaked Faith.

Her head was in a whirl. Unaccustomed to the new penitent Jonty, she was unsettled, wanting to believe that he had changed but still something held her back.

'Faith, are you all right?'

Shaken back to the real world, Faith saw Rob standing over her, one hand on her shoulder.

'Oh, hi. Yes, I think so. Has Ed gone?'

'We're about to leave but I wanted to come over and say good bye. It's a shame you couldn't join us.'

'Jonty wanted to have a talk.'

'So long as you're okay.' Rob was reluctant to go.

'Fine, fine, don't worry. I'll see you tomorrow.'

'We're still on for that meal, aren't we?'

'Of course,' replied Faith warmly. 'I'm looking forward to it.'

'Good,' Rob was relieved. 'So am I. Take care.' He strode off across the pub, brushing past Jonty coming in the opposite directions with the drinks.

'Who was that?' Jonty demanded.

'Rob, a friend from work,' Faith informed him. 'He's a really nice person.'

'Good. Now, where were we? Have you had any thoughts while I've been relieving myself?'

Faith studied his face, handsome and perhaps a little thinner than it had been. Twinkling eyes behind which lay, who knew, a real intention to change – or just the same old Jonty, searching for solace in safe, boring Faith until something better and more titillating came along? He was stroking her hand.

'Yes, I have,' Faith began slowly. 'Maybe you have had some back luck recently, but that doesn't even begin to compare with the pain and hurt that you've put me through or the distress you've caused to your father. He's given me and Ma so much help and support, I don't think we'd have managed the way we have, without him.'

'Of course – I understand all that.' Jonty, like a puppy, eager to please.

'What I can't understand is why you were prepared to risk our relationship by having an affair – if that's what you can call it – with Dawn. Did I really mean so little to you?'

'Darling, believe me, it's you I love. Dawn was nothing to me, she led me on and, like a fool, I couldn't resist.' He clutched her hand firmly, raising it to his lips to kiss it.

Faith pulled it away. 'You've destroyed the trust I thought we had in each other. That's not an easy thing to get back.'

'We can do it, Faith. I know we can. We're good together, make a good team. We need each other.'

Taking a deep breath in, Faith looked away and across the pub. 'I'm not sure that we do.'

'Darling…'

Faith found his wheedling voice irritating. 'No, I'm serious, Jonty. I think it's better if I go home now. Thank you for the drink. It was nice to see you and have this chat. I feel it's cleared the air, don't you? I really hope that you and your father make up.'

She stood up and looked around for her coat which had fallen onto the floor, rather ruining the haughty exit she had mentally planned.

Jonty caught her arm. 'You just need time to think. I've rushed you. Silly of me, but I was so excited to see you, I couldn't contain myself. Drive very carefully, my darling, as it's icy out there. I'll hope and pray that I see you soon.'

Faith gave him a last quizzical look and walked off, letting out a huge sigh when she was hit by the cold night air. On edge lest he was following her, she ran to her car and drove off recklessly, paying no heed to the scattered icy patches that glistened in the glow from the street lamps.

Faith did not sleep well that night, tossing, turning, fighting with the bedclothes, throwing them off, wrapping them tightly around her, striving to get comfortable and relax.

Jonty – whatever was she going to do? He was a rat of the first order and that was being kind. Firstly he had frightened the life out of her by being stupid and thoughtless, appearing like that out of the dark. Then his performance in the pub, that took some beating. Had he really expected her to be taken in by his sob stories? Thank goodness for Dawn and her insatiable libido. It would have done Jonty good to be let down by someone and realise what it felt like. Faith hoped that he had felt just a fraction of the despair that she had.

Glenda was right in her character assassination. Jonty was untrustworthy, dishonest and despicable. Faith congratulated herself on her calm, cool performance, not allowing any of his attempts at persuasion to permeate the tall, impenetrable barriers she had put up.

But he did say that he had changed, learned lessons and wanted forgiveness, not just with her but also his father, which must mean that he was aware how much damage he had done to the two of them. He had come across this evening as repentant and compliant, sounding as if he really meant what he said.

Everyone makes mistakes in life. The importance of these is to learn from them then put them behind you and move on. Jonty had sounded as if he was genuinely yearning to do this. Didn't everyone deserve a second chance?

Faith thought hard, imagining his face as she had left him. Her heart still skipped a beat at the sight of him and those butterflies still danced ecstatically within her stomach when he touched her, two definite symptoms that led to the indisputable diagnosis that she was still in love.

With a shudder, she remembered her last words to him. On reflection, they sounded so cold, so final. It was terrifying to think that he may be pondering on these words and taking them to heart, accepting that they were finished as a couple and severing all ties with her. To get in touch with him was imperative, to let him know that he was right, that she did love him, very much needed him and was prepared to give things another try. Never mind what Glenda's reaction would be. This was between Faith and Jonty, it was their lives and their future happiness.

Bleary eyed and kick started into action by strong black coffee, Faith tried to phone Jonty as soon as she got to work, arriving early with this mission in mind. Her call was diverted to voice mail, unsurprising as he had never been a particularly early riser unless there was a horse event to go to. For a second she contemplated leaving a message but rang off, leaving no more than a pregnant pause and some rather heavy breathing for him, which would bemuse him later. Instead, a better idea would be to go and see him in person, then they could talk more, but this time start to cement over the cracks in their relationship and reaffirm their status as a couple. The idea stayed with her all day, growing in magnitude the more time she gave to it.

By lunchtime, she had them walking into the sunset hand in hand; by the middle of the afternoon, they were kissing passionately on Simon's sofa and by the time she left the surgery, the third finger on her left hand was aching to have the engagement ring put back on it and they were eloping by dead of night, far the most romantic time of day to do such a thing, with only a full moon to guide their car across the sinuous one-track lanes of the Yorkshire Dales.

Unfortunately, though Faith was of the opposite opinion, Glenda was out when she got home and the quickly scribbled note on the kitchen table informed her that the dogs needed their tea and she would not be back until late. Had Glenda been there, Faith might well have not opted for the course of action that she did.

Dogs fed and thus happy, Faith chose with care a pair of skinny jeans, which paid homage to her current rather underweight state, a light fawn polo neck jumper, brown suede boots and a brown leather jacket. Approving her own appearance, which she liked to think made her look casually chic, she was generous with an application of perfume, rather more reserved with her make-up, wanting to go for the natural look, and then ran downstairs. At this point, feeling guilty, she rang Rob, was overjoyed that there was no reply and left a message to say that unfortunately, she really felt as if she was about to come down with something and so felt that it was better if they cancelled their 'date' that evening. Catching sight of the time on the kitchen clock, she calculated that he may have already set off, having promised to pick her up in a taxi, ignoring her protests that there was no need. So she needed to hurry; there was a big risk of him coming to see how she was if he got the message and was on his way.

Grabbing her bag, keys and throwing some bone-shaped biscuits down for the dogs – a far more generous helping than her mother ever allowed them – she locked up and jumped into her car.

Simon lived about twenty minutes away. She had often been there with Jonty, each time feeling awkward as Simon had tended to ignore her and devote his attention to the male species. He lived with a couple of other work colleagues in a modern flat, large and open plan, with lots of angular furniture and white paint, a staggeringly big flat screen television and occasional bursts of colour in the form of scarlet lamps or cushions. Uncharacteristically, for three unmarried men, their home was spotless. There was never a pile of washing-up to be done, no papers left strewn around the polished wood floors and the bathroom was always polished to within an inch of its life. Often Faith had thought that the atmosphere was cold and clinical rather than homely, not something that she had ever felt truly able to relax in, never quite being able to get over the feeling that it was more like a show flat than somebody's residence.

It was still early, so there was an excellent chance that Jonty would be in. Under normal circumstances, it was unheard of for him to stay in on a Friday night but if he was as upset as he had appeared, then he might be licking his wounds, preferring solitude to the bonhomie of his mates. Looking up at the flat, Faith saw that lights were on – encouraging. She had rehearsed what she was going to say as she was driving, over and over again, making a few alterations which she thought sounded better. The thought of telling him how she felt and his reaction was electrifying.

Swallowing hard, she ran up the steps to the communal door and pressed the buzzer. The door opened. Before getting into the lift to the third floor, Faith combed her hair and checked her lipstick, making use of the conveniently placed mirror in the hallway. Time to go up.

The door to the flat was opened by a young woman holding one towel around her body and with another wrapped around her head. Drips on the floor suggested that Faith had disturbed her in the shower. She had cherubic cheeks and large dark eyes. For one horrible moment she thought it was Dawn but quickly realised that there was little resemblance.

'Yes?' she asked.

Faith smiled her best smile. 'Hello, I'm Faith. Is Jonty in?'

The girl poked a corner of towel down her ear.

'No, he and Si have gone down to the pub on the corner for a pint while I get ready. I was late in from work. I doubt they'll be long. Do you want to come in and wait?'

Faith bit the inside of one cheek. 'I don't think so. But thanks for the offer.'

'Okay. See you then.'

The door started to close. Faith pushed against it with her hand. 'Which pub have they gone to?'

'The Moon and Stars. At the end of the road, on the corner. You can't miss it.'

'Thanks! I know exactly where it is.'

Faith walked briskly down the pavement. No point in taking the car and they would be coming back to the flat anyway, she expected.

There was something very inviting about the pub, which radiated a rosy warmth as she approached. The smell of fried food hit her in the face as she pulled open the heavy double doors, reminding her that she had not eaten all day and would very much like some food. She decided she would offer to take Jonty out to eat. It would be far easier to talk intimately in a corner of a restaurant than in Simon's flat where people would doubtless be in and out, poking their noses in, wondering what was going on.

At first she didn't see him, surprised at how busy it was and how noisy. There was music blasting from an old-fashioned juke box and in order to make themselves heard the customers had all raised their voices accordingly. Better though, this way, for her to creep up to him and surprise him. How good it would feel to be wrapped in his arms again.

Faith saw Simon first, his signature hair, gelled up into spikes, unmissable. He was, as was customary, chatting up a girl who had small, petite features, masses of tight blond curls and a pneumatic bosom. Typical, but hardly the behaviour expected of someone who ought to be trying to console a friend. Not for the first time Faith wondered why on earth Jonty had chosen Simon as his best friend; she failed to see any similarities between them.

Jonty was sitting to the left of Simon, on his own, looking forlornly at his half- empty pint glass, swilling the contents around in circular movements. Faith's heart went out to him. She had been so idiotic to believe that there was any way that her life would go on without him. Feeling her pulse accelerating, she fought her way

248

through the standing customers, getting stuck behind a corpulent man in a pinstriped suit who was regaling his colleagues with some interminable story of what had happened at work that day. Faith had to ask him politely if he would mind moving several times before he gracelessly shuffled forwards a minimal distance to let her wriggle past. Her jacket caught on his arm and she had to turn and pull to free it.

With a final wrench, she turned to greet Jonty with her much practised opening line but froze on the spot. Gone was the supposedly sad and grieving lover, in his place was his laughing, leering alter ego, with his hand up Dawn's blouse, caressing one of her breasts as she sat squirming with unbridled sexiness on his knee.

The fat man spilt wine down his front and choked as Faith sent him flying forwards into his friends, oblivious of the ructions she left in her wake. She didn't know if Jonty had seen her, nor did she care.

Mortified and overwhelmed, she gulped in the night air erratically as she did her best to run in high-heeled boots. One heel broke off, her jacket got trapped in the car door and ripped. The engine refused to start and she punched the steering wheel with alarming anger before collapsing in tears.

She had been prepared to give up everything for him. Everything, in order to give him a second chance, confident that this was all he needed, duped by the award-winning performance he had entertained her with the night before. Ready to forgive, try to forget, she had been about to offer herself on a plate as he had fooled her into believing that he felt the same. The antipathy she felt towards Jonty was only superseded by the disgust she felt for herself.

For someone who, on a daily basis made decisions about her patients' lives, she had an unparalleled penchant for retaining ingenuousness about matters pertaining to her own. It seemed that she never learned.

Sniffing unpleasantly and wiping her nose ineffectively on the back of her sleeve, she started off on her journey home, alternately crying and uttering growls of anger.

Hoping that the roads would be quiet and thus her journey quicker than usual, Faith put her foot down on the accelerator and urged the car to go faster, paying no attention to speed limits or dangerous bends.

Once back in the warm, she absent-mindedly patted the dogs, who were overjoyed to see her, used to constant human presence and hating being on their own. They followed her closely, afraid she would leave again and watched her every move as she automatically made two slices of toast and poured a glass of juice. The toast turned to cardboard in her mouth and was fed to the dogs. Somehow her oesophagus seemed to have been tied in a knot as the juice refused to go down either.

The drawing room, where she had gone to eat, looked sad and empty without the Christmas tree. It had been up for barely two weeks but had instantly become part of the décor. Telltale green needles still lay on the carpet waiting to be hoovered up, together with tiny strands of tinsel.

A poor substitute for the decorations was the stack of boxes of chocolates, still pristine, wrappers intact. Not thinking what she was doing, Faith reached over and ripped one of them open. By chance, the patient had picked the sort she liked best – truffle fillings, dark and rich. The smell was almost erotic. Her fingertips played over the small, indulgent treats, two layers of them, each one with a dusting of cocoa. A chocoholic's paradise. It would be so simple to have just one, then another and another and another…

Faith sat back. The anger had left her, the space remaining devoid of emotion. She wished that her mother was there with her, not across the village eating, or more likely drinking with friends, having a good time. Something had changed in their relationship, barely discernable but still of utmost importance. Her recent support, the evening she had spent listening and the tenderness she had exhibited made Faith realise how close they really were, that they were not just two women living in the same house, they truly were mother and daughter and, best of all, friends. From now on, she must cultivate this newly found closeness and let it blossom.

And there were two other things she needed to do.

She pushed away the chocolates, stood up and with one move of her arm swept all the boxes into a rubbish bag and threw this into the dustbin, slamming on the lid. Part of her begged her not to take such drastic action, to retrieve the chocolates and gorge on them but somehow she resisted, went inside and locked the door.

The dogs smiled at her and she hugged them, whispering to them what she was going to do next. They wagged their tails in

FAITH HOPE AND CLARITY
Cover Design: Alerrandre Zeto

Published by:
   Editions Dedicaces LLC
   12759 NE Whitaker Way, Suite D833
   Portland, Oregon, 97230
   www.dedicaces.us

Library of Congress Cataloging-in-Publication Data
   Tetlow, Carol Margaret.
   Faith Hope and Clarity / by Carol Margaret Tetlow.
   p. cm.
   ISBN-13: 978-1-77076-461-3 (alk. paper)
   ISBN-10: 1-77076-461-5 (alk. paper)

Carol Mar

Faith Hope and Clarity

Fiction

Editions Dedicaces